DEAD TO GET READY—AND GO

A Dead Detective Mystery

by Peg Herring

Published in the United States of America

ISBN# 978-1-944502-06-5

Chapter One

Bored was an impolite term, considering the wonders of the Afterlife, but that's what Seamus was. Perfect meals, endless entertainment, and unfailingly pleasant companions bored him.

There was something else, too, but he didn't know what to call it.

Seamus regularly and purposefully relived the last moments of his earthly existence. Each time, he was shaken and confused at the outset, overcome by dread somewhere in the middle, and at the last moment, blessed with a kind of fatalistic acceptance.

It was always the same. He emerged from a cocoon of pain, unable to move, speak, or see. His feet were bound tightly at the ankles, his hands behind his back. The ropes bit into his wrists, and his hands felt like bricks at the ends of his arms. It was bitterly cold, and he lay against a fish-scented wooden surface. A thin coat of ice stung the spot where his cheek rested. It hurt, but he recognized that what came next would be far worse.

Vague impressions circled his mind, but the pain stopped him from sorting them into usable bits of information. *Think!* he ordered, but his brain couldn't obey.

Water lapped around him. Thumps sounded, and movement beneath rolled him gently back and forth. He was in a boat. A familiar voice spoke above him, and it seared his soul to hear it in this time and place. "Is Seamus dead?" she asked.

He wanted to say something, but all that came out was a muffled groan. A burst of noise assailed his ears, and his weight shifted abruptly. His head struck against something, and he lost the ability to think for a while.

The chug of a motor coming to life brought awareness back. Seamus felt the tug of movement, backward a few feet and then forward, slowly at first but picking up after a few minutes. The motor whined as unseen hands guided the boat around a few slight turns. The air became even colder, and the ice under his cheek burned like a blowtorch. After perhaps ten minutes, the irritating whine lessened and the boat slowed. The growl became a purr, and movement all but stopped. They'd reached their destination.

By then Seamus knew what would happen next. His body tensed as hands grasped his ankles and the shoulders of his coat. Unwilling to submit to death without a fight, he scuttled sideways, trying to find refuge. There was none. He was lifted from his resting place by ungentle hands. He was rocked back and forth a few times to build momentum and a voice counted down. "One, two, three!"

The hands released him. He felt a brief sensation of flying, followed by a jerk at his ankles. Something heavy had been attached to his feet. He felt its pull as it hit the water first and began its descent to the lake bottom, dragging him with it. When the icy waters of Lake Michigan closed around him, Seamus was already half dead. It didn't take long for what was left of his life to be sucked away.

Coming out of the waking nightmare with a violent shiver, Seamus gasped for air he no longer needed. He gripped the heavy railing with both hands. It felt solid and real, though that was an illusion. The ship was an illusion provided to those traveling from life to What Comes After. He was as dead as everyone else on board, immune to the "thousand natural shocks" the living face each day. Here there was no fear, no pain, and little real emotion. Existence was comfortable, reassuring, and luxurious.

But it wasn't Life.

Seamus stood on the deck, facing a view he'd never been able to put into words. The ship appeared to sail through color itself—more than that—the *essence* of color. Like staring into a burning fire or a rushing waterfall, their surroundings were soothing yet intense, as if a person's whole being were centered in his eyes. A guy didn't just look *at* it. He was *part* of it, part of what comes after death.

Wrestling with his thoughts, Seamus tried to ignore the people behind him who strolled the deck or sat chatting in lounge chairs. Things they engaged in were life-like, or maybe life-*ish*. Someone called a cheerful greeting. A waiter asked if he might refill a drink. A muted splash sounded from the pool. The interruptions bothered Seamus, reminding him where he was and what he was.

The ship was a bridge, a sort of mirage created to help the dead get used to the idea of being in the state none of us can truly imagine. When an individual was ready—when he felt adequately rewarded or recovered from whatever life had done to him—he went on to the next step, which was beyond human understanding. No one was forced or even nudged in that direction, because it was a big decision. Taking that step meant giving up everything a person had been. Going on was glorious, but guests were welcome to stay on the ship as long as they wanted to. Most went on after a reasonable amount of time.

Most.

Roughly a third of the dead delayed taking the Next Step, according to Seamus' reckoning. Despite the prospect of indescribable glory, some preferred the familiarity and comfort of the ship. Others were fearful, confused, or unable to trust what they were told. Some doubted their own worthiness. Whatever the reason, those who stayed for any length of time were given tasks suited to them, mostly to provide them with a sense of purpose. The ship's management, technically angels but practically normal, were good at finding just the right slot for each client.

Seamus had stayed on the ship for more than half a century, though that measurement of time had little meaning here. Following the occupation he'd pursued in life, he left the ship periodically as a *cross-back*, a detective who helped murder victims find out who'd killed them and why. Crossing-back was frustrating, since it required hitch-hiking with someone still living. Seamus didn't care as long as he could see the world again. He wasn't ready to let go of Seamus Hanrahan, private detective. Not yet.

"Seamus?"

He turned, half curious, half irritated. Few on board knew him by name; fewer still sought him out. He was a solitary soul, he thought to himself with a tiny smile at the precision of the idiom.

The woman who'd spoken his name was young. Seamus amended his thought. She'd *died* young, perhaps just out of her teens. She wore tight, bright blue pants—he thought they were called leggings—and a multi-colored shirt that might have included all the colors there were. Her hair was cropped close to her perfectly-shaped head. With skin the color of coffee and eyes several shades darker, she brought Lena Horne to mind. With that air of self-possession, this one wouldn't scare easily.

"Ronnie." It wasn't a question, and she smiled, showing slightly crooked but very white teeth.

"I thought you were going to find me when we got back."

Seamus shifted his feet on the metal deck. He'd encountered Ronnie on his last case, as they'd solved separate crimes that turned out to be related. She'd suggested they meet in person when they returned to the ship. At the time it had seemed like a good idea.

Once he was back on board, however, Seamus had hesitated. In his experience people were complicated, whether living or dead. Would Ronnie become tiresome without a case to solve? Would she find him stodgy, irritating, or even pitiful? In the end he'd decided it was best to leave the interlude in the past, where he left all questions relating to human interaction. That way the case they'd solved together was a pleasant memory that couldn't tarnish due to the rub of familiarity.

Watching the colors around the ship shift and dance in never-repeating patterns he said, "You don't owe me anything, Sister."

Ronnie made an impatient gesture. "I thought we made a pretty good team, but—" She finished in a burst. "If you don't hang with people like me, just say so."

Judging from the angle of her head, Ronnie had taken his avoidance as an insult. That brought a smile, which for Seamus was the brief quirk of one cheek. "You think I don't associate with Negroes?"

Her wince reminded him that wasn't what they were called these days, and of course he knew better. He'd visited the world of the living often enough to comprehend the changes since his death. Still, he didn't correct himself. He was a product of his time, as she was a product of hers. Another reason they should go their own ways.

Ronnie's jaw protruded a little. "You knew I was female, so you aren't one of those men who think women's heads are full of fluff. I held my own in the case, so it isn't my ability that makes you hesitate. But my skin color? If that bothers you, just say so."

Seamus' cheek quirked again. "In the war I saw black, white, red, brown, and yellow people die, and you know what? On the inside they looked exactly the same." Meeting her gaze he finished, "I have no objections to you at all."

"Good." She joined him at the rail, leaning her forearms against it and presenting her rear to the passersby. "Mike got a kick out of hearing how we ran into each other."

Feeling safer discussing the past, he said, "You did good work back there."

"Thanks." She focused her gaze on the colors. "I was looking forward to seeing you again."

Seamus rubbed his bottom lip with his thumb. "What's it supposed to lead to?"

She turned, one brow arched almost to her hairline, and her long earrings dangled as she wobbled her head side to side. "What does anything lead to? People get together and they talk."

He shrugged. "I'm not much of a talker."

Her head swayed again, harder this time. "I get that, but I thought we could bounce ideas off each other."

That made him chuckle. "You're going to share from your vast store of experience?" When she didn't reply he asked, "How many cross-backs have you done?"

Her tone turned sulky. "That was my second—the first on my own." She gave him a sideways glance. "I want to be good at this cross-back thing, and word around the ship is you're the man." He guessed she was smiling as she added, "Probably because you've been around forever."

The other cross-backs talked about him, of course. His skills were respected, but he was also a bit of a joke: antisocial, taciturn, and hopelessly set in his ways. In his ever-present brown suit with wide lapels, fedora, and wing-tips, Seamus was one big cliché, and he knew it. But his clothes weren't part of some pose he'd adopted. They were what he was comfortable with, what he was used to. Why should a guy become someone new just because he was dead?

Ronnie continued her argument. "I thought—I got the impression—" She faltered but finished, "I'll listen when you're in the mood to talk, and I won't blab to the others."

Seamus thought about that. The only person he spent time with now wasn't actually a person. Mike, the angel in charge of client satisfaction, often joined Seamus for lunch. Through interaction with people, Mike had come to enjoy things like eating fried cod with tartar sauce and salty fries with ketchup. Seamus found him easy to talk to, but an angel couldn't comprehend what it was like to actually *be* human, to have doubts, to long for the past, to wonder, "What if—?"

"What exactly do you want to know?"

"I won't ask how you died, if that's what you're worried about. They say you don't talk about it, and that's your business."

Comparing How-I-Died stories was popular dinner conversation, but he'd never seen the point. They could say he was hiding something if they wanted to. It didn't matter.

"That's right. Mine and nobody else's."

She didn't take offense. "My story's pretty simple. I was swimming off the coast of Florida, and a shark came along. I tried to get away, but—" She grinned ruefully. "As you can see, I didn't make it."

Seamus turned slightly toward her. Though her voice was steady, he sensed she was lying.

Her business. If she doesn't want to tell me the truth, she doesn't have to.

He'd liked Ronnie on the case in Toronto, and he liked her now, even knowing she'd lied. She wasn't the kind of friend he'd ever imagined. In fact, she was the exact opposite of the last person he'd called friend. Grant had been white, male, and forty, and Ronnie was none of those things. Still, she was smart, with a bit of a smart mouth, which he liked in a person. "You had lunch yet?"

"No."

"I know a spot most of them don't go to. You willing to try it?"

Ronnie let out a breath she probably wasn't aware she'd been holding. "Sounds good to me.

Seamus led the way down one deck, to the end of a passageway, and opened an unimpressive door with a hand-lettered sign: ARTIE'S. Inside were a half dozen mismatched tables, a row of battered booths along one wall, and a low counter where three men sat, an empty stool between each one. At one table two plain-looking women sat, heads bent over their plates as they shoveled in mashed potatoes and roast pork. At another table a man dipped toast into an over-easy egg yolk and took a large bite, dribbling yellow onto the table. Behind the counter a rotund man with very little hair held an oversized spatula like a scepter. His face lit when he saw who'd come in.

"Seamus, how they—" Noticing Ronnie behind him he finished, "—treatin' you?"

"Good, Artie. Thought I'd give you another chance to give me ptomaine."

Artie chuckled. "Can't poison a corpse."

Seamus gestured at his companion. "This is Ronnie."

Nodding in a way that said he was reserving judgment, Artie said, "Hey, Ronnie."

"S'up."

They chose a table, and Ronnie took a plastic-coated menu from behind the salt and pepper shakers. "What's good here?"

Seamus shrugged. "I never had anything bad, but I'm not exactly a gourmet. Artie does stuff I'm used to eating the way I'm used to eating it."

"Burger and fries?"

He took the menu from her and dropped it back into its slot. "You won't be disappointed."

Artie came over to the table, a hitch in his step betraying a bad hip. Though no one had pain here, the bodies they were given on the ship roughly approximated a person's last healthy day. Those who'd had infirmities in life often continued to behave as if they still had them. Sometimes when he forgot he was no longer alive, Seamus himself favored the shattered knee he'd dealt with the last few years of his life, a souvenir of WWII.

Once they'd ordered and Artie shuffled off, Ronnie asked, "What's his story? He could have a nice restaurant and lots of help, but he runs this little joint all on his own?"

Seamus spread his hands, palms up. "You get what you want here, right? Artie wants this place." Opening the silverware set wrapped in a paper napkin, he set the knife and fork on the table, wide enough for a platter to fit between. "Artie started out running a diner, but his wife insisted they 'better themselves.' They kept buying bigger and fancier places, and they ended up with one of those fine dining establishments where the waiters walk around with their noses in the air. Artie was known as 'Arturo,' and he made dishes with foreign names for people with big egos. He hated every day of it. When he got here, he asked if he could go back to feeding ordinary people normal food. This is what he got."

Ronnie looked around the homey little place and sighed. "That's cool." She leaned forward, setting her long earrings swinging wildly. "How did you picture the Afterlife when you were back there?"

Seamus sniffed. "Didn't think about it much."

"Okay, then what made you decide to become a cross-back?"

He didn't answer for a while, because Artie appeared with heavy ceramic platters filled to overflowing. Each contained a burger, a huge pile of fries, a crisp dill pickle, and a small paper cup overflowing with coleslaw. Over one arm he'd hung a basket of extras: squirt bottles of mayonnaise, mustard, and ketchup, extra napkins, and a jar of pickle slices with a tiny fork protruding through a hole in its lid. Ronnie and Seamus took a few seconds to pass condiments to each other, loading the burgers with their favorite choices before taking their first bites.

Ronnie moaned with delight. "This is like a place I used to go to in high school. All grease and no class, but still heaven." Realizing what she'd said, she grinned self-consciously. "Heaven. Who knew?"

They ate for a while, interspersing bites of burger with fries. "The best thing about being dead is not having to worry about what's going to kill you," Ronnie remarked, but the question she'd asked earlier hung in the air.

Seamus finished his burger and wiped his fingers on a napkin. "I was murdered."

Ronnie stopped chewing for a few seconds, but apparently no suitable response came to mind.

Eyes focused on his remaining fries, he went on. "I wanted to be a cop like my dad, and for a while I was. Then the war came along, and from that I got a bum knee, a small pension, and no job. One of the guys in my outfit, a lawyer, suggested I go into private investigation. He promised me work and even offered space in the building where he had his offices."

Taking up a fry, Ronnie dredged it in ketchup and ate, waiting for more.

"I guess that's why I became a cross-back," Seamus took a bite of pickle. "I like helping people find answers."

"Were you killed on a case?" Ronnie laughed as soon as she said it. "Oops! I promised I wouldn't ask. It's just that when you said you were a detective, it made me think—" When he didn't say anything she went on, "I'm sorry. It's none of my business."

"Yeah." His tone revealed there was more he might have said, but he changed both the tone and the topic. "Now eat all those fries, or Artie will be offended. He's a real believer in the Clean Plate Club."

***

The Last Night—March 12, 1953

"Where are you going?" Lee asked when he called to tell her he'd be out late.

"I'm meeting someone who's got information for me."

"Where?"

"Downtown."

"What case are you working on?"

"It's not really a case yet, just possible illegal activity." Seamus' throat felt tight. It was hard to lie to his wife.

"Where is this illegal activity taking place?"

Any other time he'd have given details without her asking. "At some nightclub."

"A nightclub where they break the law." Lee's voice was hard. "Big news."

"We're meeting after the place closes, so don't wait up for me."

"Seamus, be careful. Those places don't attract nice people."

"I'm always careful, Honey Girl. And don't be so hard on nightclubs. That's where we met."

"I remember. But you're the only good thing I ever found there."

Chapter Two

Ronnie and Seamus took to meeting for lunch each day at Artie's. He waited for her to turn nosy or whiny or silly, but she didn't. In fact, he began looking forward to sharing things he'd learned in his many experiences. Ronnie got what crossing-back was really about, and she had none of the self-congratulatory attitude of some cross-backs he'd met, the daredevil types who bragged about their exploits and belittled their clueless hosts. With Ronnie, Seamus talked about practical things: how to deal with the pain of the crossing, how to adjust to the heaviness of a living body after the lightness of being dead, and how to conduct an investigation from inside the mind of a living person who could be coaxed but not controlled.

"All my life," he told her one day over a large bowl of chili, "I wanted to know *why* people do what they do. Long division problems or how atoms combine means nothing to me, but murder—that's something worth figuring out."

"I know," Ronnie agreed. "How does somebody become willing, even determined, to take the life of a fellow human being?"

"I like tracking it down until I understand—at least, what there is to understand about taking a life that doesn't belong to you."

"It's like solving a puzzle, but you're helping people, too."

When they parted after lunch, Seamus returned to staring into the void that surrounded the ship. He hadn't shared with Ronnie his recent restlessness, but with himself he was honest. Solving other people's problems was never going to resolve his own.

Those who knew how they'd died accepted their changed state fairly soon. It wasn't hard to understand that drinking and driving could end a life, and for someone who'd endured years of suffering, dying was often a relief.

It was different for murder victims. Their lives had ended on someone else's timetable, and that felt unfair. *Why?* and often *Who?* weren't idle questions. They were essential for accepting that Life was gone forever. Helping those people had always been gratifying for Seamus.

It was no longer enough.

At the end of the day he returned to his stateroom, which contained only a bed, a seldom-used TV, and a couple of chairs. He slept, setting his concerns aside with the power of his formidable will. The next morning he woke with the same concerns, and the sense that they had to be faced was stronger than ever. Seamus spent the morning staring at the wall across from his bed, rubbing his face occasionally, and listening to the silence.

When his inner clock stirred him to action, it was close to noon. Though time didn't exist anymore, the illusion of it helped the dead feel normal, just as the feel of having a body and the sense of needing to eat and sleep did. Seamus glanced at the calendar, which had days but no month or year. Thursday said, Ronnie-noon. So did Friday and Saturday and Sunday.

She was already there, and she'd ordered the grilled cheese sandwich with macaroni and cheese on the side. "Can't go to my booty," she remarked as Artie set the plate down before her. Seamus ordered the corned beef, foregoing comment on women and their figures. When Artie grabbed a coffee pot black with age and waved it, Seamus turned his cup right side up and pushed it toward the table edge.

"The food's wonderful, Artie," Ronnie said.

"Thanks." With a glance at Seamus Artie added, "Some of my customers keep mentioning ptomaine, but I think I do pretty good."

"I'd know ptomaine," she said. "That's what I died of."

Artie's watery blue eyes widened. "Really?"

She shrugged. "Well, I never heard the actual diagnosis, you know? But I ate at this new restaurant down in the French Quarter. Afterwards, I got this funny feeling in my gut then I started throwing up, really violent spasms. I got so weak I couldn't stand up. I remember lying on the kitchen floor, trying to reach my phone to call 9-1-1. That's the last I remember." She stirred her Diet Coke with her straw, adding, "Whatever it was, it was quick."

Seamus frowned, but a twinkle in Ronnie's eyes kept him silent. When Artie moved away, he said, "You're something, you know that?"

She grinned impishly. "Just keeping things interesting." She wiped her mouth with the napkin. "Now, what are you going to teach me today? We've covered the crossing, the best ways to pick up what's floating through a host's mind, and jumping from one host to another without missing and making a mess. I know we have to be careful not to let them know we're in their heads."

"A trainee I took along once couldn't accept that." Seamus' expression turned reflective. "She kept talking to the host, who finally said out loud that the voice in his head had to leave. When they do that, we have to obey. I mean, they've got free will, and they don't have to put up with us."

"I'd never upset a host. It wouldn't be right." Ronnie's eyes sparkled as she pretended to ponder her next question. "So what could you possibly reveal to me that you've never told anyone else?"

With comic disgust he said, "You want to know about the rat."

Ronnie leaned toward him. "Everyone wants to know about the rat, my friend."

He sighed. "It wasn't a choice, okay? My host got hurt, and I had to get out, because you know—"

"—If a host dies before you can jump to someone else, you're stuck between Life and the ship." She shivered. "Lost forever."

"I thought my guy was dying, so I jumped to the nearest living thing. It happened to be a rat."

"But you might have been stuck in some landfill for eternity."

He chuckled dryly. "My wife used to say, 'You gotta do something sometimes, even if it's wrong.'"

Ronnie blinked. "I never thought about you having a wife or kids, Seamus—or even a last name."

"No kids, and the name's Hanrahan." He'd never told anyone about Lee, but having brought her up, Seamus took another step forward. "As for my wife—not much to say except that she and her boyfriend are the ones who murdered me."

***

The Night They Met: February 11, 1950

Standing in the shadows, Seamus watched the entrance to Danny's Place, trying to get a sense of the club and its clientele. Shielded from

view by larger buildings, the nightclub offered its patrons plenty of privacy. The block where it sat was triangular rather than square, since the Chicago River took a turn there before heading for Lake Michigan. Two of the triangle's sides were streets lined with buildings, while the river traced the third. In the open space in the middle was a one-and-a-half-story building that had once been a warehouse, a hundred yards back from the water on higher, firmer ground. Someone, presumably Danny, had turned it into a nightclub. Entry and exit were made via two narrow, alley-like streets that led to larger but still secondary streets, one of which connected to Wacker Drive. Walled in by larger buildings, the club was a tiny island of dark and relative quiet in the midst of the city, a private spot visitors had to be aware of in order to find it.

The upper level was dark, but Seamus noted a metal fire escape at the back corner that allowed entry to the second story from the outside. On the main floor, one window near the back showed light, but along the front half of the place, the windows had been covered with heavy shutters. That would be where the action was, he figured. A flashing neon sign atop a pink-and-black, flat-roofed portico announced Danny's, offering COCKTAILS! and ENTERTAINMENT NIGHTLY! Beneath it, double doors opened and closed as customers entered, letting out light and strains of tinny music.

Crossing the parking lot, Seamus joined a well-dressed group obviously looking forward to an evening of booze and fun. A burly man at the door regarded them gravely, nodding in polite but hardly warm greeting. He was there to prevent misbehavior, and he didn't need to speak to get that message across. In the foyer Seamus separated from the group and stood off to one side as if waiting for someone. Within a minute he'd noted that the hat-check girl was cute, the décor was overdone, and the burly man was watching him. He moved through the curtained doorway and into the main room.

The object of his current case was a missing man, Arthur Jameson, whose wife reported he was last seen at Danny's Place. "I took him there for our anniversary," Mrs. Jameson had said when she hired Seamus. "I found the club a little gauche, all red velvet and gold paint, but Arthur loved it. He went back often, and he said since I didn't like it, he wouldn't force me to go along."

That struck Seamus as an excuse, and from her tone he guessed she knew it. Mrs. Jameson, who was one smart cookie, knew why her husband had returned to the club alone. Still, she seemed genuinely perplexed by his disappearance. Judging by their tasteful home, the spacious garage, and Mrs. J's well-maintained exterior, Seamus guessed old Art had a lot to lose. It followed that his absence wasn't voluntary.

Since Jameson had gone to Danny's the night he disappeared, Seamus had come to see the place. The police had been there, of course, but the employees who remembered Jameson's visit claimed he'd left around twelve, right after the second show.

The place was crowded, but Seamus pointed to a small table on the far wall that nobody had taken, probably because the view of the stage was partially blocked. The hostess led the way, skirting tables as Seamus limped along behind her. Soon he was seated, behind the pillar and against the wall. That was fine, since he hadn't come to watch the show. Seamus asked for a Cutty Sark on the rocks and sat back to observe the room.

The band was on break, and the low hum of conversation was broken periodically by laughter, sometimes low-pitched, other times high and musical, like vocal exercises. Danny's was popular with those who had a little extra cash and wanted to be seen spending it. Elegance was the norm. Most of the women wore tightly-fitted dresses that looked glamorous but probably made sitting and walking difficult.

When the girl brought his drink, Seamus asked if the place was always this busy. "I guess." She looked him over appraisingly, and he imagined himself as she saw him, not that good-looking and not that well-dressed. She moved off. Bigger tippers than he'd ever could be found at other tables.

A flourish of music drew the crowd's attention, and an emcee stepped through the heavy red curtains. Seamus couldn't see all of him because of the pillar, but he heard the spiel, which was basically "Welcome, welcome—Here's tonight's show—Headliner Lili Moreno." Seamus paid little attention as he tried to decide if Jameson might have disappeared from this place and if so, why.

Then the curtains opened, the music swelled, and the singer began her first song, "The Tennessee Waltz." The song's inherent sadness came through in her voice, which was sweet but strong, soft but compelling. Intrigued, Seamus leaned around the pillar to get a look at Miss Moreno.

She was beautiful, with long, black hair and round, dark eyes. She stood alone on the stage in a simple blue dress with only a rhinestone clip at the shoulder for decoration. Seamus moved his chair into the aisle in order to get a better look at her.

The room quieted as Lili sang, and when Seamus managed to pull his gaze away for a moment and scan the faces turned toward the stage, every man there seemed mesmerized. He could see why all the tables were full. Danny's, not the ritziest club in town, had a real crowd pleaser in their headliner. Ignoring outraged grunts from the guy behind him, Seamus leaned to one side, watching until Miss Moreno bowed gracefully and disappeared. A half-dozen lively girls danced onstage to the strains of "I've Got My Love to Keep Me Warm." It was a good thing they had love, he thought wryly, because they weren't wearing enough to keep from catching cold in the middle of a Chicago winter.

Seamus sat back, letting the man behind him get an eyeful of the bobbing dancers. Peering between the pillar and the wall, he watched the tiny slice of stage he could see, impatient for the moment when the dancers would finish and Lili Moreno would return and sing again. He told himself she'd be less impressive a second time, but that wasn't true. When Lili came back for a two-song set, Seamus fell completely under her spell until she again bowed and retreated. He had to remind himself he'd come to Danny's Place on business.

The show went on, but nothing interested Seamus once Lili's part was over. When the last dancer tapped her way off-stage, Seamus gave the waitress a sizeable tip to ask Miss Moreno if he could speak to her for a few minutes.

"She don't have nothing to do with customers." Her tone was slightly disapproving. "You'd have better luck with one of the others."

"Please tell her I'm investigating a missing person and need her help." It was partially true, though the singer had probably already been interviewed by the police.

Sniffing as if to say it was a hopeless task, the girl put the money into her cleavage and went off. A few minutes later she was back, her wide eyes signaling surprise. "Lili says you can come backstage."

He followed her along the side wall and up the steps to the right of the stage. Behind the curtain, Lili Moreno stood waiting. Women in costume and men with set pieces moved around her, but she hardly noticed. They glanced at Seamus, no doubt wondering why a gorgeous creature like Lili waited for him with such an eager expression.

Up close she was even prettier, and he became tongue-tied in a way he hadn't been since high school. Apparently used to that reaction, Lili said, "You wanted to speak to me, detective?"

Though he struggled to gather his scattered thoughts, Seamus realized she thought he was from the police. Should he tell her the truth? When her dark eyes met his, he couldn't lie. "I'm Seamus Hanrahan, Miss Moreno, a private investigator. I—uh—I'm working on a case."

"Gail said it's a missing person?"

"I guess the police already talked to you about him."

"Oh." She was disappointed. "I thought—" She didn't finish the sentence but said instead, "I never met that man they're looking for."

He didn't know what to say next. "I appreciate your time, Miss Moreno."

Now it was she who was nervous. "I wonder—" She lowered her voice, though the backstage shuffling made it difficult to hear. "Do you help the police solve crimes?"

Something in her tone signaled worry, and he figured Danny's Place had secrets the police might want to know about. Illegal gambling, maybe, or drugs for a few choice guests. "I'm only here to find out if anyone knows where Arthur Jameson went when he left here," he said, trying to reassure her. "I've got no interest in what else goes on in this place."

Instead of relief, he saw her disappointment deepen. "It's one of the dancers. She hasn't come to work since the night Mr. Jameson disappeared."

His interest quickened. "Someone else is missing?"

Her slender shoulders rose and fell. "Danny says she probably got a better job. It's just that she had a costume idea for me, and she said she'd bring in a sketch the next day." She leaned toward him, her brown eyes earnest. "Why did she say that if she meant to quit?"

He could think of a half-dozen reasons, but he was so thrilled to have Lili's face close to his that he kept them to himself. "Maybe we could meet somewhere tomorrow and talk."

She backed away abruptly, a raised brow betraying annoyance. "I don't think so."

"If you're worried about your friend—"

"She isn't my friend." Her voice had gone cold. "I made a mistake, Mr.—"

"Hanrahan. Seamus Hanrahan."

"Mr. Hanrahan. It was nice meeting you." The words were mere politeness.

He'd played it wrong. "I'd like to see you again. If you're free for dinner some night, I mean, you've got to eat, right? We could—"

"I don't think we'll see each other again."

She walked away, her spine straight. As he watched her graceful movements, the back view every bit as nice as the front, Seamus promised himself that Lili Moreno was wrong. They would meet again.

Chapter Three

Mike was breaking in a new clerk at the ship's clothing store. Because of the constant coming and going of personnel, he was almost always breaking in a new person somewhere, but he didn't seem to mind. He was, as one might expect of an angel, patient, kind, and encouraging. What some didn't expect, but was true nevertheless, was that he was also fun to be around and occasionally sarcastic.

When Seamus entered, Mike was showing a woman whose badge said BRENDA how to locate clothing a client wanted or needed for any occasion. There was no secret to it, and guests could have done it themselves, but Mike said a human presence reassured newcomers. Seeing Seamus, Brenda stepped forward and asked briskly, "How can I help you?" Mike said something, and she stepped back again.

"Thanks for coming to meet me, Seamus," Mike said. "It's been a busy morning."

"No problem. Is the case you mentioned a go?"

His smooth forehead crinkled in regret. "The lady has decided against knowing how she died. I think she's afraid you'll find that her son poisoned her in order to inherit her money."

"And was it him?"

"What goes on back there isn't our concern." Mike punched Seamus playfully on the arm. "We leave it to guys like you to find answers our clients need, while we look ahead." He glanced at Brenda, who was practicing with the huge conveyer belt behind the counter. She pressed the start button, stopped it to look at something that caught her eye, then started it up again. The soft whir of the moving rack kept their conversation private.

"You've been restless lately—more restless than usual, I mean. Is there something we should talk about?"

There was no way to explain ennui, regret, and general malaise to an angel. Mike would try to understand, and given his experience with eons of humanity, he would comprehend on some level. But even inside Seamus' head, his complaints sounded whiny. *I can't decide what to do, even after all this time.* That was it, but said out loud, it sounded ridiculous.

Despite his claim to Ronnie, there were things Seamus didn't know about his own murder, and he was afraid he didn't *want* to know. Like the client who'd decided not to engage his services, Seamus was afraid of the answers.

"I tell you what, Mike. When I'm ready to talk, I'll come to you."

Seamus found Ronnie on the deck, talking to a couple of cross-backs he knew slightly. "Rayburn, Keuchel, how's it going?"

"Good, Seamus," Keuchel replied. "Ronnie says you've got a case?"

He shook his head. "I guess the lady decided against it."

"Chicken, huh?" Rayburn huffed in disgust. "Scared of the truth."

Noting the glare Seamus cast on him, Ronnie stepped in. "Everybody's got his own pace, right? We help out when they're ready."

"I can't see how avoiding the facts helps." Keuchel rolled his shoulders in a characteristic movement. "I died in Afghanistan because I wasn't careful enough, but I faced up to what happened. I accept it."

"Then why are you still here?" Ronnie said. "What are you waiting for?"

"Lunch, mostly." He shifted his feet and did the shoulder shrug again. "I'll admit I miss the world. I didn't get much of a chance to experience it, you know? Going back is a little like being alive." He frowned. "Wouldn't let them send me back to a war zone, though. That would be bad."

"Yeah," Ronnie said. "I wouldn't want to go back to Everest, either."

"You died on Mt. Everest?" Rayburn's expression was disbelieving.

"My dad was a climber." Ronnie's tone was casual. "We were doing okay until we got caught in a storm two days' trek from the top." She bit her bottom lip. "I just hope Dad made it back down."

"Yeah," Keuchel said. Rayburn nodded solemnly. Seamus examined the support post beside him.

"Well, we have someplace to be," Ronnie told them. "See you guys around."

As they rode down in the elevator, Seamus thought Ronnie was waiting for him to call her on the lie, but he didn't. She avoided the truth. So what? He couldn't face his own unpleasant past. Why should she?

When they'd ordered Artie's special of the day, stew with cornbread on the side, Seamus said, "I'm thinking about crossing-back on my own account."

She'd been unwrapping her straw, and she stopped with the paper in one hand and the straw in the other. "You mean your murder?"

"Yeah."

"But you said your wife—" Plunging the straw into her drink, she finished, "You said she was involved. Are you sure you want to go through that?"

"I need to know all of it."

Artie approached and set down two bowls of chili, a plate of hot cornbread, and a container of whipped butter. "Anything else, you two?"

"We're good," Seamus assured him, and Artie retreated to the kitchen.

Ronnie kept her eyes on the slab of cornbread she was buttering as she offered, "I could do it for you."

"I appreciate that, but I have to go." He tried for levity. "It's not like I'm new at this."

"No, you're not." She took a bite of bread, added a spoonful of stew, and chewed for a few moments. "You know how difficult it is being there but not really there. It's hard to find stuff out." She met his gaze. "It would be especially hard to jump around in the heads of people you liked—or loved."

He pushed her arguments aside with a gesture. "You heard what Keuchel said. It's over now. I should be able to face it."

Ronnie took another bite, chewed, and swallowed. "That doesn't mean it'll be easy."

"Maybe so, but I have to do it."

"Okay." She took a breath. "Why don't I go along?"

He paused with the spoon halfway to his mouth. "You mean we'd work together again?"

"When we get there, you could pick somebody you don't know and stick with him, a cop, maybe. That will get us information on the official inquiry. I could host with people you knew." She tried for a joke. "You won't have to hear what they think about your bad breath and all."

"What would you know about my breath?"

"You drink coffee all day long. You used to smoke too, I bet." She paused, distracted for a moment. "I wonder how they take away the craving for stuff like cigarettes here."

He could have told her that for some time he'd insisted on continuing to smoke as a way of holding onto the person he'd been. Only recently had he admitted it was an empty rebellion.

Returning to her point, Ronnie said teasingly, "Coffee all day. Cigarettes. You *had* to have bad breath, and you probably used Sen-Sen to cover it up."

He chuckled at her blunt honesty. "I'm surprised you've even heard of that stuff." Sobering, he considered her proposal. Ronnie was smart, and she might keep him from doing something stupid, like interfering with the lives of those he'd left behind. She'd find out things he was ashamed of, but he knew her well enough to know she'd be discreet about it.

"You're probably right." He pointed his spoon at her. "I'd say I've been waiting for someone like you all my life, but—"

Ronnie grinned as she finished the joke. "But really, you've been waiting for a girl like me all your death."

Peg Herring

***

Their Second Meeting: February 12, 1950

The day after they met at Danny's Place, Seamus was waiting when Lili Moreno entered the inexpensive restaurant where she usually ate her dinner. He rose from the wooden bench seat, watching her surprised look of recognition shift to irritation. She was as lovely in a navy blue skirt, white blouse, and plain, long brown overcoat as she'd been in an evening gown the night before.

"How did you find me?"

"I'm a detective, remember?" He pointed to the seat opposite him. "Won't you sit down?"

A brief mental argument showed on her face. If she walked away, he could simply show up somewhere else. Resigned, she sat down, put her hands on the table, and folded them into a knot. "You have the wrong idea about me." She spoke carefully, as if thinking about each word before she said it.

Meeting her gaze with all the earnestness he could muster, Seamus replied, "I don't have any ideas about you, Miss Moreno. I like your singing. I like you. If we sit here, have a meal together, and talk, we might learn we have things in common. If that's not the case, I'll take my hat and go, leaving you alone forever." He picked up his hat from the bench beside him and set it comically askew on his head to demonstrate the truth of his claim. "What do you say? Just dinner, and then you go off to do your work and I go off to do mine."

She sighed. "All right, but my name is Lee, not Lili. And you have to promise you won't show up at Danny's anymore."

"That's easy." He took off his hat and returned it to the bench. "My case got solved, so I have no reason to go there again."

"You found Mr. Jameson?"

"Not me. The police." He lowered his tone, speaking gently. "You were right to be concerned about the girl. She was in the car with him when they slid on the ice and went into the river. It'll be in the papers tomorrow, but a friend on the force called to let me know."

"Oh no!"

"I'm sorry."

Lee bit her lip. "Thank you. We weren't close friends, but Tina was nice to me. Most of them—" She didn't finish.

"—Are jealous cats who go out of their way to make your life miserable?"

She didn't answer, but he judged from her silence it was true.

"The police think Tina and that man were on a—" She fumbled for the proper word. "—a date?"

"That's what it looks like. She didn't mention she was seeing him?"

"We only talked about costumes." Lee was clearly ready to drop the subject, and she turned to the approaching waitress with what looked like relief.

By the time the meal was over, Lee had agreed to see Seamus again, though he had to plead a little. Repeating her admonition that he not come to the club, she agreed to meet him at the theater on

Sunday, her only night off, to see *She Wore a Yellow Ribbon.* "John Wayne's one of my favorite actors," she said.

He would have paid to watch kittens napping if it was something Lee wanted to do.

Seamus thought Lee liked him a little, but she wasn't a woman who trusted easily. She told him almost nothing about herself, asking questions instead. Seamus told her about his childhood in Jefferson Park, his career as a cop, interrupted and later ended by the war, and his present arrangement with attorney Len Dobbleman, who'd served with Seamus in the Philippines. "I do investigations for him in lieu of rent," Seamus explained, "and I earn the groceries doing my own."

Brown eyes regarded him intently. "And that's what brought you to Danny's."

"Right. Mrs. Jameson hired me when her husband went missing."

"Poor woman!" Lee said. "Not only did she lose her husband, but there'll be a scandal surrounding his death."

Seamus was less than sympathetic. "I think she'll weather the storm. The lady's got lots of reasons to keep her chin up, and they're all in the bank."

Though he tried not to dominate the conversation, his questions for Lee brought only minimal answers. He learned she was twenty-two (fifteen years his junior, but he tried not to think about that), alone in the world, and not particularly thrilled with being a nightclub singer.

"I need the money," she said when he asked why she'd taken the job. "Singing pays a lot better than slinging hash." She glanced up to make sure the waitress hadn't heard her.

"But you're good," Seamus told her. "Really good."

She sniffed. "So are a thousand other girls in Chicago, including at least three in the chorus at Danny's who hope I break a leg or get pneumonia." After the waitress refilled Seamus' coffee cup for the third time, she went on, "You have to really want to be a hit to make it in show business, and honestly, I don't." She fingered the silverware next to her plate. "Mostly I want to be out of there for good."

Seamus fought the urge to immediately offer her freedom from the job she hated. Though it was too soon to tell her so, he was certain Lee Moreno was the woman he'd been looking for his whole life.

What did she see when she looked at him? A guy with more than a decade on her, a bum knee, and a face that had never been compared to Barrymore's. *Take it slow*, he cautioned himself. *This girl is something, but if you're going to have any chance with her at all, you have to be patient.*

Keeping that in mind, Seamus spoke only of cases he'd had, friends he'd known, and minor scrapes he'd gotten into as a kid. He made Lee smile several times, and she even laughed once when he told a story about a comrade in France who'd unearthed a cache of wine and tried to finish it before anyone else found out. All in all, he considered his first dinner with his future wife a huge success.

Chapter Four

Seamus and Ronnie went to Mike and explained their plan. Though sympathetic, Mike referred them to Gabe, head of operations on the ship. "It's unusual, going back to investigate your own death, but Gabe allowed it before, right?"

"He let a woman go with me to investigate her own murder."

"And you've got a chaperone." Mike smiled at Ronnie. "Can I talk to Seamus for a second?"

She backed away, giving Seamus an encouraging look. "I'll wait outside."

When she was gone, Mike asked, "Why now, Seamus? Why after all this time?"

Seamus couldn't lie to Mike. It wasn't magic or any kind of trick. He was just a guy—not a guy—a *being* he had to be straight with. "I've started forgetting things."

Mike nodded soberly. "It amazes me you've kept your memories this long."

Seamus ran his fingers along the brim of the hat he'd politely removed when entering Mike's presence. "I work at it."

"Most people forget anyway."

Seamus grimaced. "I had a lot of incentive."

With a sigh Mike said, "Okay, I'll tell Gabe to expect you." As Seamus turned away, he added, "Be careful back there. I understand it's different when the experience is personal."

Dead to Get Ready—and Go

***

The Courtship: Winter/Spring, 1950

Seamus began arranging his schedule to leave the afternoons free. He showed up wherever Lee was, insisting it was Fate that had guided him there. She tried to be stern and resist his invitations, but he wracked his brain to come up with proposals she couldn't refuse. When the air warmed, he packed a picnic basket and took her to Grant Park for bologna sandwiches and chocolate chip cookies. They watched graceful sailboats dance on the lake, discussing what it would be like to slice through the water with the wind in their hair. Another time he took her to a Cubs game, where he taught her the finer points of judging balls and strikes. They rode the ferries that traversed the river, pointing out landmarks as they leaned on the railing. He bought her flowers.

Lee was different from other women Seamus knew. Listening to her thoughtful comments on social issues, he came to respect her intelligence and unique perspectives as much as her beauty and talent.

After several months, he was no closer to understanding what made Lee tick. It was clear she hated her job—the smoky club, the raucous crowds, the spiteful women who wanted to be in her place. Still, she did her best, spending hours rehearsing with the musicians and making her costumes herself. With a grim chuckle she told Seamus, "I'd much rather make my own outfits than wear anything Danny Proust would choose for me."

Lee never spoke of her past, her people, where she came from, or what she hoped for the future. She seemed to look no farther than the next show, though he noted with pleasure that after a few weeks she revealed anticipation for their dates, not overtly, but with hopeful comments for fair weather and no unforeseen impediments. Their relationship was odd. For all Seamus knew, Lee had been born yesterday and might be gone tomorrow.

In addition to being reticent, Lee allowed no physical intimacy. If Seamus touched her arm to guide her on the street or help her onto a bus, she flinched. When he put his hand on hers, she pulled it away. And when he thought about kissing her full, tantalizing lips, she seemed to read his mind and turn cold and forbidding.

It drove him crazy.

She even refused to tell him where she lived. They always met at an agreed-upon place, and when their date was over, Lee waited for Seamus to walk away before going off in a different direction. The detective in him wanted to follow and learn what the secret was, but he reminded himself that Lee wasn't a case he'd taken on. She was...

What? His girlfriend?

In darker moments he fretted about what Lee would say if they ran into someone she knew. Would she introduce Seamus as her friend? Her gentleman friend? Her boyfriend? None of those sounded right, but he couldn't figure out what she would call him. It drove him nuts.

In mid-August, Seamus made a discovery that changed everything. They'd spent a Sunday afternoon together, walking through the park then window shopping along State Street. Though he pointed out interesting displays in Marshall Fields' many windows, Lee seemed distracted. She'd been quiet all day, answering his questions minimally and biting her lip the way she did when she was worried about something.

"What are you thinking about, Honey Girl?"

"Nothing." It came too quickly, and her tone was dismissive.

"If you've got a problem, I might be able to help."

Lee's smile was wistful, as if she wished it were so. After a moment she said, "There's nothing wrong. Really."

He didn't believe her, but when Lee wasn't willing to talk about something, there was no use in nattering on about it.

When they parted, he expressed worry about her traveling the streets alone, as he'd often done before. As always, she smiled away his concern. "I did it for a long time before we met, Seamus. I'll be fine."

Once he was a few blocks away, his arm brushed against something in his suitcoat pocket, and Seamus realized he still had the small change-purse Lee carried with her. Her dress had no pockets, and he'd offered to hold it while she fed the remains of their picnic lunch to some ducks along the lakeshore. Hurrying back the way he'd come, he peered down the side streets in hopes of catching a glimpse of her.

For several blocks he ducked and dived on the wide sidewalks, trying to see around the people and the colorful awnings on most of the buildings. He saw nothing until he reached the narrow street that led to Danny's Place. A figure in a long, slim dress disappeared around a building as he watched. Limping after her, Seamus paused when he neared the club. Ahead of him, Lee was unlocking the front door. Stuffing her cotton glove between the door and the frame, she kept it ajar while she replaced the key atop a decorative panel. Retrieving her glove, she disappeared inside.

Why was she at the club on a Sunday?

Knowing Lee would be angry to learn he'd followed her, Seamus waited. When she got whatever she'd come for and left, he could "accidentally" bump into her on the street and return the purse, allowing Lee to believe her secret was safe. It was a strange thing to do for a girl, but he didn't want to lose this one. That meant respecting her privacy.

He waited outside for a half hour, but Lee never came back out. Leaning against a convenient building, Seamus considered other possible ways to return the purse. He could come back when the club was open, but Lee had made it clear she wanted to keep their relationship—whatever she thought it was—separate from her place of employment. He could knock on the door and hand it to her, but then she'd know he'd followed her.

As he considered his options, a man came across the parking lot from the street on the opposite side. He brought to mind Lee Savold, the American recently named world heavyweight boxing champion. Despite a slightly flattened look to his face, he had the muscular build and tall stature women everywhere seem to find attractive. Seamus recognized him as the club's bouncer, a man named Murray. Taking a key from its hiding place, Murray let himself in, holding the door open with his foot while he replaced the key.

Jealousy reared its head, but Seamus tried to fight it. This didn't have to be a lovers' meeting. When Lee spoke of Murray, she hadn't seemed fond of him. The jealousy kept coming back. If Lee was involved with the guy, it explained why she wanted Seamus to stay away from the club. Had she been letting him pay her way to movies and buy her dinners while she saved her kisses for a man with muscles on top of muscles? Suddenly he was sure Lee considered him a chump. Her real affection went to someone younger, more virile, and better-looking than Seamus Hanrahan, gimp.

He had to know.

Though most of him realized it was a bad idea, he took the key from where Lee had left it and let himself in, taking pains to be as quiet as possible about it.

There was no one in the lobby or the dining room, which seemed downright gloomy without lights and the bustle of activity. The red draperies looked vaguely threatening, as if they might be hiding something evil, like the lies he'd been told—or at least allowed to believe.

The empty tables seemed forlorn, but that might have been Seamus' fading happiness. Recalling his initial visit to Danny's, he knew that behind the stage were dressing rooms for the girls and storage for props, set-pieces, and costumes. That part of the building was silent, but he heard footsteps above. The man trudged slowly up a set of stairs, no doubt expecting to find Lee waiting for him.

The staircase was at the left side of the stage. Recalling his previous visit, Seamus knew it led to a loft that served as the roof of the stage. Stretching across it was a balcony rail with an array of can lights attached to its base and aimed at the stage. He'd seen a man he assumed was Danny Proust standing at the railing, surveying the crowd below like a duke on the castle parapet. Concentrating on the image in his memory, Seamus remembered that a few feet behind the railing was a wall with a single door marked Private.

Setting his foot on the bottom step, Seamus looked up the stairs, where a faint shaft of light showed down a corridor that ran toward the back wall. Somewhere up there a man spoke, and a woman answered. Seamus was halfway up the stairs before he could stop himself.

He did stop halfway up, aware that what he was doing was wrong. Trespass for sure, but worse, betrayal of Lee's closely-guarded privacy. If she wanted him here, she'd have invited him.

He should leave.

There were a dozen reasons why she might meet a fellow employee at the club. He tried to think of one that satisfied his jealousy.

There was none.

If he confronted her this way, it meant the end of their relationship. Lee would never forgive him for spying, for embarrassing her, for thinking what he was thinking. He was angry, he was jealous, and he was irrational.

He had to give his emotions a chance to cool.

Rationality won. Seamus wanted to act from conviction, not emotion. He'd ask Lee about it later and use his observational skills to see if she was lying.

He'd be a man about it.

Turning, he started back down the stairs. He'd leave the purse on the counter in the coat-check room. Lee had mentioned the girl who worked back there was as close as she had to a friend at Danny's, so she'd see—

That's when the noise from upstairs changed. There was no scream. It was more like an involuntary objection. The man's voice rose, taunting in tone. Lee said something back, angry but at the same time fearful.

He was up the stairs in seconds. Down the hallway were two doors, each standing open. The first room was empty, and Seamus caught only the impression of a masculine presence. In the second he found Lee. Murray held her by the shoulders, grinning as she fought to free herself. Neither of them noticed Seamus until he spoke. "Let her go!"

"Seamus!" Lee's expression revealed surprise, alarm, and relief.

The bouncer pushed Lee away so hard she staggered against the bed behind her. "Who are you?"

"Lee's friend. I don't think she wants your company."

Looking him over, the big man came to a conclusion. "Mind your own business, pal, or you're going to get hurt."

Seamus rubbed at his jaw as if he were thinking about it. Actually, he was considering how he'd go about taking the man-mountain down. After a moment he said, "Sorry, friend, but I can't mind my own business in this case. You see, I like this girl a lot."

In answer Murray took a swipe at Seamus that would have sent him to the floor if he hadn't been ready. Ducking the oversized fist, he stepped in quickly and delivered two quick blows, one to the bouncer's gut and one to his jaw.

Murray hardly noticed.

Seamus stepped back but the big man followed, landing an uppercut that made his head spin. Seamus managed to remain on his feet, but a follow-up blow to the ribs sent the air whooshing from his lungs. He staggered backward, raising his hands in an attempt to appear ready to defend himself. Actually he was coming to terms with the idea he was probably going to be beaten to death right then and there.

Murray stood back for a second, savoring Seamus' suffering. Then he wasn't standing at all. He swayed, his eyes rolled upward, and he collapsed like a dropped shirt, unable to save his jaw from hitting the floor.

Behind him Lee held a lamp in both hands, ready to strike again if necessary.

"Are you all right, Seamus?"

He was just getting his breath back. "I think so."

"What are you doing here?"

He stammered like a schoolboy caught cheating. "You, um, you forgot your purse and I thought, um—was afraid you'd need money for the streetcar."

"And how did you get in?"

He gestured at the man on the floor, dazed but already stirring. "Shouldn't we discuss this somewhere else?"

"You're right." Snatching up her coat Lee said, "Can you walk?"

Seamus nodded, though he still wasn't getting much air into his lungs. He guessed he'd cracked a rib, but since he'd already been rescued by a woman, he wasn't about to admit it, nor how much the beating had hurt.

Lee took his arm, helping him down the stairs and out of the club. It was cold, and already the sky was turning dark. "There's a

Chinese restaurant close by that's open on Sundays," she said, pointing north. "We can go there."

The place was almost empty, the patrons mostly Asian. Leaning on Lee more than he wanted to, Seamus half-collapsed onto the oilcloth-covered bench seat. Taking the seat opposite him, Lee ordered tea for them both. Once the owner went to fetch it she said, "Tell me how you got into the club."

With her dark eyes focused on him, there was nothing Seamus could do but tell the truth. As he spoke, trying desperately to make himself sound like something less than a complete heel, Lee's face revealed nothing. Did she blame him for sneaking around after her? Despise him for his inept attempt to save her from Murray the Bouncer?

You've done it, he thought. *You had a great thing going with a wonderful girl, and you ruined it.*

Which made it all the more surprising when Lee began to cry.

Seamus moved to her side, and before he knew it she was in his arms. Ignoring the stabs of pain from his ribs, he held her, trying to comprehend phrases uttered between sobs. "I—didn't—anywhere to—live!" came from the vicinity of his breast pocket. "My mother— (indecipherable something)–tramp!"

When Lee calmed a little, she was better able to tell the story. She'd taken the job as a nightclub singer in order to provide for her mother and four siblings. Danny had offered more money than she'd ever imagined, and a friend had urged her to accept, claiming her fortune would be made. She'd rise in the entertainment world. She'd be the next Rosemary Clooney.

It hadn't worked out that way. Though she was a popular draw for the club, it wasn't a nice place to work. Her co-workers were unfriendly; some of them were dishonest. The females were jealous of her, and the men gave them cause to be. And worst of all, when her mother found out where the money was coming from, she'd called Lee horrible names and thrown her out of their home.

"That's not fair," Seamus objected. Lee shook her head.

"You don't know my mother." Sitting up, she took the handkerchief Seamus offered and wiped her nose and eyes. "Danny just laughed when I told him. He said I could stay in one of the rooms upstairs." Seamus had a vague memory of a couch, a battered night stand, and a few hooks on the wall with clothing on them.

"Did the offer come from his kind heart, or are there strings attached?"

Lee licked her lips. "Danny Proust does nothing out of goodness, and he has no heart. It was mostly because he didn't want me to quit the club. People were starting to hear about me, and he was making lots of money." She pressed her lips together. "When he offered the room, Danny didn't mention that Murray lived next door."

"And he gives you a hard time."

She shrugged. "Before today he only said things. He'd 'accidentally' touch me when we passed in the hallway but he was afraid I'd tell Danny if he did more than that."

"What changed today?"

Her gaze slid to the tabletop. "I don't know."

Tears came again, and Seamus waited, wondering irrelevantly how someone could be so beautiful with red eyes and a runny nose. When she calmed a little he asked, "That's why you hate Danny's Place—because of Murray?"

"He's part of it." She paused then said merely, "It's a terrible place."

He thought of the men who came to Danny's to leer at Lili Moreno and fantasize about taking her to bed. That led him to wonder about Proust himself. What was his attitude toward his star singer? "Does Proust, um, bother you?"

Lee shook her head. "Danny looks at me like I'm Christmas dinner sometimes, but he's been with Patti for years, and Patti's the jealous type." She chuckled, though there wasn't much humor in it. "Danny's scared of Patti, and Murray's scared of Danny, so my virtue remains intact."

"I heard Danny's brother is his manager? Is he okay?"

"Frankie's a creep, but he leaves me alone. The rumor is he doesn't like girls."

"So the guys you work with are all crumbs, but they didn't bother you until now."

"Things have been strange lately. I've had the feeling they were talking about me, you know?"

"So what happened just now?"

She bit her lip. "I was reading. I heard Murray come up the stairs, but I didn't think anything of it. Then he opened the door without even knocking and started saying things—" Her face flushed at the memory, but she didn't repeat Murray's threats verbatim. "I told him he should leave or I'd tell Danny, but he just laughed. He said—" Again she didn't elaborate. "Then you came along." She smiled for the first time. "My knight in shining armor."

"Some knight."

"You distracted him so I could move in and whack him. We were a team."

Seamus' expression turned serious. "Lee, you can't go back there."

"I'm saving up to get an apartment of my own, but—" A third time Seamus thought she changed what she'd meant to say. "It's harder than I thought."

Before he realized it, Seamus heard himself saying, "Marry me, Lee. You won't have to sing for drunks. You won't have to fight off your boss and his hired goon. You won't have to ever see Danny's Place again."

"I can't." Tears pooled in her eyes, still wet from earlier ones.

"Why not?"

Once more he got the sense she changed what she might have said. "I'm not a respectable woman."

"Does that come from your mother? I don't know her, Lee, but she's wrong. You're as respectable as anyone I've ever met." He raised his hands, trying to lighten the moment. "Besides, P.I.'s aren't all that respectable. If I respect you and you respect me, who else do we care about?"

She blew her nose. "You're only asking because you feel sorry for me."

"I definitely do not feel sorry for you, Lee. I love you." The words hung between them for a moment. When Lee said nothing, he switched to a different argument. "You can't go back. That guy isn't going to be happy with you for hitting him over the head." Touching his ribs he added, "Thanks for that, by the way."

"You'd have beaten him." She set her elbows on the table. "I just hurried things along."

He snorted a laugh but returned to his point. "I think you should accept my offer."

Lee turned away. "You don't really want to marry me."

"That's not true." He pulled a small box from his pocket. "I've been thinking about it since the day we met. I just wanted to give you time to—to like me a little. I'm no Rock Hudson, and I'm gimpy—"

"Seamus!" She seemed genuinely surprised. "You're a wonderful man, good and kind and handsome too."

He held out the box with the tiny diamond ring nestled inside. "Then marry me."

He thought for a moment she was considering it, but she pushed the ring away. "You can't saddle yourself with someone like me. I'm—I'm a nobody. I'm worse than nobody. I'm—I'm—" She never finished the sentence, because he pulled her close and kissed her. At first she didn't respond, but when she did, Seamus thought it was a good thing he was sitting down, because his head spun and his knees felt weak. However she presented herself to the outside world, Lee Moreno was not cold. Not when it mattered.

When the kiss finally ended, Lee tried to return to her arguments, but Seamus wore her down, answering each objection with a declaration of love. He'd caught her in a weak moment, but he told himself he'd make her love him. Not as much as he loved her, maybe, but enough. She liked his company. The kiss showed she was attracted to him, at least a little. From the months they'd known each other, he knew they shared many of the same views on life. They'd make a good couple. Believing this, Seamus kept asking Lee to marry him until she finally said yes.

Chapter Five

The aura in Gabe's office was serene. The current receptionist was a middle-aged man with a pleasant manner and an Irish accent. "I'll tell him you're here," he said, and in a short time they were ushered into Gabriel's presence.

Ronnie took the lead. "Seamus feels it's time to answer the remaining questions about his death. He and I would like to go back and investigate."

"I see." Gabe was so handsome he seemed unreal, like an airbrushed photo of a fashion model. Seamus thought him likable, though more reserved than Mike. Gabe turned to Seamus, his expression interested. "You're ready to know?"

"Yes."

"And it isn't likely you'd let anyone else conduct the investigation." His tone revealed understanding of Seamus' personality. There were rules here, but there was also understanding that no rule fits all situations.

Gabe turned back to Ronnie. "What will your role be?"

She grinned. "I'm the buffer. Any host Seamus doesn't feel comfortable with, I'll take."

A nod indicated approval, but he gave them a warning. "In order to work together, it's important you're truthful with each other."

"Of course—" Ronnie spoke too quickly, and Gabe raised a hand, palm out, to stop her.

"You're aware that you only get one chance to go back on a case. Therefore, neither of you should hold back any bit of information you learn, even if it's uncomfortable to tell it."

"I understand." Ronnie glanced at Seamus, who nodded but didn't speak.

"Very well." Gabe raised his hands in what might have been a blessing or simply a gesture of finality. "I hope you find what you seek."

"Thank you." Seamus bowed ever so slightly, and they backed away.

In the elevator, Ronnie shivered in relief. "He's something, isn't he?"

"Going into Gabe's presence is a little like being called to the principal's office." He rubbed his hands together. "But he gave his okay. Do you think that means this is the right thing to do?"

"I do." Ronnie changed the subject to distract her friend from the serious decision he'd just made. "Did you know they look different to each of us? Gabe looks like Denzel Washington to me, and Mike reminds me of my Uncle Lamont. Same complexion, you know?"

That got Seamus' attention. "You see them as black men?"

Ronnie shrugged. "To make us comfortable, they let us see what we're used to." The elevator chimed softly, and the doors opened. "When should we leave?"

They stepped out onto the deck. Seamus set his hat onto his head, pulling it snugly into place. "No time like the present. Shall we?" He held out his hand. Ronnie took it, and the darkness immediately enveloped them.

The Wedding: August, 1950

Lee never returned to Danny's Place. Seamus fretted for her reputation, since they were forced to live together until they could get a marriage license. "No one can say worse about me than my mother already has," Lee joked. Sobering, she put one hand on his chest. "Let's just be us and not worry what anyone else thinks, okay?"

He nodded, aware that when Lee touched him, he'd do absolutely anything she wanted.

Theirs was the simplest of weddings. Seamus had almost no family living, and most of his friends had moved on with their lives while he was in the army—those who hadn't died in Europe, Africa, or Japan. Lee claimed she had no one who cared enough to come, so their wedding party consisted of a minister, his wife (who played "O Promise Me" on the piano in her living room), and Seamus' two friends, Len Dobbleman, the lawyer he rented from, and Grant Wellman, a cop he'd worked with before the war.

Grant was now a detective, and while Seamus was happy for his friend's advancement, there was a distance between them neither wanted to acknowledge. Grant tried too hard to overlook Seamus' limp, as if he were embarrassed to be whole when his friend was not. Always an imposing physical specimen, Grant had come through the war unscathed, and Seamus, smaller, thinner, and lame, felt self-conscious standing next to him.

Seamus had been disappointed when Grant acted more like a cop than a friend. Told of the upcoming wedding, he'd asked a lot of questions about Lee that Seamus didn't want to hear.

"What do you know about this girl—I mean, beyond that she can sing and looks good in an evening gown?" When Seamus tried to explain, it just got worse. "She's staying at your place? Doesn't she have a family?" Grant's handsome face had twisted with concern, and it looked like he was biting his cheek to keep from saying more.

Though he knew Grant was only watching out for him, Seamus resented the insinuation that Lee was somehow suspect because she had no loving papa to hand her over at the altar. His buddy was thinking like an old-timer, Seamus told himself, while he saw Lee as a modern woman who'd made her own way in the world. It was something to be proud of, in his view, and not odd at all.

Things got a little better when Grant met Lee for the first time. "She's definitely a looker," he told Seamus afterward. "And she seems nice. Not much of a talker, but what guy doesn't appreciate that in a woman?"

Still, Grant urged Seamus to wait a month or so before going through with the marriage ceremony. Seamus ignored the advice. He was eager for the wedding, both for the sake of Lee's reputation and to finally have the woman of his dreams. He slept on two chairs pushed together in a corner of his studio, suffering the agony of having Lee sleeping in his bed, only a few feet away. He tossed and turned every night, and it wasn't just from the couch's stiffness.

When they went to the registry office to apply for a license, Lee listed her current address as 1950 Lake Street, giving Seamus an impish grin. No one questioned the fictional address. To the bored clerk they were just another couple eager to become man and wife.

Seamus had approached Len Dobbleman about leasing them the floor above their offices as an apartment. It was plenty spacious for two people, it had over-long, double-hung windows that let in lots of light, and, Lee noted with satisfaction, it was miles away from downtown and Danny's Place.

As Lee and Seamus stood holding hands beside the minister's horsehair couch, he admitted to himself that Lee's agreement to marry him came at least in part from desperation. Seamus offered her safety and security, but he hoped she knew he also offered real love, something no one else in her life seemed willing to give her. Lee said she was happy, and Seamus believed her because *he* was happy. And because he wanted to.

Chapter Six

As always, the pain of passing from the ship to Life was agonizing. And as always, two things made it bearable: keeping in mind it was temporary, and groaning. Seamus began it, but Ronnie joined in immediately. The feeling of falling a great distance while at the same time being ripped apart by invisible forces made it impossible to remain silent. When it seemed he could take no more, it was over, and Seamus found himself in a dark, silent place. Ronnie moaned once more beside him, and he squeezed her hand before releasing it. Of course there was no hand there, for they were now nothing but essence. Ghosts, he supposed, though he'd always disliked the term.

Now that he'd arrived, Seamus doubted his decision even more. Was he ready to face Lee, to see her reaction to his death? Would she cry, even a little, acknowledging the love he'd given her? Did she understand she'd betrayed a man who'd have done anything for her if she'd simply asked? Or had she been playing a role all along, secretly despising him as she followed some plan he didn't understand?

Whatever the truth was, he'd know it soon.

Their first task was to find a host. Since Gabe's plans were always well made, a living human would be near their landing spot, close enough to jump to. It had to be immediate, because without a host, they'd quickly lose the power they'd been given and be forced to return to the ship.

Seamus heard a door open. "Jump!" he ordered, at the same time launching himself at the dark shape entering the room. There was a moment of oddness as his essence passed into a living being, a feeling of weight as the cumbersome body enveloped him, and finally the surprised, "Oh!" as the host felt the wave of nausea and confusion brought on by two cross-backs taking up residence in his head.

When the figure touched the holstered gun on his hip in automatic reaction to a sense of trouble, Seamus realized their host was a cop. The feel of wool on his skin meant he was in uniform. One of Chicago's Finest.

Ronnie must have settled in lightly, because Seamus felt nothing after the initial jolt of his jump. Like her, he made himself as small as possible. Having two cross-backs was a burden on a host, but if they were still and quiet, the host would function with just a vague sense of illness, like a touch of the flu.

There could be no communication until their host went to sleep, because their voices were audible to him, like whispers from inside his mind. For now they'd listen and try to learn where they were, who their host was, and what he knew about Seamus' death.

The man was slightly near-sighted, so things at a distance were blurry. Nevertheless, Seamus recognized where he was: his own living room.

A hundred memories flooded his mind. Lee sitting in the wide, brown overstuffed chair with her feet pulled up, reading a hard-backed novel she'd borrowed from the library. His usual seat was on the other side of a small table, in a battered easy chair she'd been determined to replace. As the cop's gaze swept the room, other memories rose: Lee with a cold, sleeping on the couch because she didn't want to keep him awake with her coughing. Lee leaning against the kitchen doorway, her hair frizzy from the humidity of a July day, grinning and waving two bottles of chilled beer at him. Lee adjusting the antenna on their tiny black and white TV, looking to him for a thumbs-up when they achieved the best possible picture. Lee, Lee, Lee.

The cop's movement brought Seamus back to the present. On the wall was their wedding picture, which the man examined closely.

Seamus, wearing a suit only slightly different from the one he wore these days, looked dazed and a little unbelieving. Lee was beautiful, as always, her long, dark hair done up in an elegant French twist. Her dress was a pale blue sheath he'd bought her at Sears and Roebuck, and she held a single rose.

The Honeymoon: September, 1950

Despite her objections, his half-healed rib, and his protesting knee, Seamus carried his new wife over the threshold into the almost empty apartment. Used for storage until days before, it was now a large, mostly empty room with an ancient bathroom in one corner roughly partitioned off with sheet rock. Seamus had begun installing appliance hookups in the corner that would become the kitchen, but as yet there were only holes in the plaster with hoses sticking out.

"Welcome to the home of Mr. and Mrs. Hanrahan, as well as any future Hanrahan children," he told Lee as he swept her into his arms. She'd been laughing a moment before, but when he set her down on the bare wooden floor inside, there were tears on her face.

"What's the matter, Honey Girl?"

She couldn't speak for a few seconds, but finally she said, "This is a mistake. I made a mistake."

"Lee, I don't understand."

Sobbing, she put her face against his shoulder. "It isn't your fault. It's all mine. I thought—I thought I could do this, but I—I can't. It's all wrong."

Seamus held her until she stopped crying. Patting her hair he soothed, "Whatever's wrong, Lee, you can tell me. I want you to be happy. In fact, that's all I want for the rest of my life. If there's something—if I need to do something—just tell me, and I'll try to do it. I know I'm not the richest guy, but I'll work hard so you—"

She turned her back to him. "Seamus, it isn't money, and there isn't anything you can do. It's me."

He winced at the age-old excuse people use to avoid hurting each other. "Lee, you're perfect—exactly the woman I want. We're going to be fine, I promise."

She was quiet for a few moments. "Are you sure?"

"I'll always love you, Lee, whatever you've done; whatever you do."

It seemed to be enough, for she dried her tears, pushed a wayward strand of hair away from her face, and lightened the mood with a comment. "I'm noticing your priorities, Mr. Hanrahan. We have no cook-stove and no icebox, but we have a nice big bed."

"Well," he responded, "what kind of husband would I be if I didn't plan ahead?"

Chapter Seven

The first cop, whose name was Waite, was joined by a second, which made things easier for Seamus and Ronnie. The thoughts of the living were a jumbled mess, and cross-backs often had trouble gleaning useful information from among their hosts' concerns. Waite had a tooth that was starting to ache, regrets about a comment he'd made to his father at breakfast that morning, and a choice to make about where they'd stop for lunch. Conversation with his partner focused his thoughts, and Seamus listened carefully.

"No sign of the wife," the newcomer announced. "Some of her clothes are still in the closet, but no lady stuff in the bathroom. There's an imprint of a suitcase on the bed."

Waite glanced into the bedroom Seamus had partitioned from the rest of the apartment in the early days of their marriage. When he'd finished creating a ten-by-ten room, Lee had wallpapered it in a bright yellow floral. For him it had been the closest place to heaven on earth.

The double bed they'd shared was neatly made, but a rectangular dent demonstrated the truth of the cop's words. Seamus recalled buying a suitcase for Lee as a gift their first Christmas together. Inside it he'd put two train tickets to South Haven, Michigan, for a delayed honeymoon. She'd been thrilled—at least he'd thought so at the time. He was certain of nothing anymore.

Waite sighed. "She took off."

"Looks like it." The other cop sucked at his teeth. "Think she gave her old man a Lake Michigan bath before she left town?"

"Could be." Circling the room, Waite picked up a photo of Seamus and Lee at Burnham Park. It had been a sunny but windy day, and he'd had to chase her wide-brimmed hat across the grass several times. He recalled teasing, "Why don't I just hold onto it? I'll still love you if you get a freckle or two on your nose." In answer she'd given him an odd look he'd noticed before but could never decipher.

"Pretty woman, eh, Joe?" The younger cop was peering over the other's shoulder. "Them's the ones you gotta watch out for."

Waite took the photo from its frame. "Here, Malloy. See if anybody in the building can tell us where she might have gone."

The younger cop snickered. "My guess is she's travelling with the fellow who's took this guy's place."

As Waite moved around the room, Seamus caught a glimpse of his host's face in a small wall mirror. He hadn't met many Negro cops in Chicago, but Waite was as black a man as he'd ever seen. Malloy seemed perfectly at ease with having a Negro partner, perhaps because he was younger and less experienced. In fact, his belt and holster were so new they squeaked when he moved.

Feeling a slight tremor in Waite's body, Seamus guessed Ronnie had jumped to Malloy. He approved, both because it would be easier on Waite and because they'd glean more information from two hosts. While the men slept, he and Ronnie could compare information telepathically, which their hosts would interpret only as odd dreams.

Seamus was both eager and anxious about what they would learn. The police officers' suspicions were the same as his, and they didn't know the half of it. When she learned the details of his death, Ronnie would no doubt pity a man whose wife had wanted him dead so much she'd taken action to achieve her desire. Still, he was determined to face it, to find out everything. What Ronnie or anyone else concluded was of no consequence. He wanted the whole truth.

Seamus observed as Officer Joseph Waite meticulously noted details of his search of the apartment. When Officer Malloy returned from interviewing the others in the building, Waite entered the meager bits he gleaned neatly into the same small notebook. Finished, the two men returned to the station, and Waite climbed the stairs to the second floor. There he approached a bored-looking detective whose nameplate said GRULKE.

"I've got the preliminary information you asked for on Seamus Hanrahan, Detective."

Grulke glanced at the stack of folders on his desk. "That the guy they fished out of Lake Michigan yesterday?"

"Yes, sir. The body was weighted but the rope broke, and a fisherman hooked it near Navy Pier."

"And the boys at the 18th pushed the case onto us." Grulke didn't sound pleased. "They can preach interagency cooperation all they want. Everybody in this town screws everybody else."

Waite suppressed impatience at the detective's lack of interest in a murder case the younger cop would have been happy to investigate. "The guy lived down here, so it's ours. Mr. Hanrahan was a private investigator."

That brought a derisive snort. "Stuck his nose into some bedroom and got killed for it, no doubt."

"His wife is missing, sir. Packed a suitcase and left."

"Ah." Rubbing his chin, Grulke switched theories. "Maybe he should have been watching his own bedroom." He wheezed a sigh that hinted at allergies. "I've got three other cases going, but leave your notes. I'll look into it." He turned away without offering thanks for the work Waite had done to save him time and effort. Seamus felt a rush of anger from the young patrolman, but it faded quickly. He was used to being on a lower rung, at work and almost everywhere else.

As Waite hesitated, not sure if he'd been dismissed, Seamus took the opportunity to jump to the detective. Enthusiastic or not, Grulke was in charge of the case, and information would flow to him. The man winced as the weight of Seamus' presence hit, and he tapped his diaphragm with a fist.

Guessing he was free to go, Waite left, his expression blank. When Grulke finished the report he'd been preparing, he turned to the notes Waite had provided. Seamus listened eagerly, but the detective asked himself no questions as he scanned the information. Another detective who was passing the desk paused to ask, "What you got there, Pete?"

"Just what I needed." Grulke shoved the notes aside. "The guy they pulled out of the lake yesterday was murdered, and his wife is missing. Want to bet she talked some idiot into taking her husband for a night-time boat ride?"

"The joys of marriage, hey?"

"When we track the wife down, we'll find the killer toting her suitcase and opening doors for her."

The other man shook his head. "Did you hear about the detective that got shot downtown?"

That piqued Grulke's interest. "What happened?"

"From what I heard, he was driving along in his car and somebody shot him."

"He didn't see who it was?"

"He's unconscious. They're not sure he's even gonna make it." He gestured at the files on Grulke's desk. "Better get your cases squared away. Everybody'll be expected to help out, since it's an attack on a cop."

Grulke made a dismissive gesture at the notes before him. "This one won't be much. I just have to track down the Widow Hanrahan and find out who she was sleeping with besides Mr. Hanrahan."

Seamus bit his tongue—at least metaphorically. He hated his death turning into a cuckolded husband joke.

What a dope. He trusted his wife.

Poor schmuck missed all the signs.

He hadn't missed them. He'd simply refused to face them.

***

The ride to the police station was nerve-wracking for Ronnie. Malloy didn't buckle his seat belt when he got into the car, which she realized was because there was no belt to fasten. As they rounded corners and stopped at intersections, Ronnie felt jostled and slightly naked. *Don't people in this era know how dangerous it is to ride around all loose like that?*

She waited downstairs with Dean Malloy while his partner went up to report to Detective Grulke. Malloy told his fellow officers about the day's events, gratified to have something to talk about other than traffic stops and petty thefts. He milked it a little, describing the dead man's injuries, the couple's apartment, and the signs that the wife had packed a bag before leaving.

"You can't trust women," he concluded. "Guy ends up floating in Lake Michigan and his wife is nowhere to be found."

"Is that why you're staying single, Malloy?" one cop asked. "Afraid your wife will do you in when she gets tired of you?"

"It's possible!" he answered. "But why settle for one when there are so many girls out there?"

"If I had as much luck with the ladies as you do, I woulda never got married," another man put in. "What you got lined up for this weekend?"

"It wouldn't be the weekend without a date, now would it?" Malloy pretended to consider. "I think her name is Carole—with an *e*."

As the listeners made appreciative noises, Ronnie felt a wave of something pass through Malloy's mind. It felt like guilt.

"Just be ready to tell us all about it," the first guy ordered. "If I can't play the field no more, at least I can relive my glory days through your stories."

Malloy made a "can-do" gesture. "Sure thing, Bobby."

The guilt-like sensation passed again, and Ronnie realized the precinct Romeo wasn't as sure of himself as he pretended to be. He left the building, pulling his coat collar close against the cold March wind. "Carole with an *e* is quite a dish," he muttered as he headed for his car. "Too bad she doesn't know me from the Fuller Brush man."

Seamus grew frustrated that evening as Detective Grulke dozed off in his chair several times, jolting himself awake a few minutes later with his own snoring. Just after eleven, Grulke finally rose and went to bed, leaving his wife engrossed in a magazine called *Agonizing Love.*

As soon as his breathing slowed, Seamus put out a cautious call to Ronnie. "Here," she answered immediately.

"Are you still with Malloy?"

"Yeah. Nice kid, but he spends most of his time thinking about his looks and how to build his image as a ladies' man. I plan to jump back to Waite first chance I get."

"He seems the most interested in the case of anyone we've found so far."

"Joe Waite wants to become a homicide detective."

"That won't be easy for a black man in 1953, but his chances are better in Chicago than in most places."

"Still not easy," Ronnie opined.

With a grunt that signaled agreement, Seamus described the lead detective on the case. "Grulke isn't stupid, but he's no ball of fire. He's already made up his mind about what happened."

"And you haven't?" Her tone was challenging.

"What do you mean?"

"You say your wife planned your murder, but I haven't heard what makes you think that."

Remembering he'd promised to be honest with Ronnie, Seamus told his partner what he'd never told anyone before, living or dead. "When I met Lee, she was singing in a nightclub. She only accepted my marriage proposal because she wanted out of there."

Typically, Ronnie was direct. "Did she tell you that?"

"No, but I know she regretted marrying me. Sometimes she'd cry for no reason and say she'd made a mistake."

"Has anyone ever told you you've got an inferiority complex, Seamus? Why assume this mistake had anything to do with you?"

"I told you. She hated working at the club, and I offered her a way out. Once she married me, she wished she hadn't."

"If it was so bad at this nightclub, why did she take the job in the first place?"

"A friend of the family talked her into it, said she'd make lots of money and be the next big singing star in Chicago. He was right about her being popular, but within a few weeks Lee knew it wasn't for her."

"So she didn't want to be married and she didn't want to be famous. What did she want?"

"How would I know?" Grulke twitched in his sleep at the angry sound of Seamus' response. "Lee hated the club and just about everybody there. Once I convinced her I really wanted to marry her, she left and never went back."

"How long were the two of you married?"

"Two years—almost three."

"And things were okay between you?"

"I thought so at first. Lee got more relaxed after she left Danny's. She laughed more often. She even got so she teased me sometimes."

"But she had secrets."

"I didn't talk about the war. Lee didn't talk about her past. I figured that was how it had to be."

"Was she a good wife?"

His voice warmed. "The best. She took over a lot of the office stuff. She answered the phone, kept the books, and dealt with clients when I wasn't around." He spoke faster as good memories came to mind. "She was good around the house, too. She could make a meal from almost nothing, and she made the place look nice." He chuckled at the memory. "I didn't know my life was missing doilies until she started adding them everywhere."

"I noticed how cute your place looked."

"Lee made the curtains, refinished some end tables she got at a church rummage sale, and trimmed the lampshades with braid to make them match the furniture. They look like they came right from the Fair, don't they?"

"They do." Ronnie might have been suppressing a smile, but he went on anyway. He hadn't thought enough about the good times.

"She got the local Watkins man to sell her some liniment they thought would help my knee. She saved the containers the cottage cheese came in because they made pretty drinking glasses. She got a whole set of flatware by collecting Green Stamps. One day I came home to find she'd taken this wooden rack someone had built apart, because it blocked the light from one of our windows. She was always trying to make things better for us."

"It sounds like your wife *was* happy, Seamus."

His mood shifted. "Happiness is just something we let ourselves believe in when things are going good."

"What do you mean?"

He didn't answer for a while, but finally he said, "It's like all the stuff on the ship, the activities, the clothes, the food and everything. As long as a guy accepts it, it's good, right?"

"I guess most of the people back there are pretty happy, considering they're dead."

"Exactly. For me, reality keeps sticking its nose in, and that destroys the illusion."

"You're no romantic," Ronnie said wryly. "I think you might have been for a while, when things were good between you and Lee." After a moment she prompted, "What went wrong?"

"Little things." He was delaying, but Ronnie didn't let him get away with it.

"Give me an example."

"One day when I got home, I asked Lee what she'd done all afternoon. Just making conversation, you know?"

The image came to life in his mind. She'd been frying ham in a skillet, and on the counter beside the clunky old gas stove, a serving plate sat ready. On the back burner, a pan of potatoes bubbled, a wooden spoon laid across the top to prevent boil-over. In a bowl on the table were celery sticks, the fresh vegetables required by diet experts. Seamus recalled feeling like a happily married man as he took one and munched on it.

"Lee told me she'd gone to the office supply store to get some stuff we needed."

She hadn't turned from her cooking when she spoke. Planting a kiss on the back of her neck, he'd opened their secondhand refrigerator, noting that ice an inch thick had formed around the tiny freezing compartment. He promised himself he'd tackle it soon. Lee shouldn't have to chip away at it for hours. She was such a tiny thing—

Recalling that Ronnie was waiting, Seamus went on with the story. "I said to her, 'You must have seen the fire,' and Lee said, 'What fire?' She didn't know anything about it."

"It was a big fire?"

"The bus driver told me three crews fought it all afternoon."

He recalled his wife's profile, how her jaw had tightened at being caught in a lie.

"Lee said she forgot about it," he told Ronnie. "I laughed and asked, 'How do you forget a three-alarm fire?' She just shrugged, like it wasn't worth remembering."

Lee had said, "I got a new book from the library today, *My Cousin Rachel* by Daphne du Maurier." Her voice had been unnaturally high, and the words came out in a tumble. That had been the first hint there was something wrong with his marriage.

"She was nervous," he told Ronnie. "I knew she'd lied about where she went."

"So she didn't want to admit she strolled through Saks Fifth Avenue and drooled over expensive dresses and shoes," Ronnie said. "Not that big a deal."

"That was just the first time. After that it happened at least three more times. I'd ask about her day and she'd answer, but I could tell she was lying."

"Maybe—" Ronnie didn't finish. One lie she could dismiss, but many lies—no.

"She got more and more distracted, too. Once when I asked what she wanted me to bring home for dinner, she said, "Probably not the Cubs.""

"Something on her mind."

"Right. Then one day I stopped at the newspaper stand down the block, and the proprietor leaned over the counter confidentially. 'Pretty smart, Hanrahan,' he said, 'using that pretty wife of yours for undercover work.' Before I thought about it I said, 'My wife?' I saw right away he knew something I didn't."

That scene came to mind, the array of papers laid out for sale: the *Chicago Daily News*, the *Chicago Sun-Times*, the *Herald Examiner*, the *Chicago Herald-American, Chicago's American*, and others. Terrance had pushed his cap back, eager to tell what he'd seen. 'You should get her a different partner, though. It's too easy to tell the big guy is a cop.'"

Feeling Seamus' hesitation, Ronnie encouraged him to go on. "He'd seen Lee with another man."

"Not just another man. My former partner on the police force." His tone turned mocking, but it was himself he mocked. "My friend."

"Maybe they had a good reason for being out together."

"Then why did Lee lie? When she realized Terrance had seen them, she gave him some phony story about helping me out on a case."

"What did you do about it?"

Seamus' laugh was harsh. "What everybody does—at first. I decided there had to be a logical explanation. I reminded myself that Terrance was the neighborhood gossip, always adding a little bit to make a story juicier. Then I went to see Grant."

"Your friend?"

"Grant Wellman. He works out of the 18th. I stopped in like I was in the neighborhood, you know. After we talked for a while he asked, 'How's Lee?' When I said she was fine, he said something like, 'We should all get together some weekend.' I said, 'You haven't seen her lately?' Grant stopped, like he'd been caught. It was pretty clear he didn't want to answer."

Grant's face had frozen, the file in his hand forgotten. "Finally he said, 'No. I haven't seen her.' I don't think Grant had ever lied to me before that day, but he was lying then."

"Why do you think your friend would sneak around with your wife?"

Seamus sighed. "Grant's one of those guys women can't resist. It's not just that he's good-looking. There's something else—charm, I guess you call it. They flock to him."

"But if he was your friend—"

"They both lied, Ronnie, and it wasn't just once."

"Maybe they were planning something you weren't supposed to know about—a surprise birthday party or whatever."

"It was January. My birthday's in August." Seamus' voice softened, as if he spoke only to himself. "They were evasive, both of them, and it wasn't like they had a funny secret they'd tell me when the time was right. They were afraid I'd find out."

Ronnie hesitated, unable to explain but unwilling to give up. "It doesn't have to mean what you think it means. There could be another explanation, something we don't know about yet."

Though he appreciated her efforts and her implication they were in this together, Seamus didn't answer. He was dead. He accepted that. What was harder to accept was that he'd been murdered at the instigation of his best girl and at the hand of his best friend.

Chapter Eight

On Tuesday morning, Seamus accompanied a grumpy Grulke to work. At breakfast there'd been a set-to with his nine-year-old son, who wanted to wear his coonskin cap to school. The boy's mother said it wasn't appropriate, the boy insisted, and Grulke had been called in to mediate. "Leave the damned thing home," he told his only child bluntly. "Do you want people to think you're an idiot?"

Grulke began his investigation convinced that Lee Hanrahan and some unknown man had murdered her husband and fled the city together. While Seamus agreed, in fact could have given the man's name, he quickly became frustrated with the detective's lack of real interest in the case. He whispered, "Find them," several times to encourage Grulke's curiosity, but there wasn't much there to begin with.

Though Grulke was reluctant to expend much energy investigating the Hanrahan case, he knew his job. He sent officers to ask train and bus station personnel if they'd seen Lee Hanrahan, but he didn't have much hope of success. Grulke thought her boyfriend probably had a car, which meant they might be anywhere from Florida to Canada. After finishing the most pressing tasks on his other cases, he drove to Macken Street to see the victim's home and office for himself. He spent little time in the apartment, having read Waite's carefully detailed notes. He took more interest in Seamus' office on the ground floor, mostly out of curiosity about the work of a private detective. He searched the files, the desk, and even the pockets of Seamus' extra coat hanging on a hook by the door. Nothing there but an indecipherable list that might have been for groceries and several matchbooks from different businesses.

For Seamus, it was embarrassing to watch someone rifle through things that had mattered to him. Hearing Grulke's dismissive thoughts as he worked made his life seem petty and inconsequential. The detective sniffed in derision at the old case files, which were almost empty. It had been Seamus' policy to give his clients everything he'd gathered, keeping only copies of the financial documents he needed for tax purposes. Slamming the last desk drawer closed Grulke muttered, "Wasted trip."

As he left the office, the detective looked into Len Dobbleman's reception area. The lawyer's secretary sat at her desk, her rabbit nose actually twitching with curiosity. Showing his star, he said, "Detective Grulke, miss. I'm investigating the death of Seamus Hanrahan."

"I'm Miss Flint, Geraldine Flint." She tried to form a pleasant expression but couldn't hide her ravenous curiosity. "Is it true his wife killed him and ran off?"

"I can't comment on that." Noting the woman's eagerness, Grulke used it to his advantage. "Are you aware of any trouble between Mr. and Mrs. Hanrahan?"

Miss Flint scrunched her eyes, searching her mind for some tidbit of gossip to share with the detective. She came up with nothing.

"Anything unusual happen in the last few weeks?"

Again she searched for something that might impress him, but in the end her mouth twisted in disappointment. "No." He turned to go.

"There was that Negro man." When Grulke paused she went on, "Kind of a sharp-looking fellow with a nasty scar on his cheek."

"Interesting." The lover could be a Negro. Grulke had seen stranger things.

Miss Flint saw that she'd hit on something. "I asked him, 'Are you taking Negro clients now, Mr. Hanrahan?' and he said, 'I guess I would, if one came along.' He was always saying funny things like that. Sometimes I had trouble figuring out if he was kidding." She paused as if still trying to puzzle it out. "Anyway, I said somebody thought he had because of that man coming in, but he told me I was mistaken." She leaned toward Grulke, her eyes wide. "*She* told him no one had been in all afternoon."

"What did Mrs. Hanrahan say about the guy with the scar?"

Miss Flint's brow lifted. "She doesn't talk to me much. Some people think they're too good for other people, you know?"

"She's disagreeable?"

Her chin dropped as she considered her answer, making her horse-like face even horsier. "I can't say she was ever rude, but it's just 'Good morning' and 'Good afternoon,' you know? Never anything like a conversation."

Grulke thought he might avoid Miss Flint, too, if he had to work opposite her all day. "So you saw this guy leave Hanrahan's office, but the missus denied he was there?"

"To tell you the truth, I was relieved," she said. "I have nothing against those people, but I think we all feel a little safer when they stay in their own part of town."

Grulke didn't comment, though Seamus felt his agreement. He had a moment's pity for the unknown black man, judged and found wanting by a woman who'd only seen him in passing and a man who'd only heard him mentioned.

Shortly before the end of his workday, Detective Grulke was told a woman wanted to see him about a case. When the officer manning the front desk escorted a young black woman in, Seamus felt Grulke's wave of distaste. He failed to rise from his chair, nor did he ask her to sit down. "What do you want, girl?"

The "girl" was Lee's age, maybe a little younger, with African features and skin the color of cinnamon. Her hair was covered by a colorful scarf, but kinky tendrils peeped from the edges, rebelling against restraint. Her lips twitched briefly at the hostility in Grulke's tone, but her answer was neither submissive nor disrespectful. "My name is Lincoln Cole. They said you're the one looking into the murder of Mr. Hanrahan."

"You knew him?"

Her eyes shifted to a spot on Grulke's desk. "I know his wife, Lee."

"I see." Grulke shifted in his chair. The case he didn't want might easily be closed if this woman could help him locate the main suspect. "Do you know where she is now?"

"No, and it worries me. Lee would have come to me if she was in trouble."

"Even if she had something to do with her husband's death?"

Miss Cole shook her head vehemently. "She wouldn't."

Grulke leaned forward, glaring up at her. "She packed a bag and disappeared on the night the man was tied up, taken out past Navy Pier, and dropped over the side of a boat."

Before she dropped her gaze to the front of Grulke's desk, Seamus saw her anger. "Lee's no murderer."

"How do you know what Mrs. Hanrahan would do?" The detective's tone was scornful. "You her best friend or something?"

"I used to work for her mother." Her chin lifted. "I know Lee better than anyone, least I used to."

Seamus tried to recall Lee ever mentioning a woman named Lincoln Cole. He couldn't, but she was obviously a domestic of some sort. Her hands were rough from physical labor, and she clutched the handles of a battered, overstuffed shopping bag that probably held some sort of uniform. A single, rumpled apron string dangled over the top. The shoe he could see at the side of the detective's desk was scuffed and creased from wear, and her dress had been washed so many times it was hard to tell what color it had originally been. Lee had never spoken of having servants, but then she hadn't shared much about her life before she met him.

He focused on the interview, hoping to learn more about his wife's background, but Grulke's only interest was finding out if Linny knew where she was now.

"I don't know where she could be," she insisted when he asked a second time.

"She's dodging a murder charge. You don't want to be arrested as an accessory, do you?" Linny opened her mouth to repeat her denial, but Grulke demanded, "When did you last see her?"

Her expression turned troubled. "I haven't actually seen her for three years."

The detective looked disgusted. "So you don't know if there were problems between her and her husband."

"I didn't even know she got married," she admitted. "Not until I saw her picture in the papers with the name Lee Hanrahan." She licked her lips. "Mama didn't like me and Lee getting together."

"Might your mother know where Lee is?"

Lincoln's gaze fell. "Mama got the cancer, and it took her real fast. When I went to the place Lee used to work to tell her about it, they said she wasn't there no more and they didn't know where she went."

Grunting in disgust, Grulke shoved a piece of paper and a pencil across his desk. "Write down your name and address," he ordered, "in case I need to talk to you again."

As she wrote Lincoln asked, "Will you let me know when you find her?"

"This is the Chicago P.D., lady. We've got better things to do than tell—" Catching himself, he finished, "When we catch her you can read it in the papers, like everybody else."

A narrowing of Lincoln's eyes revealed she'd guessed the term he almost used. "If you're looking for Lee because you think she killed somebody, you're thinking the wrong way. She's not like that."

Grulke returned to the report that lay before him, clearly indicating it held more interest than anything more Lincoln Cole had to say.

***

When the two young officers met at the station house before their shift began, Ronnie jumped from Dean Malloy to Joe Waite, hoping for thoughts about more than body-building, women, and the possibility of becoming famous. Their day was spent on patrol, and neither man even mentioned Seamus' case. By afternoon they'd spoken with a store owner about a woman known for shoplifting, a pedestrian about a car that almost hit him in an intersection, and three separate groups of young men who were obviously ditching school. Though she learned the term *junking*, the practice among teenaged boys of picking up discarded items and selling them to earn petty cash, she decided that overall, a day in the life of a Chicago cop in 1953 was far less exciting than she'd imagined. Ronnie resolved to find a new host at the first opportunity.

When their shift was over, Malloy parked the car while Waite started inside to sign them both out. As he approached the outer doors, a young woman burst through like an angry wind. Waite jumped aside to avoid the door striking him in the face. "Hey! Watch it!"

"I'm sorry." Her apology was distracted, and her eyes shone with unshed tears.

"Are you all right, miss?"

"I came here for help." Her tone was bitter. "Nobody in there is interested in helping someone like me."

Ronnie got a kick out of Waite's reaction as she experienced interpersonal attraction from the male point of view. Though Waite's innate kindness made him willing to help others, this woman's pretty face and shapely figure amplified his good intentions. "Sit down over here and tell me about it," he said, indicating a bench near the doorway. He brushed a light skiff of snow from the seat. "Maybe I can do something to help."

That was how Officer Waite met Lincoln "Linny" Cole, who poured out her story of a missing friend and an uncaring police detective. Waite knew well how Grulke treated people he considered inferior, and in addition, he recognized the name Linny mentioned, Lee Hanrahan.

"I know a little about that case." He neglected to mention his belief that Linny's friend had almost certainly been involved in her husband's death. "They haven't located Mrs. Hanrahan yet?"

Linny met his gaze. "They think she killed her husband, but Officer, Lee wouldn't kill nobody." Her eyes filled with tears again. "I have to find her!"

As Linny composed herself, Ronnie considered her options. Should she stay with Waite or jump to the woman in order to learn more about Lee Hanrahan? In the end she decided to stay where she was. Linny admitted she hadn't seen Lee for years. She hadn't even known her friend was married. Better to stay with the cop, especially now that he seemed to have discovered a reason to investigate. Waite offered, "I could maybe look into it for you."

Linny seemed to see him clearly for the first time. "You mean you'd help me find Lee?"

He scratched at the side of his face. "I can't promise anything, you dig?"

"I understand." Linny turned to look at the street before them, as if hoping Lee might appear and end her worry. "I didn't know what to do, so I came here."

Waite fished a notepad out of his uniform pocket. Tearing off a sheet, he wrote his number down and gave it to her. "You can call me at home if you hear anything that might lead us to her. Do you have a telephone?"

When she shook her head, he handed her the notepad. "Give me your address then, and I'll contact you if I find out something."

Linny obeyed, her quick movements revealing gratification that Waite was actually interested in what she had to say. Handing back the notebook, she smiled shyly. "I'm grateful to you, Officer—um, Officer—"

"Waite," he supplied. "But you can call me Joe."

***

Seamus was intrigued by Lincoln Cole's visit to Detective Grulke's desk, and he listened with interest as Ronnie told him while their hosts slept that night what had happened after Linny left Grulke's desk.

"The names *Lincoln* and *Linny* don't ring any bells," he said when she'd finished her account, "but *Cole* sticks in my mind. Once when I came into the office, Lee was on the phone. Her back was to the door, so she didn't see me at first. She was talking to Grant Wellman about someone named Cole. She said, 'He's still hanging around, Grant, and it scares me.'"

He paused as his mind conjured a picture of Lee, her knuckles white on the receiver. She'd turned, seen Seamus in the doorway, and hurriedly ended the call.

"When I asked who was hanging around, Lee said I'd misunderstood. She insisted I was trying to find out what she'd bought me for Christmas."

At the time he'd believed her explanation because he wanted to. He'd told himself it was good that his wife and his best friend had gotten to know each other well enough that Lee could call Grant to ask for gift suggestions.

"We're going to find out more about Linny Cole," Ronnie said. "Joe Waite is taken with her and wants to help."

"But he's just a patrol officer, and a black man at that. He can't go around asking questions." With a huff of disgust he went on, "The guy who's actually in charge has other cases he finds much more interesting."

"Maybe you could move to the partner."

Seamus searched his memory for a name. "Malloy?"

"We can work on the two of them, press our agenda a little." After a pause she added, "But you'll have to work to get his attention."

"What do you mean by that?"

"Malloy's a little obsessed, and it isn't with the welfare of others."

"Conceited?"

"He's not a bad guy. He just needs some incentive to think outside his own interests."

"You know we can't control what a host does."

"No, but if Malloy and Waite both have the urge to investigate—"

"They might keep each other going. Good thinking, Ronnie."

"Can you get from Grulke to Malloy in the morning?"

"Shouldn't be hard to work my way through the ranks."

She snickered. "They'll think the flu is going around." As Waite stirred and began to wake, she said in a teasing tone, "No matter what the cops do or don't do, don't you go hosting with rats."

Chapter Nine

It took only two moves to get to Dean Malloy. When Grulke entered the station house Wednesday morning, Seamus jumped to the man at the front desk. After that it was simply a matter of waiting until Malloy went by and moving to him.

As a host, the young cop was a refreshing change from the detective. His vision was excellent, his outlook bright. As Ronnie had said, he was a little overly concerned with the impression he made on others, but it was generally harmless stuff. He wondered if each person he met was impressed by his musculature, his haircut, and his carefully practiced smile. Malloy's dream was that a Hollywood scout would ask him to star in a television show about police work. In each episode he'd solve some heinous crime. Like Jack Webb, only much more hip.

He'd been partnered with Waite as part of a move to integrate the Chicago police force, and it pleased Seamus to learn that Malloy liked Joe Waite and looked up to him. With two more years' experience on the force, Waite had developed many of the essential cop instincts Malloy hoped to nurture in himself.

Waite was in the common room, setting his blue cap firmly over his close-cropped hair, when Malloy joined him. There was a light in his eyes that hinted he had something to tell his partner. "Something going on, Joe?"

"Not much." A wag of his head said he'd elaborate later, outside the building.

Once they were in their squad car, Waite told Malloy about Linny Cole and her interest in Lee Hanrahan's disappearance. "You promised you'd find this woman for her?" Malloy's brows rose.

Waite made a helpless gesture. "She's really cute, and you can guess how Grulke treated her. I figure it can't hurt to look into it, as long as it's on my own time." He bit his bottom lip before adding, "I could use your help, though."

Malloy was doubtful. "We're going to chase juvenile delinquents by day and hunt for some dame who killed her old man after hours?"

"And whoever helped her," Waite reminded him. "She couldn't have done it by herself."

Malloy chewed at a hangnail. "Yeah. She definitely would have needed help."

"Linny says Lee used to sing in a night club downtown called Danny's Place. A couple of years ago, she left there without a word to anyone. I took a look at marriage records before I went home yesterday, and that's about the time she married Hanrahan."

Malloy scratched his head then checked the car's mirror to make sure he hadn't messed up his hair. "So she met Hanrahan, maybe at this club, and married him. She put up with his cheap apartment and barely-in-the-black business for a while, but then she met a guy she liked better. They killed old Seamus, dumped the body, and left town."

"Why kill him?" Joe asked. "Why not just leave?"

"He was a P.I. They were probably afraid he'd find them no matter where they went." He wriggled his brows. "Or maybe she just wanted him dead. Women are like that."

"You're a cynic, you know that, Malloy?"

"Only where the fairer sex is concerned." He started the car. "Where do we start?"

"Nobody in their neighborhood knew much about Mrs. Hanrahan. They certainly didn't know she used to be a night club singer." He thought for a moment. "We could visit the place where she used to work. Girls talk to girls, so maybe one of the women there can tell us about her."

Shifting into reverse, Malloy released the clutch and backed out of the parking spot. "Are we going to tell Grulke what we find out?"

Waite sniffed. "Like he'd be interested in what I've got to say."

"If it makes you feel any better, I don't think he'd listen to me either."

"When we get something good, we can go to him together." Waite rubbed his jaw before asking, "You willing to nose around a little after our shift?"

"At Danny's Place?"

"Yeah. Ever been to a nightclub before?"

"Sure." Malloy was lying, and Seamus wondered if Waite knew him well enough to realize it. "Lots of times."

"Good. You'll get more answers there than I would."

"That's because I'm better-looking than you by a mile."

Waite chuckled. "Now that's a lie, but you do have the right complexion for the job. What do you say?"

Malloy put the car into first gear. "Always wanted to work undercover."

As he drove home, Malloy's mind boiled with doubt. He'd sounded enthusiastic when Waite proposed the visit to Danny's Place, and he'd been enthusiastic at the time. But doubts crept in as he navigated the slushy streets. *What should I tell them? What if they don't want me to?*

"They" turned out to be Malloy's parents. When he entered the comfortable, two-story house, his mother was in the kitchen, her back to him as she stirred gravy for the potatoes that boiled on a back burner.

"Hi, Deanie," she said as he kissed her cheek. "How was your day?"

"Good."

As if by magic, Mrs. Malloy picked up something in his voice. "What happened, dear?"

"Nothing, Mom." She waited, the spoon poised above the pan, her expression expectant. "I—Joe Waite wants me to help him with something tonight."

Her brows got closer together, but she said, "What is it he needs?"

"He's got this friend—"

"A girl?"

"Um, yes."

She crossed her arms. "I thought so."

"Anyway, this girl wants to find a friend of hers, but the friend is white, and her and Joe think—" At his mother's glance he paused. "I mean *she* and Joe think I'd have better luck asking about her in places where Negroes aren't welcome."

"This girl's family doesn't know where she is?"

Malloy scrambled for a plausible reason for a young woman to have lost contact with her family. "She's not from here. Her family's back in Boston."

"Why is she in Chicago if her family's in Boston?"

Malloy sighed, but only on the inside. "She came here with her husband, but he died."

"Oh, how sad!"

"Yeah—I mean, yes. This friend of Joe's used to work for them, and now she wants to make sure the lady is all right."

"I see. So you're going with Joe to look for her?"

"Yes."

To his immense relief, Malloy's mother nodded. "I think it's very nice that you're trying to help out a poor widow, Deanie. Just don't stay out too late. You know you have work in the morning."

Seamus was both amused and horrified. He knew some men had trouble untying their mothers' apron strings, but this one seemed to be wrapped up pretty tight.

In the next few hours, Seamus learned a lot. First, Dean Malloy was completely inexperienced when it came to night clubs and the people who frequented them. Raised in a strict, Catholic family, he'd been sheltered from what his parents and most of their friends considered the sinful side of life. While he had a young man's understandable fascination with Marilyn Monroe and Ava Gardner, for the most part he accepted his parents' contention that people who "flaunted themselves" in public were under the influence of Satan himself. Dancing was okay if it was dignified and there was daylight between the partners. The jungle rhythms played at nightclubs, combined with free-flowing alcohol, were bound to bring out a person's baser emotions. Going anywhere near them was asking for trouble.

Part of Dean's mind looked upon Danny's Place as a trap waiting to spring closed on him, leaving him a helpless slave to animal passions and reefer madness. Another part was pleased to be helping his partner and excited about the prospect of seeing an actual den of iniquity for himself. After listening to the guys he worked with, Dean had concluded it was possible his parents were a little prejudiced when it came to such things.

He changed his mind about what to wear at least three times, ending up in a dark blue suit accessorized by adding a smart felt hat with a yellow band and a handkerchief of the same shade. "Cool," Malloy told his reflection in the mirror, "but not too much."

When a nervous Malloy arrived at the entrance of Danny's Place, a big man standing beside it took note of the unescorted young man, his face a vague threat. After a moment of regret for having agreed to this, Malloy squared his shoulders and went inside.

Danny's was beginning to hum with activity. Malloy was led to a table barely bigger than one of his mother's dinner plates, where he sat watching other customers enter. After a few minutes, he noticed two men circling the room. The man in the lead, apparently the host, greeted customers as he moved from table to table. Completely bald, he wore dark glasses despite being inside at nine p.m. on a March evening. Though his eyes were covered, something in the set of his face hinted at arrogance, or at least an abundance of confidence. His clothing was black, relieved only by a large silver belt buckle and a shiny silver watch.

As he circled the room, the man didn't shake hands, in fact, didn't touch anyone. Once when a careless customer jostled him, he turned on him angrily. Recovering at a word from his companion, he gave the offender a wooden smile before moving on.

Seamus recognized the man as Danny Proust, the club's owner. He'd spoken with him briefly during his investigation of Arthur Jameson's disappearance, and he could have told Malloy that Proust's behavior matched his outward demeanor. The man had seemed convinced that nothing could or should be denied to him.

A second man followed the owner, this one taller and thickly built. His face was similar to Danny's, but with a jutting chin, a lower forehead, and less prominent cheekbones, he seemed like a half-melted version of Proust. While the owner seemed relaxed and confident, this man's eyes scanned the crowd constantly, alert for anything unusual. Seamus concluded his purpose was protection, not client satisfaction.

When a waitress stopped at his table, Malloy commented on the long, cold winter that was finally ending. The girl agreed that it would be nice when it was gone but didn't seem interested in weather forecasting. Gathering his courage, Malloy asked, "How long have you worked here?"

"About three months." Her tone hinted she'd seen a lot in that time.

"The place is pretty busy for a weeknight."

"It's always busy. Last week Tony Accardo's cousin was in here."

Malloy wasn't sure what response was appropriate. A member of a notorious gangster's extended family had visited. Was that a brag or a complaint?

The waitress gave a little wiggle of impatience. "What are you having?"

Unable to think of another question, Malloy ordered a beer. The girl couldn't have known Lee Hanrahan, and she didn't seem particularly impressed by his strong physique and charming smile. *I should have known this wasn't going to work.*

Seamus felt a little sorry for the kid. At Danny's, attractive guys with light wallets were a dime a dozen, easily spotted and pigeon-holed. The waitress moved away, and Malloy thought regretfully: *Should have ordered a cocktail. That would have impressed her more.*

Musical noodling signaled the floor show was about to start, and Malloy sat back to enjoy it. Despite striking out with the waitress, the atmosphere here was cool and he was feeling adventurous and a little cosmopolitan. Of course, if his mother found out he'd been to a nightclub, there'd be an extra trip to confession in his future. Sipping his Carling Black Label, he silently vowed, to his own mother and Jesus' mother as well, that he'd atone for his night of sin as soon as possible.

The show's opener was a dance number in which the girls in the chorus, whose black sequined costumes suggested panthers, sang about love in the jungle. When they bounded offstage, the lights dimmed and the headliner appeared, bathed in a blue spotlight. Her name was Patti LaFlame, and she drew the eyes of every man in the place like a magnet. Her first song, a torchy lament of lost love, was liberally spiced with provocative moves and languorous glances.

While Malloy felt the pull of her overtly sexual display, he remained objective enough to discern that the woman's voice was ordinary. *Some of the girls in the choir at church could do better, but they wouldn't be as sexy about it.* Seamus agreed, noting that skillfully applied makeup and carefully-chosen costumes hid Miss LaFlame's physical faults. Still, she was nothing if not seductive, and the looks she shot at nearby males practically melted the tiles between them.

When the show ended, Malloy asked his waitress to take a note to the singer, asking if he might buy her a drink. He wasn't sure that was how it was done, and the look he got signaled mild disgust, but she did as he asked. After a few minutes the stage curtain twitched a little, and he guessed someone was peeking out. He must have passed muster, because Miss LaFlame came out from the side of the stage a few seconds later and sauntered to his table. She gave him plenty of time to anticipate her visit, stopping on the way to chat with other men and often patting their hands in some sort of promise.

Arriving at Malloy's table, Miss LaFlame stopped, setting one foot behind the other at an angle said to diminish one's apparent weight. Seamus didn't recall seeing her before, but he knew the type. *A real barracuda.*

"You wanted to speak to me, Handsome?"

Malloy rose and politely pulled back the chair beside him. She was older than he'd first thought, and what his mother would call "shop-worn." There were smoking lines around her mouth, and up close, heavy makeup couldn't disguise her puffy eyes. Still, he was polite. "I'm pleased you could join me, Miss LaFlame."

"Not for long, Darling. You ain't the only one looking for company tonight." Patti waved daintily at an elderly gentleman a few tables down who practically fell out of his chair waving back.

"I'll get to it then," Malloy said. "Do you recall a woman named Lee who used to work here?"

Patti's nostrils flared. "What are you, a cop?"

"Um, no. I mean, I'm private. An investigator. A private eye."

She looked him up and down. "I met a private detective once. You're not much like him."

"We're not all exactly alike." Leaning back in his chair in an attempt to look relaxed Malloy said, "You probably read the story in the papers, so I'll just ask: Do you know where Lee might be now?"

She huffed disdainfully. "How would I know that?"

"If you were friends once—"

"That girl and me ain't friends!" Her voice was harsh. "I haven't seen Lili—okay, Lee—since the night she took off from here without telling a soul."

Malloy gestured at Patti's elaborate costume. "A lucky night for you, right?"

She shrugged disdainfully. "I got top billing back when she left, if that's what you mean."

Seamus whispered his own name in Malloy's ear. "Did she ever talk about the P.I. she married, Seamus Hanrahan?"

"She didn't talk at all." Patti's lip curled. "Miss Moreno thought she was better than the rest of us."

"But she left a promising singing career to marry him. That seems odd to me."

Patti shrugged. "The guy was cute, in a Humphrey Bogart kind of way."

So they had met. Seamus didn't remember her, but why would he?

Putting a hand on Malloy's arm Patti purred, "He wasn't nearly as cute as you, Baby." The casual caress felt practiced, and her glance flickered around the room as she said it, assessing other possibilities.

Malloy was green, but he wasn't hopeless. "He's done being cute now," he said, subtly reminding her they were discussing a murder victim.

The waitress brought two drinks he hadn't ordered, set them before them, and mentioned an amount that made Malloy swallow hard. As he paid, Patti took half of hers in one gulp. "From what I read in the paper, the cops think Lee killed him." She seemed pleased by the idea, and Malloy took a sip of his own drink before answering. He suppressed an involuntary shudder at the burn of undiluted scotch.

"They'd like to find her and ask about it." He returned to his own questions. "Did you know she'd married Hanrahan?"

Patti fluffed her hair. "It shocked the hell out of me when I read it yesterday. I mean, Lee was a real prissy type, too good to date anybody around here. A real pain in the ass, you know?"

Malloy coughed into his fist to hide his shock. Of course he'd heard women swear before, but only the lowest sort of woman, and not casually, as if cursing was a natural part of speaking. *Mom's right,* he decided: *A guy doesn't meet nice girls in low places.*

Finishing off the scotch, Patti rose from her chair. "I think you and me are done, Handsome. I didn't like the girl. I don't know where she went from here, and I don't know where she is now." With that she slunk away, stopping at the table of the man she'd waved to earlier. Malloy had been relegated to the past.

The waitress paused as she passed. "I should have warned you. Patti only likes the rich guys."

Malloy looked around at the tables full of people, admitting to himself that he wasn't like these people. He didn't know how to have fun the way they thought of it. He couldn't get them on his side with his best smile and his smoothest line. *Might as well go home.*

Seamus was frustrated at his host's decision. There were dozens of employees at the club, and he'd spoken to only two of them. "Hat check," Seamus whispered. After a few seconds he repeated it. "Hat check!"

Malloy responded to the suggestion, though half-heartedly. As he turned in the ticket to retrieve his hat, he tried his opening line on the girl behind the counter. "Have you worked here long?"

"Long enough," she replied. Short and slightly plump, she had eyes that hinted her sense of humor remained private only with effort. "Haven't seen everything yet, but almost."

Malloy leaned an elbow on the counter, emboldened by her friendly manner. "What's your name, doll?"

"Sandra." She looked at him through lowered lashes, and Malloy's body temperature rose a notch. Seamus had to remind himself there'd been days when a young woman's eyelashes could send him off the track. It did no good to be impatient with the kid.

With a little cough at the lie he was about to tell Malloy said, "I'm Jim Cooper, a private investigator." That impressed her, and she looked him over in a new way. "Do you remember Lee Hanrahan? She worked here as Lili Moreno."

"Sure. Her picture was in the paper today." Her gaze sharpened. "They made it sound like she killed her husband."

Malloy answered as he and Waite had decided was best. "I'd like to help her out if I can."

"That's good, because I don't believe she'd kill anybody."

"You liked her?"

"Better than I like most of the people here." Sandra smiled, showing deep dimples. "The help, I mean. Some of the customers are pretty cute."

When she was sure Malloy had gotten her meaning, she went on. "Lee and me didn't talk that often, 'cause I was out here and she was backstage, but one time we all got stuck in a snowstorm and had to spend the night." She gestured at the cloakroom behind her. "There's practically no heat up here in front, so I probably would have frozen to death, but Lee came out and got me. She had some Hershey's cocoa powder up in her room, so we swiped some sugar and milk from the kitchen and sat around talking and drinking cocoa until the plow dug us out in the morning."

"Did she tell you about Seamus Hanrahan?"

Sandra chuckled. "Lili—I mean Lee—wasn't the type to trade stories about boyfriends." Her lips tightened. "But she was really good on stage. Not just eye shadow and shiny dresses, you know?"

The implied comparison was clear. In Sandra's mind, the present headliner was more show than substance. "How did Lee and Miss LaFlame get along?"

"Patti was the headliner until Lee came along, and she didn't much like taking second place."

"Who said she had to step aside?"

"Danny. Everybody around here does what Danny says, but that doesn't mean she liked it. Patti's Danny's girlfriend, but he saw dollar signs when Lili showed up, so Patti went back to the chorus. When Lee took off, Patti was back in the spotlight so fast it made my head spin." Sandra's disagreement with that management decision was obvious.

"So it was a good thing for Patti LaFlame when Lee—Lili—disappeared."

She considered that. "Maybe that's why Lili left; she got tired of putting up with the harassment. Patti was jealous of Lee, and she made stuff up about her all the time. She told the other girls that Lee tattled to Danny about every little thing they did. I'm pretty sure Patti was the tattle-tale, but the rest of those dumb bunnies believed her and treated Lili like dirt." She tapped Malloy's forearm. "If *Lee* had turned up dead back then, the cops wouldn't have had to look any farther than Patti to see who did it."

Interesting, Malloy decided, but not relevant. "Did you know Hanrahan?"

"I didn't remember the name, but when I saw the pictures in the paper I remembered meeting him once. It was in February, I think, and it would have been 1950, 'cause that's when Senator McCarthy told everybody about all the communists in our government. Ain't it awful? I mean, you can't tell 'em from normal people because they look like everybody else, but they could be planning to blow up Congress with one of those Molotov cocktails, you know?"

"Yeah." He tried to forestall any further political statements. "You met Hanrahan back then?"

"Only gumshoe I ever met until now." She touched Malloy's arm again, openly flirting. "He was working for this woman whose husband was missing. Mr. Jameson was one of our regulars, but I didn't notice anything special about the night he disappeared. That's what I told the police, and a few days later I told the private eye the same thing." She leaned toward him, lowering her voice. "It wasn't much after that they found out what happened."

"And what was that?"

"There was a bad storm that night. The guy's car slid into the river, and he drowned."

Malloy could tell there was more to it. "And?"

"Tina, one of the girls from the chorus, was with him." She shivered, and her ample breasts moved under her sequined costume, distracting Malloy for a second. "It makes you wonder. What goes through a person's mind when she plunges into ice cold water and realizes she's not going to get back out?"

Seamus' thoughts went briefly in that direction, but he forced himself to focus on the present. Malloy asked, "Was Mr. Jameson Tina's—um—boyfriend?"

Sandra stroked her reddish hair. "I wouldn't exactly call him that."

Before Malloy could ask what he would be called, a couple came to the counter to collect their things. Taking two slips of paper the man handed her, Sandra stepped into the cloakroom to retrieve the woman's mink and a fine wool topcoat for the man. When she tucked the tip he gave her into her top, the man watched with interest. She gave him a professional smile, bright but not warm.

As the couple left, a woman in a costume similar to Sandra's approached, set a camera with a large flash attachment down, slid under the hinged countertop, and leaned dramatically against it, kicking off her shoes. "My tootsies are killing me," she complained, lifting one foot and rubbing it. "And it's only ten o'clock."

Malloy couldn't look away as the newcomer dug at a spot under her breasts where something in the tight bodice she wore apparently poked her. Seamus chuckled at his thought: *Must be all kinds of wires in there to push her knockers up that high.*

"Jim Cooper," Sandra said, "meet Addie Blair, club photographer."

Addie inclined her head coquettishly. "Hi, Jim. What's cookin'?"

"You take pictures of the customers?" he asked.

"When I can." She snickered lasciviously. "Some want a visual record; some don't."

"Jim here's a private investigator," Sandra said. "He's asking about Lili Moreno."

Blue eyes regarded him briefly. "The girl with the voice."

Seamus was pleased they'd found a second person who remembered Lee. Malloy asked, "She was good?"

"A little shaky at first, but she had the pipes." Addie reached under her short skirt and pulled at the bottom of her costume on either side in an attempt to cover her buttocks. Once she'd made that adjustment, she leaned against the counter again, picked up the other foot, and rubbed it. "Lili was definitely an amateur, but she was talented and really pretty, so the men were inclined to be patient with her."

"How did she get hired if she had no experience?"

Addie shifted feet again, setting the free one against the opposite calf. "There's this guy who hangs around here, Chicken Charlie. He saw Lee singing at some church and told Danny she'd be a big draw."

"Charlie was her agent?"

Both girls chuckled, and Addie said, "Charlie's a Negro. Danny gives him odd jobs so he can earn a few bucks when his gambling doesn't pay, which is most of the time."

"Why do they call him Chicken Charlie?"

Addie turned to Sandra. "I don't know. Do you?"

"I think because he always wears that big hat with the rooster feather in the brim."

"Any idea where he lives?"

"Over in the Black Belt, I guess," Addie said. "He should be easy to track down. Got a big scar down one side of his face."

Remembering Dobbleman's secretary's account of a scar-faced black man, Seamus' interest quickened.

Addie bent down, put her shoes back on, adjusted the costume again in several places, and ducked under the counter. Hefting the camera, she slid the strap over her head, tracing its length with her fingers to remove the twists. "Once more into the pit, dear friends." Wriggling her fingers, she added, "Nice to meet you, Jimmy. Don't you two do anything I wouldn't do."

When she was gone Sandra muttered, "That doesn't rule out much."

"What do you mean?"

A smile lit her face, but Seamus recognized it as her professional one. "Nothing. Just kidding around."

Taking his hat, Malloy handed her a modest tip. "Thanks for the help, Sandra. Maybe I'll see you again sometime."

The smile was more natural this time. "I'd like that, Jim."

Seamus was amused at the young man's dilemma as he left Danny's. He wanted to see Sandra the hatcheck girl again, but if he did, could he admit he was neither Jim Cooper nor a private eye? Again Malloy acknowledged his mother's wisdom. *One lie only leads to another.*

Chapter Ten

While Malloy was inside the nightclub, Waite arrived on foot and found a place out of the worst of the wind where he could wait for him. Though he wouldn't be welcome as a customer, he was eager to learn what his partner could discover. The night was cold, and the stars seemed like chunks of ice in the dark sky. As a Chicago native, Waite hardly noticed.

Ronnie noticed. She felt keenly the damp seeping through Waite's thin shoes and the draft that crept around the corner and slid up the back of his jacket. While she wondered why anyone would want to spend a winter north of Ocala, Waite passed the time imagining the moment when he told Linny Cole he'd located her friend. She was bound to be grateful, and she could hardly blame him if Lee was later arrested for murdering her husband. Linny's eyes warmed him like his morning coffee did, and he found himself wondering what it would feel like to hold her in his arms.

A door near the back of the building opened, flashing light into the darkness of the parking lot. The large man who'd stood by the club doors a few minutes earlier appeared, wrestling a dolly that had two kegs tied to it with rough twine. Waite deduced the kegs were empty, but the dolly's wheels caught on the door frame, causing him to curse softly.

Seeing an opportunity, Ronnie ordered, "Help." Waite crossed the parking lot and grasped the base of the dolly, helping the bouncer lift it over the threshold.

Instead of gratitude, he got suspicion. "What are you doing back here, boy?"

Lowering his head, Waite adopted a subservient manner. "I can take care of those if you want, mister. Just tell me where they gotta go."

The man considered. "Okay. Take them down there to the boathouse—see the trail?" He pointed into the darkness. "Put them outside, along the wall. We usually put them inside, but we lost the key."

"You got a light, Mister, so I can see the way?"

The man stepped inside and returned with a metal flashlight. "Here. Once you get rid of these, come back and get the rest."

"I can do that." Waite maneuvered the dolly into the existing track then turned back. "You got more work like this, sir? I could use a job."

"Danny's already got himself a tame nigger, but he didn't show up tonight. Just do what I said, and I'll give you four bits."

"I 'preciate it, boss."

The man didn't answer, and the door was already closing.

The primitive road to the riverbank was bumpy and unplowed. Waite struggled to keep the dolly's wheels in the ruts of former trips in the frozen-thawed-re-frozen snows of March. He heard the Chicago River before he saw it, but the flashlight finally reflected off the water's surface. Turning the beam right and left, he located an ancient, slightly crooked boathouse on his right. A dozen empty kegs already lined a wooden platform along the side wall, two rows of four topped by four more staggered atop them. He guessed the brewer came upriver periodically and took the empties away to be refilled.

Waite did a quick reconnaissance of the boathouse, mostly from curiosity. It was small, perhaps ten feet by twenty. The end that faced the river had large doors that were padlocked closed, as well as a side entry door also fitted with a padlock. There were no windows, but he pictured a wooden boat inside, protected from the elements.

Unloading the kegs he'd brought and stacking them next to the others, Waite returned to the club's back door and knocked. The bouncer answered. "You get them down there all right?"

"Yes, sir."

"Okay. I've got the others set here by the door. Do the same with them."

"I'll take care of it, sir."

"Come around to the front when you're done, and I'll give you your money." Slightly less suspicious now, he added, "I'll tell the boss you're looking for work, and you can stop by in a day or two and see if he's got anything."

"Yes, sir. Thank you, sir." Responding to a whispered word from Ronnie, Waite asked as he bent to pick up the first keg, "Mr. Proust is the boss here?"

The big man's mouth moved in what might have been a smile. "There's two Mr. Prousts. Danny owns the place, but his brother Frankie runs it." He shifted his heavy shoulders. "I fight a little, and Frankie used to, when he was young. He still likes to hang around at the gym."

"A fighter, huh? Was he any good?"

The man snuffled a laugh that hinted at a deviated septum. "The way I heard it, he didn't have no finesse, you know? Just bam-bam!" He took two playful swings at Waite, who ducked out of the way.

"I bet you win every time." Waite tried for an admiring tone. "Is Mr. Frankie the one who'll hire me?"

The man pointed a finger at Waite's nose. "I ain't promising anything, boy. I said I'd mention it." In a moment of honesty he added, "I just got hired myself."

"Well, I sure appreciate it, sir. I do." Waite went off to finish the job, not sure if he'd learned anything worthwhile but pleased with his first bit of undercover work.

When Waite finished with the kegs, the bouncer paid him the promised amount but was no longer in the mood to talk. Waite left, but once out of the bouncer's sight, he stopped to wait for Malloy. The cold had deepened, and he stamped his feet to keep them warm.

Ronnie had seldom been more miserable. *You aren't feeling this,* she coached herself. *Waite is. You can't feel anything.*

It didn't help. She felt what her host felt, and it was just plain freezing on the cold concrete.

When Malloy finally came out, he saw Waite and gestured toward his car. "Hop in, and I'll take you home."

The heater took a long time to warm the interior, but it felt better in the car than on the frigid street. Waving his hands in the tepid air from the blower Waite said, "Thanks, Dean. What did you find out in there?"

Malloy reported his conversations with Patti LaFlame, Sandra, and Addie, ending with, "I didn't learn anything that helps us find our victim's missing wife."

"I managed to ask a few questions myself."

"You got inside?"

Waite chuckled. "Not likely! I talked to the bouncer, pretended I was looking for work. He's new, so he couldn't tell me much except that Frankie, the manager, and Danny Proust, the owner, are brothers. The bouncer got his job through Frankie, who used to do some boxing."

"Frankie looks like he's been punched a few times," Malloy observed. "His nose is kind of squashed." He stopped at a light and waited, though there was no traffic to speak of. "I'd say Danny's is a dead end. Mrs. Hanrahan cut ties with those people when she left."

"So we got nothing but a couple hours' less sleep tonight."

"Oh, I don't know," Malloy said. "I met a cute little number who seems to like me, so it wasn't a total loss."

***

While their hosts slept, Seamus and Ronnie interpreted for themselves what they'd learned.

"I don't see that we got a lead on finding Lee there," Ronnie said.

"I had a sense from the first that the place was shady," Seamus said. "The fact that Lee didn't want to talk about it made me even more certain."

"But—?"

"But once I got her out of there, Lee wanted me to forget Danny's Place existed."

"What do you mean when you say it was shady?"

"Just a feeling, you know? Grant said the same thing after he went there to interview the staff about Jameson's disappearance. He asked around, but nobody on the force was aware of illegal activity."

"How did you get involved in the investigation?"

"Jameson's wife got antsy after a few days when the police didn't find her husband. Grant gave her my name, but not long after she hired me, they found the guy and his sweetheart in the river. It was the kind of accident that can happen pretty easily in a Chicago winter."

"How do you people stand it here? Snow, ice, colder than—cold."

"We're used to it, I guess." After a pause he went on. "Anyway, Lee was determined I should never go back to Danny's Place, so I didn't. It used to make me wonder what she'd seen there."

"Could it connect to your murder and your wife's disappearance?"

"I don't see how. Even if they've got some penny-ante scheme going, why would they come after a guy who knows nothing about it more than two years later?"

Ronnie considered. "And the disappearance of—Jameson. You're sure that was an accident?"

"The official word was he lost control of his car and went into the river." After a pause he added, "The wife's reaction was a little odd, though."

"What do you mean?"

"Again, just a feeling I got. When she hired me, she was kind of smug, like she knew something I didn't. But when they found her husband dead, she seemed different."

"Different how?"

"Not grief-stricken, that's for sure, but—I guess *shocked* would be the word."

"That's understandable."

"But it seemed like she'd expected one result and got something else. She wasn't unhappy about it, but she was a little—I don't know. Nervous, maybe."

"Like she didn't expect him to turn up dead?" She paused. "Where is this woman now?"

"A few months after Jameson died, I saw a wedding announcement in the *Tribune*. The Widow Jameson joined her hand and her former husband's fortune with a visibly younger, much handsomer gentleman named—" He searched his memory. "—Collins, maybe. His name doesn't matter. It just seemed to me that when Mr. J died, his wife already had somebody lined up to be Husband #2."

"You're saying Mrs. Jameson expected Mr. Jameson's death? I thought you just said she didn't."

"I don't get it either. When she hired me to find him, she seemed puzzled but not worried. She hinted he was holed up in a motel somewhere."

"Judging from the short wait between marriage one and marriage two, she might have been doing the same."

"Right. I got the sense I was supposed to catch him with his baby doll, in trouble but alive. I think Mrs. J planned on a divorce, but I don't think she expected to become a widow."

Ronnie was silent for a few seconds. "She couldn't have known an ice storm was going to remove him from the picture."

"No. She couldn't have arranged that."

"But she could have arranged the affair if she got a little help from Tina."

"The wife gets the girl to put her husband in a compromising position." Seamus' tone was disgusted. "I should have thought of that."

"But how did she find Tina? How do you advertise for a floozy to seduce your husband?"

Seamus thought about that for a moment. "That might be where somebody at Danny's comes in."

"They promise the wives evidence of their husbands' infidelity."

"If Lee knew, that explains why she wanted out of there."

"So much so that she married me, you mean?"

"I didn't mean it like that!" Ronnie snapped. "You haven't shown me a single bit of proof that your wife didn't love you."

Seamus made a sound of disagreement. "Haven't proved she did, though, have I?"

"Seamus—"

"There's one more thing you should know," he interrupted. "I've been having trouble remembering details, but when I saw that club tonight, one thing came back really clear."

"What's that?"

"Danny's Place was the scene of my death, or at least the spot where any hope for me to remain a living human being ran out."

Chapter Eleven

Dean Malloy woke early and sat up, rubbing his face with both hands to chase away the cobwebs of a too-short sleep. After pulling on a pair of shorts he left his room, tiptoeing down the stairs and by-passing the one known to squeak when pressed.

The Malloy house was large, and Seamus had already noted photos that indicated perhaps as many as eight children in the family. Apparently they were all married and gone but Dean, who now made his way through the living room, down a hallway to the kitchen, and out the back door to the garage, where the temperature dropped to about forty degrees.

When he flipped on the light switch, Seamus saw Malloy's purpose for rising early. In one corner of the room was a collection of exercise equipment: barbells, boxing gloves, a punching bag, and a jump rope. On a stand in the corner was a book, and Seamus recognized the name of fitness expert Jack LaLanne.

Without consulting the book, Malloy put himself through a set of exercises, working his legs, arms, stomach, and back muscles with practiced efficiency. As he counted, he thought about what he'd learned the night before. He hadn't found anyone who'd seen Lee Hanrahan lately, but overall he was pleased with his first foray into the world of night clubs.

With a healthy male twenty-something's natural optimism, Malloy forgot Patti LaFlame's rejection and focused on how he might get to know the hatcheck girl better. As he worked on his thrice-weekly regimen, he imagined Sandra's apartment: pink, maybe, with silk sheets on the bed and little Cupid statues in the corners. A woman much worldlier than he might teach him the things he'd been pretending to know for months. As Malloy switched from barbells to jumping rope, Seamus shared his naïve daydreams of sexual conquest. Being worldlier than his current host wouldn't be very difficult.

Malloy's reputation as a ladies' man was something he'd encouraged and even cultivated when he came to work at the 8th a few months earlier. The other cops, unaware of the sheltered life he led, had assumed their good-looking, single co-worker was a magnet for women. He'd begun dropping hints about his dating habits, letting his tone of voice imply that he could have said more if he weren't a gentleman. The others ate it up, and even Joe seemed impressed by the number of female friends his partner mentioned casually in conversation.

His fellow cops didn't know that the girls Malloy talked about were mostly friends of his sisters or girls from church who'd known him all his life. They treated Dean more like a little brother than a hot dating prospect, and they abetted his family's well-meant but irritating oversight of every aspect of his life—except work. His parents were both proud and puzzled by their youngest son's job choice. While they were pleased he wanted to make the world a better place, they didn't understand why he couldn't do good deeds in a safer environment, like his father's plumbing store.

Malloy liked being a cop. He liked the manliness of it, and he saw himself as heroic, even if what he'd done thus far on the job was pretty mundane. He liked the uniform, he liked the way shopkeepers spoke to him respectfully, and he liked the guys he worked with. He just wished he hadn't laid it on quite so thick about the women he knew and how well he knew them. What had started as fun had become a problem, since the gap between Malloy's real and supposed sex life grew wider each day.

I need to get laid, but I'm never going to as long as Mom and Dad keep watching me like two hawks. Last night his father had expressed displeasure with his son's "gallivanting until all hours when you've got work in the morning." As Malloy switched from arm curls to neck stretches Seamus heard: *If he says, "under my roof" one more time, I'm going to explode.* The rhythmic movements continued, but the thoughts that went through his head came in spurts. *I'm almost old enough to vote. Fourteen, fifteen, sixteen. I should be able to stay out past midnight without a lecture. Thirty, thirty-one, thirty-two: I've got to get my own place—soon!*

Part of Malloy's disquiet came from the slip of paper he'd found inside his hat. On it was a name and a phone number followed by a heart. Sandra wanted to spend time with him.

Seamus fought his irritation, trying to remember what it was like to be young. Malloy had little interest in looking for Lee. If he kept chasing after dreams of fame, adulation, and real, live sex, Seamus' time with him would be wasted. He decided to remain with Malloy until after his date with the hat-check girl. Maybe Sandra would recall something that might lead them to Lee, though he didn't doubt her claim they hadn't met since Lee left Danny's Place.

Guessing Sandra slept late, Malloy waited until after his shift to call the number she'd given him. Sandra herself answered, which he took as a good omen. Often girls' fathers answered the telephone, which led to questions about who the caller was and what he wanted.

Sandra was pleased he'd contacted her. "I can't stay away long, but I could meet you somewhere for a while." She mentioned a drug store close to her home where they could talk without "big ears hearing every word." Malloy took that as a good sign, too. Sandra had things to say to him she didn't want anyone else overhearing. Still, it meant she didn't live alone, which dimmed his hopes of seeing her boudoir with the cupids and such.

When Malloy got to the drug store, she was already seated at the counter, talking to a soda jerk with a bad case of acne. Taking the stool next to hers Malloy said, "Hey, Good-Looking, can I buy you a banana split?"

Giggling, she slapped his arm playfully. "I have to fit into that god-awful costume, remember? A lime phosphate, please, Teddy."

"The same," Malloy added, and Teddy turned to the array of bottles and glasses behind him, squirting, measuring, and shaking the ingredients for their drinks. The over-the-shoulder looks he gave Sandra as he worked betrayed hopeful devotion; the single glance he spared for her date was pure malevolence. When the drinks were ready, Malloy paid, deftly caught the change the kid practically threw at him, and asked, "Would you like to move to a booth so we can talk?" With an apologetic smile for the glowering Teddy, Sandra nodded.

Taking their glasses, they chose the booth farthest from the counter, sitting opposite each other. As they sipped their drinks through paper straws, Malloy learned that Sandra was twenty-four (more than three years older than he), a high school graduate, and a Capricorn. He told her he was also twenty-four (to make her feel better), an orphan (it made girls sympathetic), and unaware of his birth sign. After asking his birth date, she informed him he was a Libra. That was good for a private detective, she said, because Libras liked balance and fairness.

Seamus tried to move the conversation in a more interesting direction. "Danny's!" he whispered. "Danny's!"

Malloy was a suggestible host. "Working at a night club must be interesting."

Sandra's left eyebrow rose. "You'd think so, but it's just like anyplace else. There's good people and not-so-good ones, and you have to figure out who's who."

Malloy licked his straw, already going limp from soaking. "Who's on the not-so-good list?"

She shrugged as if unwilling to say, but having an interested listener seemed to spur Sandra to confidences. "Murray, the guy who used to be our bouncer, would chase after a camel if it was wearing a skirt. He quit last weekend, and the jury's still out on the new guy, Herb."

"What about the manager?"

"Frankie?" She lowered her voice and spoke with exaggerated lip movements. "He don't like girls."

"Wow." Malloy knew of such things only from passages of Scripture he'd read, and his understanding was vague.

Sandra rolled her eyes. "At least he isn't always backing me up against a wall like Murray did."

"And the boss? Danny?"

Her brows rose eloquently. "Me and the Proust boys grew up in the same neighborhood. They're older than me, but our mothers used to be good friends. When my mom asked their mom if they'd give me a job, they kinda had to do it." She rolled her eyes. "Of course, our mothers have no idea what Danny's is really like. Mrs. Proust thinks her boys run a nice supper club with waiters in tuxedos and Big Band music."

"She wouldn't approve of girls in skimpy costumes dancing under colored lights?"

Sandra grinned. "She's from the old country, and she can make you wish she was back there, you know?"

"Sounds like she's got them under her thumb."

With a sly smile she admitted, "My mother's never seen the outfit I wear at work, and she never will." Sandra sighed. "You wouldn't get it, being an independent person. You can do what you like."

Malloy made a vague sound, understanding parental pressure better than Sandra suspected. "So the Prousts gave you a job."

"And now they can't fire me, because I could tell their mother all kinds of things she wouldn't like."

"Like what?"

She waved the question away, tracing a scratch on the tabletop with a poorly-enameled fingernail. "Somebody went to Danny and told him you were asking about Lili—I mean, Lee. Probably that mouthy Addie."

"Miss LaFlame might have. I talked to her too."

"Like either of them should be minding anyone else's business." Leaving the scratch, Sandra began making circles on the tabletop with the moisture from her glass.

"Why do the Prousts care if I asked about a woman who quit a long time ago?" When she merely shrugged in answer he added, "It's nothing to me, but it makes me mad that someone tattled on you."

She smiled, pleased at his concern. "Frankie asked if I'd heard from Lili lately. When I told him no, he wanted to know what I told you about her. I said the same as I told him, because it's the truth." Her lip curled. "Then he said *somebody* noticed it took me an awful long time to tell you nothing."

"Wow," Malloy said. "I guess you're right about having to watch your back at that place."

"It's a real snake pit." Sandra's chin lifted. "Those girls got no right tattling on me, not with their sugar daddies and all."

"Sugar daddies?" Malloy frowned. "You mean Danny's is a brothel?"

Her eyes widened. "No! I wouldn't work there if it was. But some girls date the married men that come in, and that makes trouble."

"Not trouble for you, I hope." Malloy gave his well-practiced smile, and in response Sandra curled her shoulders like a kitten.

Malloy had deduced that Sandra's world consisted mostly of Sandra. *Maybe he does have the makings of a ladies' man,* Seamus thought, *if he ever gets his parents off his back.*

Licking her lips, Sandra said, "I try to look the other way, you know, but I can't help noticing."

"Noticing what?"

Wriggling her rear on the wooden seat, she leaned in to give him the lowdown. "Remember when I told you about Tina and Mr. Jameson? Well, they weren't the only ones. A lot of the girls do things with the customers that aren't right, if you know what I mean."

"Pretty girls and wealthy men go together, I guess."

Finishing the phosphate with a tiny slurp, Sandra apparently had an alarming thought. "I don't want you to think we're all like that. Me, I do my job and go home."

The primness in her tone revealed that Sandra wasn't the worldly woman Malloy had imagined. *She knows the score*, he concluded, *but she doesn't play the game.*

"It sounds like Danny's isn't a good place for a decent girl to work."

She shrugged. "The tips are good." Apparently feeling that wasn't enough explanation, she added, "My mom's crippled. My brother stays with her at night, but he's got a nine-to-five job at Kresge's, so I work nights."

Malloy was seeing a clearer picture of Sandra. Despite the skimpy costume she wore at the club, she was an ordinary girl trying to keep her family solvent.

"I get it. No sugar daddies for you."

"My little cubbyhole keeps me safe." Her tone was righteous, a good girl who remained above the sins she was forced to observe.

"Lili!" Seamus whispered in Malloy's head. He dreaded the answer, but he needed to have the question asked. "Lili!"

"Did Lili Moreno have sugar daddies?"

Sandra's eyes widened. "Lili? Heck, no! She wouldn't have anything to do with the men who came to the club. It's another reason Patti and the rest hated her so much."

"Miss LaFlame—um—dates married men?"

"I know--it's crazy. She's Danny's girl, but he doesn't seem to care when she goes off with some man."

"And a lot of the other girls do this—this flirting?"

"Five or six, I'd say." Sandra met Malloy's gaze. "Now, me? I was taught that marriage is a holy institution."

"Me too." Malloy thought of his parents, happily wed for forty years. "How about Addie?"

Sandra paused, perhaps considering the wisdom of saying what was in her mind. In the end her eagerness to tell secrets to her handsome companion overcame her sense of discretion. "Her job is being on the other side of the camera, get it?"

"Oh." Malloy was shocked, but Seamus realized he and Ronnie had been correct. There was an organized scheme at Danny's Place. Arthur Jameson wasn't the only man who'd been caught in a trap there.

Malloy eventually got it too. "Addie photographs the men misbehaving with the girls, which leads to the trouble you mentioned."

She nodded gravely. "Patti's been named as the other woman in a couple divorce cases, and some of the other girls have too." Fidgeting with the empty glass before her she said, "I'd die of shame if that happened to me, and then my mother would kill me again, just to be sure. But those girls? They keep right on doing it."

"What does Mr. Proust say about his employees breaking up marriages?"

Sandra rolled her eyes. "He's all for it."

"What?"

"When I first went to work there, Frankie said I could make a little extra if I was nice to men they picked out for me."

Malloy was barely keeping up. "They *wanted* you to—"

Sandra slapped the table with red-tipped fingers. "Brother, I told him they could find another girl! Since then we're kind of at a standoff. The Proust boys can't fire me because of what I know, and I can't quit because I need the money."

"That's a sorry state of affairs." Malloy was unaware of the pun.

Flipping her hair back, Sandra shrugged. "Mostly it's okay. The work is easy, I get to meet a lot of people, and nobody bothers me, especially now that Murray the Creep is gone."

Malloy nodded. "It's good that you get to keep your job and your, um, integrity."

She liked that. "I'm stuck with the hats and coats, but at least back there, nobody can pinch my a—my behind."

Seamus sighed in frustration as Malloy's thought ran briefly to Sandra's very pinch-able behind. He remained a gentleman though, turning the subject to a possible ice-skating outing on Sunday. She agreed that would be nice, then rose to go. "Momma can't get out of bed on her own anymore," she explained, "so we don't leave her alone for long."

He walked Sandra to her home, just a few blocks away, and she offered her cheek when they reached her front door. Malloy kissed her lightly, seeing her inside before he turned back to where he'd parked his car. Sandra wasn't the world-wise woman he'd imagined, but she was pretty and easy to talk to. He couldn't wait to drop into the conversation at work that he was dating a girl who worked at a night club.

As Malloy pondered Sandra's sweet-smelling hair, Seamus' thoughts remained on what she'd said about Danny's Place. Women at the club were encouraged to seduce married men. Blackmail was a possibility, but evidence of wrongdoing had to remain secret for blackmail to work. Sandra had mentioned that Patti LaFlame had been named in several divorces. Such things were public, especially if the parties were wealthy. Seamus whispered a single word to Malloy: "Library."

Once again, the young cop was suggestible. Driving to the public library, Malloy requested access to Chicago newspapers for the last year. He was a little daunted when the librarian showed him to the stacks, where hundreds of them lay in neat piles, most untouched. Gamely, Malloy waded in and took an armload before heading to a table.

He paged through one by one, hardly knowing what he was looking for. Seamus whispered encouragement from time to time so he wouldn't give up the search. Finding a name he recognized, Malloy said aloud, "Huh. Look at that." He skimmed the article, talking to himself in a low tone. "Milton Cameron was sued for divorce by his wife, Meredith Cameron, when she learned he was involved in an 'adulterous relationship with Patti LaFlame, a singer at a downtown night club.' Skipping to the end of the article, he saw that Mrs. Cameron had received a divorce and a generous settlement.

Jotting the names and dates down in a notebook, he moved on and a few minutes later found another. "Eli Mendenberg, sued for divorce by his wife," he muttered as he wrote. Mrs. Mendenberg had charged adultery, naming "an anonymous employee of Danny's Place, a local night club." In this article, the reporter claimed he'd tracked the

Other Woman down but got only a "No comment." He had, however, convinced a court clerk to show him a picture of Patti LaFlame sitting on Eli's lap.

In the hour before closing time, Malloy found a third case naming Patti LaFlame as the cause for divorce between a wealthy man and his wife. Along with that were several other references to Danny's Place. The settlements always favored the wives and were without exception sizeable amounts.

Hoping his partner was at home, Malloy went to the pay phone in the library foyer and called him. Relaying what he'd learned, he ended with, "They're setting these poor slobs up, Joe."

Waite gave a derisive snort. "I doubt they're *poor* in either sense of the word, and they cheat on their wives. I don't feel sorry for them."

"But why would Danny and the women who work for him go out of their way to get their customers in trouble?"

Joe thought about it for a moment. "If they're deliberately leading men into compromising situations, it's so their wives can divorce them and still get a healthy slice of their income."

"Geez." Malloy's Catholic faith made divorce an almost unmentionable topic at home. If they had to speak of it, his parents lowered their voices, as if the word itself were sinful. "I'm not much of an expert on that."

"In order for a divorce to be granted in Illinois," Waite explained, "someone has to be at fault. Adultery's a legal cause for divorce that's pretty easy to prove."

"With photographs, hotel records, stuff like that."

"Or the admission of one of the parties involved in the adultery."

"Which could be arranged."

"So here's what might happen: a man meets a girl at Danny's. After a lot of flirting, she agrees to go to a motel with him. Someone, possibly that photographer you told me about, snaps photos of the happy couple. The judge has someone to blame, a divorce is granted, and everyone's happy."

"Except the guy, who gets to pay through the nose."

Waite sniffed. "He broke his vows. The law says he has to pay."

"And you think this is all set up ahead of time?"

"Could be."

"Why would Proust do that? What does he gain from it?"

Waite paused to collect his thoughts. "The wife can't be involved. She needs a third party to arrange things."

"And night club is a perfect place to start trouble."

"Some liquor, a good time, and a pretty girl who's interested in him. The guy's halfway to divorce court before he knows it."

"Sandra says Lee Hanrahan refused to play along," Malloy said. "It might be why she quit the club."

"It doesn't tell us where she is now, though." Waite sighed. "I think Danny's Place is a dead end."

Since he'd gone to Danny's on the last night of his life, Seamus couldn't agree. Still, it wasn't Danny Proust's voice he'd heard asking, "Is Seamus dead?" That had been Lee.

"What did you find out about Charlie the Chicken?" Malloy asked.

Waite chuckled. "It's Chicken Charlie, and I haven't tracked him down yet. No one I spoke to has much good to say about him, and nobody seems to know where to find him at any given time."

"So what are you going to do?"

"I got a lead on where he'll be Saturday night, so I'm going to try again then. How about you?"

"I'll go back to Danny's Place. Now that I know what to look for, I might see things differently."

"Didn't we just decide the club's probably got nothing to do with Lee's disappearance?"

"Yes, but the boys in bunco might want to know what Frankie and Danny Proust are up to. I'd like to find out what kind of guys set other guys up for money."

Chapter Twelve

"Explain it to me," Ronnie said once Waite snored softly in his bed. "What weird way of thinking in your day would cause a woman to hire one of Danny Proust's girls to seduce her husband?"

"You have to understand the times," Seamus replied. "Divorce was a big no-no."

"I've heard. All that White Anglo-Saxon Protestant morality stuff."

"Right. The surest way to end a marriage is for one party to accuse the other of adultery. As long as a woman has evidence, like photographs, and as long as she hasn't been adulterous herself or encouraged her husband's adultery—"

Ronnie snickered. "How does one partner encourage the other's adultery?"

"She withholds sex, maybe. Then he's—"

"Wait a minute. A guy sleeping around is okay if he isn't getting sex at home?"

Seamus made an irritated sound. "I'm not defending the fifties. I just lived there."

"Okay. A wife gets a divorce if she can prove she's a good girl and he's a bad boy."

"Since the courts look at a woman as pretty much useless without a husband to support her, she gets a nice settlement."

"I'm starting to get it. A woman wants to ditch her old man. She hears about a guy who can arrange a little mischief for him and enough evidence for her to obtain a divorce with benefits."

"For a fee."

Ronnie's next comment seemed to be a shift in topics, but they both knew it might not be. "I think it's time you told me about your wife, Seamus. All of it."

"It's water under the bridge."

"Remember what Gabe said? We have to be honest with each other if this is going to work. I know the cops think Lee is involved in your death, but you loved her. Why do you think she killed you?"

She waited a long time, but finally he spoke in a low voice. "Like I told you, we met at Danny's Place. She wanted out, and I wanted her, so we got married. Over time, Lee told me a little about her family, how her mother raised five kids pretty much by herself. When the offer of a job at Danny's came along, Lee saw it as a chance to let her younger siblings finish school. But her mother disagreed. When she learned Lee was a night club singer, she threw her out."

"Harsh. But if her mother didn't want her at Danny's and she hated working there, why didn't Lee quit?"

"She was kind of vague about that, but I think she kept sending money to her family even after her mother disowned her." Seamus' voice seemed to come from far away, and Ronnie imagined the times when, alone in his stateroom or leaning on the ship's rail, he'd tried to figure out how it all went wrong. "Lee had been Danny's headliner for over a month when we met, but she never had more than a few nickels in her little change purse. Eventually I learned that she lived upstairs in that smoky, dingy club like a mouse in a hole, eating leftovers and sewing her own costumes."

"Not what I'd picture for a rising star."

"I think her pay went to her family."

"The mother took money from the daughter she'd tossed out?"

"I doubt it. Lee must have found a way her mother didn't know about."

Ronnie mulled that over for a moment. "Okay. If Lee's family needed her income so much, why did she quit Danny's Place to marry you?"

"I could say it was my natural charm, but I doubt you'd believe that."

"Stop disrespecting yourself and tell me what happened," she said brusquely.

"Okay, okay." Seamus chuckled softly then turned serious. "One night I found Lee struggling with Murray, the club's bouncer. It wasn't a sexual attack—at least, it wasn't all sexual. We got out of there, but we both knew she couldn't go back again."

"So you offered her an alternative."

"First, I promised her the love of a slightly damaged ex-G.I. Second, I described a quiet life in a part of Chicago where she didn't have to ever be Lili Moreno again. And third, I said she could have the check I got from Uncle Sam every month to spend however she wanted."

"You offered the girl money to marry you, Seamus?"

"It sounds bad when you put it that way, but I was considered partially disabled because of my knee. It didn't keep me from earning a living, so I figured Lee could have her own income and do whatever she wanted with it."

Ronnie chuckled. "You were a pretty advanced male for your day, Hanrahan. Do you know how she spent the money?"

"No, but it wasn't on herself. Lee would never have had new clothes if I hadn't bought her things."

"She never told you where it went, even after two years of marriage?"

"I guessed it was something to do with family, and everybody has family stuff they'd like to keep private. We weren't starving, and we were happy—at least I thought we were."

Ronnie's sigh was audible. "So what changed, besides Lee fibbing about where she spent her afternoons?"

The answer came slowly, as if he had to drag it up from some hidden place in his mind. "Money came up missing from the business account."

"Oh."

"When I asked about it Lee said it was a mistake. I knew she was lying, because she was a wreck."

"And that added to the other lies, like where she spent her afternoons."

"Yeah."

"How much money did she take?"

"Nothing we couldn't handle, but Lee wouldn't explain. She just hung her head and said she was sorry."

"Sometimes people overspend. It isn't right, but—"

Seamus spoke over her argument. "One day when Lee was out, I got a phone call. A woman said she could tell me the truth about my wife. She claimed I'd be shocked to find out what she was up to." His tone went flat. "I should have told her to drop dead, but I didn't."

"You agreed to meet her."

"At Danny's Place, after closing on Saturday."

"Oh." Ronnie's voice sounded odd. "That was the night you—"

"Yeah."

"You said you'd forgotten what led up to the end of it."

"Well, I remember the call. This woman claimed she knew Lee from before I met her, and she said she knew what was going on with Lee and me." His voice was almost inaudible. "I'm not proud of it, but I thought I had to know."

"And what did this woman have to say?"

"It was a trap." His tone was bitter as he added, "The end of Seamus Hanrahan, not-so-clever private eye."

"I'm sorry."

He sniffed, and she imagined him shrugging her condolence away as if he actually had shoulders. "It was a long time ago."

"I don't see why you're so sure Lee and Wellman are responsible for your—" She reworded the comment. "If they did it, then who called you offering dirt on Lee?"

"I think she asked one of the girls she used to work with to lure me to Danny's after everyone else went home."

Ronnie had been thinking the same thing, but she kept that to herself. "Why Danny's?"

"The river's not far, and there's a boat they could use to—to transport the body out into the lake."

Though it couldn't help, Ronnie said again, "I'm sorry."

"I was an idiot to respond to an anonymous call," he said. "In my defense, I went there early and did some reconnoitering."

"Good idea. What did you find?"

With an investigator's precision, Seamus described the scene. "I got there as the last of the patrons were leaving. I found a spot to wait by some sheds that sit along the west wall, across from an access road to the river. In half an hour or so, the help left and the club went dark, at least the downstairs. The parking lot did too; in those days nobody lit empty spaces. The only light that showed was upstairs.

"It was a cloudy night, with just a slice of moon showing through every once in a while. Once everybody who was leaving had gone, there was just a black sedan left, parked between me and the club. Its engine was cold and there was snow on the windshield, so I guessed it hadn't been moved in a while."

"Sounds like you did what you could to check the place out."

Seamus' chuckle was sardonic. "I was aware I wasn't acting rationally, showing up in a dark place in the middle of the night. I went all the way around the outside of the building. I'd brought a flashlight, and I shined it into all the corners. There was nobody hiding back there, nobody with a big knife ready to stab me in the back. The place seemed deserted."

"You thought maybe you'd been stood up?"

"For a while, yes. But when I came around to the front again, I saw a car pull up."

Ronnie was trying to get a mental image of the scene. "Where was your car parked?"

He sniffed disgustedly. "You think everybody in Chicago owned a vehicle in 1953? I took the El to Wacker and walked the rest of the way."

Ronnie went silent, trying to absorb the idea of people without personal transport. Seamus went on, "When I looked out from the shadow of the building, I saw Grant's Chevy about twenty yards away. I could tell there were two people inside, a man and a woman. When the driver's door opened, I saw it was Lee in the passenger seat."

"Maybe—"

Seamus interrupted Ronnie's objection loudly enough to make both their sleeping hosts shift in their beds. "I heard them talking, Ronnie!" He waited for the hosts to settle back to sleep, and when he resumed his account, the tone made Ronnie's heart ache.

"Grant got out and came around the car. Lee rolled the window down. I heard every word, as if they were standing next to me. Grant asked, 'Are you sure this is the best way, Lee?' and she said, 'Seamus is the kind of man who won't leave it alone until he finds out the truth. I have to end it tonight.'"

"Oh!"

Ronnie wasn't aware she'd made a sound until Seamus said, "Yeah, 'Oh.' Grant told her to wait in the car, said he couldn't be worrying about her safety while he looked for me. Lee said, 'Hurry, or we'll miss the train.' Grant started for the club, and I saw he had his .38 in hand, ready for action. He went around the opposite side of the building from me, checking things out just as I'd done a few minutes earlier."

"That's when you concluded they planned to kill you?"

Seamus sighed. "Up to the point when I saw the gun, I'd been telling myself they intended to confront me so they could tell me they were in love."

"What if—"

"Whatever you can think of for an explanation, I tried it," Seamus interrupted. "Why did Grant have his gun out? Why did they call me downtown to that empty spot and then show up together? What other reason could they have except to get me away from any possible source of help?"

She had no response to that. "What did you do?"

"A dozen half-baked ideas went through my head, but in the end I realized the smartest thing to do was get out of there."

"Were you armed?"

"No. I'm not the Sam Spade type with a .38 at my waist and a spare strapped to my ankle. I gave Grant a few seconds, and when I thought he was as far from me as he was going to get, I started across the parking lot. I figured in the dark I could get away without either of them seeing me."

Ronnie wanted to say something encouraging, but what had Lee been doing at the scene of Seamus' murder if she wasn't aware of what was going to happen—if she wasn't involved in it?

Instead she said calmly, "Knowing how this ends, I guess you didn't get far."

"No. Something hit the back of my head, and I went down hard. After that things get blurry. There were sounds, I felt someone moving beside me, but nothing was clear. When I had a somewhat coherent thought again, I couldn't move my arms and legs." With a grim chuckle he added, "My brain wasn't working too well either."

"You probably had a concussion."

"Yeah. I opened my eyes, but my vision was messed up, like a movie reel that got too hot and melted in spots. It was snowing those tiny flakes that are almost nothing but cold. Two people picked me up and tossed me into the trunk of a car. I think I hit my head against the edge, because things got even fuzzier."

"But you're sure it was a car trunk?"

"Yeah. I could smell the rubber of the spare tire and the greasy rags inside. I heard a clunk as the lid closed over me, and the night got even darker."

"Horrible!"

"Yeah." After a few seconds he went on. "The starter ground a few times, but the engine wouldn't turn over. Someone—a man—said, "Don't flood it." Then I heard someone farther away holler something, maybe 'Please!' There was a lot of noise for a while, and then it went quiet. I heard whispering, and the starter ground again, longer this time."

"And then?"

"The car started and the driver shifted into first. The ride was bumpy, and the tires crunched through snow, so I knew we were off the pavement. When the car stopped, the driver just sat there waiting."

"For what?"

"I don't know."

"Are you sure—"

It was as if she hadn't spoken. "I don't know how long it was, because my head was killing me and I drifted in and out of consciousness. I think I might have slept for a while."

"You slept?" Ronnie was doubtful.

"I suppose that's not what you'd call it, but I was in and out, you know? It seemed like people were talking, but that could have been my imagination. At one point I thought I was at home with my mother. She told me things would be okay."

"She was right," Ronnie said. "People think death is the worst thing, but it isn't."

Seamus made no comment on that. "I was face down, so I didn't see who lifted me out of the trunk, but it was only one person this time. He dragged me down a wooden walkway, and I knew we were at the river from the smells and the way sounds echoed like they do. He dumped me into a boat that was floating in the river. It was quite a drop, and when I landed my head hit something. Everything went black again.

"I woke up in the boat, and I heard Lee's voice asking, 'Is Seamus dead?' A man answered, but I couldn't hear what he said. Then there were gunshots—two, maybe three. Something hit me hard, and I lost consciousness again."

His voice became even softer. "The next time I was aware of what was going on is the last thing I remember. The cold. The boat motor whining and the smell of gas. The ropes cutting into my wrists. And then the water."

Ronnie was silent for a while. Then she said, "It wasn't right, Seamus. You didn't deserve to die like that."

He cleared his throat brusquely. "I got over it—most of it. But I don't know why Lee wanted me dead. If she'd asked for a divorce, I wouldn't have stood in her way."

"Then we'll keep looking," Ronnie said. "It's odd that the whole thing started and ended at a place Lee hated so much."

"Like it or not, Danny's is a great spot to stage an ambush. We need to know more about who Lee might have stayed in contact with there."

"Or who might have had something against her or both of you." Ronnie wasn't ready to give up on the idea of an alternate explanation. "Linny Cole claims she was close to Lee once. I'll work on getting Joe Waite to find out a little more about how they knew each other, and how well."

Seamus chuckled. "From what you told me about their first meeting, I doubt it will be difficult to convince that young man to seek out Miss Cole again."

Chapter Thirteen

Friday was spent on activities Seamus remembered from his own days as a patrolman. He'd planned to encourage Malloy's interest in solving his murder, but the young officer was so embroiled in police duties there was no time to do so. One small disaster followed another. A truck tipped over when it took a corner too fast, dumping boxes all over a busy intersection. No sooner had they dealt with that mess than a fight broke out several blocks away. It started when one man became angry over a neighbor's wandering dog, but others joined in on both sides, and soon there were two screaming mobs involved. Wading in to try to stop it, Malloy's jaw connected with a flying elbow, and he spat blood for several minutes. Once the melee was under control, they were called to a third scene where a young woman teetered on a ledge, threatening to end her life. It took over an hour of sidewalk counseling before finally she agreed to let Malloy help her back inside the building.

At the end of their shift, Malloy and Waite practically staggered to the station, wrote out their reports, and went to their separate homes, unable to do much more than feed themselves and collapse into bed. Seamus knew it was useless to pester his host, and he guessed Ronnie would leave Waite alone as well. The officers had the weekend off. That would be a better time to encourage them to look further into their off-duty case.

Young and healthy, Malloy awoke refreshed and, Seamus was happy to note, curious. During his research at the library, he'd listed all the names he could find in the newspapers of wives who'd divorced their husbands due to affairs with girls from Danny's. He'd been considering interviewing one of them, and Seamus approved the idea.

Unfortunately, Malloy had committed to helping his mother sort clothes for the upcoming church rummage sale. As he folded old sweaters and tuned out her chatter about church events, he argued the pros and cons of his idea with himself.

On the one hand, it could get him into trouble. A rookie cop lying about who he was at a sleazy night club was one thing, but lying to an upright citizen who might file a complaint with his superiors was something else. On the other hand, what were the chances the woman would connect a cop named Malloy to Jim Cooper, private eye? Seamus added his urging to his host's natural desire to find answers, and by the time the sorting was completed, the balance had tipped in favor of taking the chance. Seamus also helped Malloy choose which woman from the list he'd see.

In his 1947 Ford coupe, Malloy drove to Evanston, unaware of his secret companion's satisfaction with his persuasive powers. Seamus was eager to see his former client's reaction to the possibility that her involvement in Danny Proust's schemes might become public. Hoping the young cop wouldn't overplay his hand, Seamus murmured from time to time, "Be cool." Malloy was receptive, repeating aloud: "I gotta play it cool. Real cool."

Malloy had dressed in his good suit again, but this time he toned down the outfit with a white handkerchief in the jacket pocket and a plain brown hat borrowed from his father's extensive collection of plain hats. His father's woolen winter coat, more dignified than Malloy's leather Eisenhower jacket, felt overly warm by the time he arrived in Evanston.

The Collins home was much grander than Malloy was used to, and he sat out front for a few seconds, gathering his courage. The sight of the imposing red-brick facade didn't help, so he forced himself to leave the car, step briskly to the wide front door, and ring the doorbell. When he heard it chime a dignified, low-toned alert to the inhabitants, his nerve almost deserted him. Once more Seamus voiced encouragement. "Cool. Be cool."

A woman in a plain gray dress answered the door, and Malloy asked if he could speak to the lady of the house concerning a missing person investigation he was conducting. Though he stammered a little, Seamus thought he made a plausible case. The maid listened with a blank expression, told Malloy to wait, and left him on the doorstep, closing the extra-wide oaken door firmly in his face.

As he shuffled his feet on the fat-pillared portico, Malloy coached himself. *Confidence! If you get in, project confidence.* He tried to recall salient points from two books he'd been studying, *The Power of Positive Thinking* and *How to Win Friends and Influence People.* He planned to apply the books' principles to his meeting with Mrs. Collins, if he got that far. Seamus went silent, figuring the kid had enough advice with the likes of Dale Carnegie and Norman Vincent Peale in his head.

The maid returned with the same blank expression. "Mrs. Collins will see you." She turned and walked away, apparently expecting he would follow.

Malloy entered a foyer with a ceiling as tall as his parents' whole house and trailed the maid through the space, which had no apparent purpose other than ambiance. On the other side of it were three steps that led to a sunken living area with a television, two couches, chairs that looked like no one ever sat in them, and an assortment of mostly bare tables. There was not a single doily to be seen, and he imagined his mother's disapproval. On the walls were examples of what he assumed was art, but there wasn't much he could identify in any of them. One had part of a person in it, but he, or maybe she, looked to Malloy as if the artist had gotten tired and quit before he finished it.

Dead to Get Ready—and Go

A woman stood looking out one of a line of windows that made up a whole wall. The garden she observed was still wrapped for winter, the shrubs burlapped and tied, the smaller plants covered with overturned pots. Though it wasn't particularly pretty now, Malloy guessed the view was spectacular the other three seasons of the year.

She turned as Malloy entered, and he again coached himself as he strode toward her. *Use her name. Smile. Project confidence.* "Mrs. Collins. It's good of you to see me."

Wilma Collins looked much the same as when, as Wilma Jameson, she'd hired Seamus to investigate her husband's disappearance. In this very room she'd told him gravely that the police weren't getting anywhere, and a more focused investigation might get results.

For a woman in her thirties, she's still pretty attractive, Malloy was thinking, and Seamus winced mentally at the callowness of youth. Wilma was certainly well-maintained. She wore an elegant white dress he thought they called a sheath, and her hair was arranged in a sophisticated French twist. Bright red lipstick and nail polish matched her shoes, and bracelets—*Real gold,* Malloy judged—jangled at her wrists.

"Bridget says you're a private investigator, Mr. Cooper."

"Yes, ma'am. I'm hoping you can help with a case I'm working on."

"I hope so, too," she said, meeting his eyes for a second longer than was necessary.

Her frank gaze startled Malloy. *She looks at me the way a hungry man looks at a chicken leg.* When he took an involuntary step backward, Seamus whispered, "Cool."

Responding to the command, Malloy tried to cover his retreat by setting a hand casually on the back of the couch. At that moment the maid brought in a tan overcoat and laid it across the arm. Getting out of her way meant moving back toward Mrs. Collins, who regarded him wryly, aware of his discomfort. After the maid laid a multi-colored headscarf beside the coat, her employer said, "Thank you, Bridget. You may go."

Bridget disappeared, and Mrs. Collins' gaze grew warmer. "Tell me what you're working on, Mr.—What was your name again?"

"Cooper, ma'am. James Cooper." Malloy felt ill at ease under her knowing look, and suddenly the idea of getting to know an experienced woman didn't seem so attractive. *This one's definitely experienced, and I doubt I'm up to her speed.*

Taking a package of cigarettes from a table beside her, Mrs. Collins shook one out, tapped the end on the tabletop, and waited, staring pointedly at him. Realizing belatedly what he was supposed to do, Malloy took the lighter from its matching ashtray and lit her cigarette. When she'd taken in a lungful of smoke she asked, "How can I help?"

"Well, ma'am—"

"Wilma." She blew the smoke out, not really at him, but she didn't turn away, either.

"Ma'am—uh, Wilma, I wonder what you can tell me about a club called Danny's Place."

Her manner went from warm to cold in an instant. "Nothing, I'm afraid."

Seamus hoped the kid didn't blow it by accusing her of anything, but Malloy merely asked, "I'd like to know your impression of the place."

"I only went there once." Squashing the almost-whole cigarette in the ashtray, she picked up the coat, signaling imminent departure.

Malloy took the garment from her and held it, as a gentleman should. "I've discovered that some of the women there actually set men up for trouble," he said, keeping his tone informative rather than accusing.

Her shoulders felt stiff as he slid the coat on, but her voice remained cool. "What makes you say that?"

"Over the past year, seven wives who divorced their husbands for adultery named a woman from Danny's Place as—" Malloy couldn't think of a polite word. "—assistants in infidelity."

Mrs. Collins took some time with her coat, looking down as she fastened the oversized horn buttons. "Really," she said when she'd finished. "That's very odd."

"The girl who died in the accident with your husband had been named once before in divorce proceedings. We—I think someone at the club pays the girls to commit adultery with rich men."

She turned to a decorative mirror as she settled the silk scarf over her hair. With deliberation that might signal care for her appearance but might also have been stalling for time, she wrapped the scarf at her throat, tied it at the back of her neck, and pulled the coat collar upright to cover the knot.

"I can only tell you what happened in my situation," she finally replied. Her tone was casual, as if she answered as a good citizen, not because her experience was germane. "My husband took me to Danny's for our fourth wedding anniversary. One of the girls—Tina—flirted outrageously with him. The next night he went back without me, and after that he was a regular visitor. He never spoke of what went on there. Then one night he didn't come home."

"You reported him missing?"

Slightly more comfortable with the facts of the case, she nodded. "When the police could find no trace of him, I hired an investigator. I had to know what happened."

She hadn't seemed worried for her husband's safety, Seamus recalled, only puzzled. He'd guessed she was unwilling to wait for the resolution of a missing person case that might drag on for years.

"The P.I. was Seamus Hanrahan?" Malloy asked.

"Yes. He'd barely begun to investigate when they found Arthur's body in the river."

"With a girl from Danny's."

A raised brow told him she didn't like being reminded of that. "I have an appointment, Mr. Cooper. Bridget will see you out." She hadn't raised her voice, but Bridget appeared in the doorway, her hands folded in front of her.

"Thank you, Mrs. Collins—" Malloy began, but she'd already turned away. As he followed Bridget out, Seamus whispered, "Look back."

Malloy glanced behind him and saw that, despite her claim of having to leave, Wilma Collins had taken up the telephone and was dialing a number she read from a small book. Glancing up, she saw him watching and turned away, removing an earring as she put the receiver to her ear.

"Did you work for Mrs. Collins when she was Mrs. Jameson?" he asked the maid as they navigated their way to the front door. Though Seamus approved of Malloy's attempt, Bridget acted as if she hadn't heard the question.

"Have a pleasant day, sir," she said, opening the door. It closed behind him almost before he was clear of it. Letting out a breath of mixed relief and frustration, Malloy headed for his car.

Next Malloy searched out a pay phone and called to tell his mother he'd be late coming home. He sounded like a little kid asking permission to eat dinner at the neighbors' house, and Seamus heard his thought: *If I don't let her know I'll be late, she'll start calling my friends to ask if they've seen me.*

"Where are you going, Sweetie?" his mother asked.

He tried to shut her curiosity down. "Out with a friend."

"Which friend is that?"

Malloy suppressed a sigh. "Joe."

"It sounds like you and he are becoming good friends." A pouting tone entered her voice. "I wish we could meet him. You're our baby, Deanie, even if you are all grown up. Your father and I want to get to know the people you spend your time with."

"You will, Mom. When Joe gets to know me better, he'll want to meet you."

"Well, tell him he's welcome anytime." She paused. "You don't think he's nervous about being—a Negro. I mean, you told him we don't mind, right?"

"I told him, Mom."

"That's good. Now where are you and Joe going?"

Malloy bit his lip as he concocted a lie. "Um, somebody he knows is reciting poetry at a café. We're going to go listen."

"Oh, is he a beatnik?"

"It's a she, and no. She's a student at Northwestern."

"So Joe's dating a college girl? That's nice. Maybe she has a friend for you."

Almost off the hook. "Maybe."

"Well, you boys have a nice time, and I'll leave the key in the usual place so you don't have to wake us up to get in."

Though irritated at the delay, Seamus couldn't help but be amused by Malloy's troubles with his mother. Having seen him with the other cops, he couldn't help but compare the illusion of the young man's active love life with the fact that the kid could barely get ten feet from his mother before the leash tightened.

Malloy didn't let his mother, and the guilt he felt for lying to her, stop him from heading to Danny's Place. As he drove, he promised himself he'd be more aware of undercurrents than he was before. He was sure his experience would be very different this time.

For his part, Seamus allowed himself to hope Malloy's visit would contribute to the solution of his murder. He might recognize a voice he heard as the woman who'd lured him to Danny's. Malloy might find someone who'd seen or heard something that night. He didn't know how the club figured into Lee's affair with Grant and their escape from Chicago, but he was determined to find out.

Danny's Place was again busy. Men in dark, vested suits escorted well-dressed women in fur coats and jaunty little hats through the doors, held for them by the square-built man Sandra had identified as Herb. When Herb noticed Malloy getting out of his car, he turned to speak to someone inside. By the time Malloy reached the entrance, Frankie Proust had stepped outside. He and the bouncer stood side by side, blocking the way. *Uh-oh*, Seamus thought. "Cool, kid. Be cool."

When Malloy reached them Frankie said without preamble, "Herb here tells me you're a private eye."

Malloy sensed a threat he didn't understand. "Yes, I'm looking for a woman you knew as Lili Moreno."

"And why do you think she might be here?"

"I don't think she's here. I'm looking for someone who knows where she might be."

A look passed between the two men. "You already asked your questions," Frankie said. "Did you find out anything?"

"Careful!" Seamus warned.

Malloy remained cool, at least on the outside. "Nothing concrete."

"Then I suggest you look for Miss Moreno someplace else."

Seamus whispered, "Quiet!" but it did no good.

Ignoring the hint that he should leave Malloy said, "Then I'll just go in and enjoy the show."

"You ain't welcome here," the bouncer said.

Frankie took a step toward Malloy, using his index finger to poke him in the chest. "Listen, kid. We ain't seen that girl for years, and the boss don't want you hanging around, keeping the employees from doing their work."

"It's a free country—" Malloy began. He gasped in surprise as Herb picked him off his feet, hustled him around the corner of the building, and slammed him against the wall.

"Show some respect, you little worm. Frankie told you how it's going to be."

"You can't—"

"I can't what?" There was a metallic snap, and Malloy felt the chill of a blade at his throat. Herb's eyes bored into his, and he realized the man was willing, even eager, to use it on him.

Frankie spoke from behind Herb. "If I was you, I'd listen to reason."

"Let him go," said a third voice. Herb stepped back, holding the knife loosely in his hand. Looking past the bouncer's angry glare, Malloy saw that Danny Proust had joined his brother. He was again dressed all in black, but this time he wore no necktie and had left the top two buttons of his shirt undone.

"What's your name, kid?"

Shaken, Malloy had to think for a second to recall his false identity. "Cooper. Jim Cooper."

"Mr. Cooper, I'm sorry if the boys were rough on you. They're very protective of the club's reputation." Turning, Proust told the other two, "Give us a minute."

When they were gone, Danny reached out and straightened Malloy's tie. He used his left hand, and when he patted the jacket in a gesture of completion, his face twisted a little, as if the movement caused him pain. Touching his opposite shoulder briefly he said, "I read in the newspaper that Lili and her boyfriend killed her husband then left town. You got reason to believe that isn't true?"

Malloy answered honestly. "Not really."

"Well, then. It's a tragic story, but not a new one." Proust licked his lips, and Seamus thought of a python he'd once seen at a circus. As if the thought had just occurred to him, Proust said, "I'll tell you what. If I find out where Miss—Mrs. Hanrahan is, I'll call you. And if you should happen to find out where she is, bring the information to me. I'll pay half again what your current client offered." He frowned. "Who's the client, by the way?"

"It's my policy not to provide that information."

Proust smiled thinly. "Family, I think. Lili never talked about them, but I guessed they were out there." He patted Malloy's chest, again using the left hand. "More money for you if you tell me when you find her. Get it?"

"Why do you care?"

Proust's mask slipped for a split second, revealing anger. When he recovered his smile, the image of a snake returned to Seamus' mind. "Let's just say I believe in justice."

Malloy recoiled at hearing that word from the lips of someone he suspected was far from just, but Proust didn't seem to notice. "Do you understand what I'm saying, Mr. Cooper?"

"Yes." The word came from lips that didn't want to agree.

"Herb." The man appeared immediately. "Escort Mr. Cooper to his car, please."

With a grunt of assent, Herb followed Malloy to the parking lot. As he bent to open the door, Herb spun him around, pressed him against the vehicle, and raised his knee sharply into Malloy's groin. Seamus felt Malloy's pain as if the groin were his own.

"Don't come here again unless you got what the boss wants." Adjusting the suit jacket over his massive shoulders, the big man turned and walked back to the club, not sparing another glance for his still-gasping victim.

Though Seamus knew his host would live through the effects of the blow, Malloy wasn't sure if he wanted to. His mind buzzed with pain, anger, and surprise. Having never been the victim of such casual violence, Malloy's first thought was *I'm in way over my head.*

Seamus was sorry he'd urged Malloy to come, but how could he have known it was dangerous for his host to ask questions about someone who'd worked there so long ago?

When Malloy could finally stand straight, he got into his car, started the engine, and sat for a few minutes, recovering his breath and his courage. To Seamus' surprise he muttered, "Mr. Proust, you're going to be sorry you messed with Chicago's Finest."

Seamus wanted to pat the young cop on the back. What might have scared him away had instead turned his curiosity into a burning desire to see Danny Proust's secrets exposed. "We'll see how much you really want justice," Malloy said as he drove away. "I'll bet he won't be such a fan when the justice is focused on him and his thugs."

Chapter Fourteen

Everywhere Joe Waite looked in the seamier spots of the Black Belt, people knew Chicken Charlie, but no one could say at a given moment where he'd be. "Charlie live here sometime, there sometime, know what I mean?" one man said. "Lotsa times he can't go back where he been, 'cause he don't pay."

Finally Waite learned that Charlie played poker in the back room of a chair factory most Saturday nights. When he asked how he might get into the game, the man laughed and said it would be a cinch if a guy had a few dollars to put at risk.

The place wasn't easy to find, but the directions Joe had been given were good. On a street lined with dilapidated buildings, a sign advertised, Quality Wooden Chairs. In a dusty window display was an assortment of ladder-back, bow-back, and harp-back chairs, along with a few rockers and some stools.

Going around to the side, he found an alley that led to a side door so scarred it seemed unlikely to keep out stray dogs much less full-grown adults bent on theft or mayhem. He knocked six times, three short, three long, as he'd been instructed. The door opened a crack, revealing a wary face.

"Moe said there might be a game here." After an unabashed examination from Waite's feet to his hair, the man stepped back, allowing him entry into a storeroom. Five more men sat around a battered table, most of them in their fifties. Each had brought along something to drink: three bottles of beer, a liquor flask that smelled like whiskey, a Coca-Cola, and one glass of milk set beside a small thermal jug. Overhead, a single light bulb hung from a black-coated wire, its light unshaded and glaring. One of the players wore a visor to shield his eyes from its brightness.

The harsh glow of the light cast the rest of the room into darkness, but Waite sensed its smallness. It smelled of sweat and wood shavings.

Six faces regarded Joe, some with curiosity, others with suspicion. He'd dressed in pleated gray trousers, a white shirt with a knitted vest over it, and a charcoal gray wool coat that wasn't new but kept out the biting Chicago wind. Two of the men rolled their eyes, possibly at his youth, before returning to the study of their cards. No one objected to his inclusion in the game, and the man who'd answered the door kicked an empty chair away from the table in a casual invitation to sit.

"I'm Pickles," he said. "The rest you'll get to know, I guess."

Ronnie recognized Charlie Cole right away by the scar that traced his cheek from eye to mouth, a poorly-healed memento of some long-ago disagreement. Unlike the others, he was sharply dressed, in a black dress shirt and a white tie. His finery was slightly shabby, but the purple felt Panama with a rooster feather bowing from the brim to the back of his head made a statement.

"Do we know you, son?" the man in the visor asked Waite.

"You maybe knew my daddy, Prince Blair. He worked at McCluskey's till his heart gave out a few years back."

"What he do there?"

Waite chuckled. "Why, he was the manager, of course."

There was a pause, then one of them got the joke and snorted a laugh. Once the others joined in Joe went on, "Daddy did the sweeping up and lugged barrels of beer around. What else a Negro man gonna do at a white man's bar?" There were nods around the table, and he finished, "When Daddy died in McCluskey's back room, I quit school and went to work downtown to feed the family." It was all true, though not for him. Joe had taken on the identity of a friend from high school.

"I heard about that," one man said. "Took McCluskey half a day to notice Prince was missing. Sorry, son." The others nodded, their faces touched with sympathy this time.

"It's all over now." Waite plunked down a wad of bills, signaling he'd come ready to play. That was apparently introduction enough, and he was dealt into the next hand.

Waite played moderately, having learned the game from his father and uncles. He bet enough on each hand to interest the others, but not enough to seem flashy. He lost a little, but as near as Ronnie could tell, it was an honest game. Waite was observant, and once he realized the guy across from him was a sandbagger and the guy on his left would peek at his cards if he didn't hold them close to his chest, he relaxed and let the hands play out naturally.

Chicken Charlie sat to Joe's right, with two men between them. Charlie, a talker, kept up a running commentary when it was his turn to deal. "Five card draw, gentlemen. Now who needs cards? All right, two for my favorite cousin Pickles, and two for Matthew. The new kid takes two, good luck with those, young man. One for Billy—are you drawing to an inside straight again, Bill? Two for Abraham. Sammy don't want no cards; he likes the ones I gave him. And me, I'll take two, and Lord Above, make 'em two good ones." When he looked at his new cards, Charlie's face didn't reveal whether he was pleased or dismayed. "Now, gentlemen, who's going to start this mess?"

As the game went on, the players casually picked information out of Waite. "Who told you about this game, son?" the man named Matthew asked.

"I do appliance repairs, and I got called to this place over near 33rd." He paused, as if recalling. "Funny name, the woman had—Lincoln. Ain't that odd for a girl?"

"Nothing wrong with a man naming his children after eminent Americans, son," Charlie said. The others around the table smiled knowingly.

"Anyway, I had to wait for her to get home, and while I was standing in the foyer, I talked a little to a couple of guys there, and the subject turned to poker. Moe said this was an honest game, so I thought I'd see if I could win me some money." He gestured humorously at the small pile of bills in front of him. "I wish you gentlemen would do better for the new man."

Everyone laughed except Charlie, who asked, "Would that be Lincoln Cole you was working for?"

"Yes, sir," Waite replied. "I fixed her stove, but I felt bad for her. Someone she knows real well came up missing, and she's awfully worried." Ronnie could have hugged Waite—if she'd had the ability. The guy was good undercover, sliding subtle bits of information into his responses.

"Lee," one of the men said. "The papers say she killed her old man and split." He made a wave-like motion with his free hand, simulating flight.

"Lee, yes. That's the name she said."

Charlie's face had gone pale, making the scar stand out even more. "Lee's missing?" He tried to sound casual, but his tone betrayed anxiety.

"It's a good thing her mama's gone to her reward," Matthew said. "She always said the girl was trashy. At least Victoria don't have to see her first-born child go to prison for murder."

Sammy clicked his tongue in agreement. "She broke her mama's heart, sure enough."

There was general discussion of Lee's character faults, apparently defined by her mother to anyone who'd listen. Ronnie found herself feeling sorry for Lee. She couldn't have been trashy, because then Seamus wouldn't have loved her. He just wouldn't.

Charlie didn't join the discussion of Lee's supposed sins. In fact, when he recovered from the news that had obviously shocked him, he ordered everyone back to their cards with a terse, "Whose bet is it? We ain't got all night here."

The game broke up just after one. Waite thanked the players for including him and left.

"Wait!" Ronnie ordered, but she needn't have said anything. Waite stepped into the shadows at the first opportunity, eager to see where Charlie Cole would go next.

It wasn't long before he emerged from the building, body bent forward as he hurried away. Waite followed. They traveled some distance, but in the end Charlie turned down a street Ronnie recognized, the one that led to Danny's Place.

The last of the guests were leaving the nightclub, some laughing, a few supporting friends who'd overindulged during the evening's festivities. Charlie paused in the parking lot, shivering in a March wind that must have gone right through his thin coat. When the doorway was clear, he approached the oversized doorman, his manner obsequious.

Watching from some distance away, Waite strained to hear what they said but caught only phrases. Charlie asked a question, and Ronnie heard Lee's stage name, Lili. The man shook his head. When Charlie asked a second question, the other made shooing gestures. Charlie persisted, and the doorman gave him a shove of dismissal. He staggered back a step but didn't give up. His voice rose, and Ronnie caught the words, "—wouldn't have told him."

This time the shove was harder, and Charlie almost fell. The doorman said in a voice loud enough for the hidden listeners to hear, "We don't know where she went. Now get lost!"

His anger was enough to deter Charlie. As he turned to go, the doorman assisted him with a kick to his backside. Charlie stumbled and fell. He tried to protect his face with his hands, but they slid on the ice and he hit the ground hard.

Laughing, the big man called, "Don't want to be putting your nose into a white girl's business, boy. It ain't healthy."

Charlie didn't answer. He rose, brushing the front of his coat and wiping dirty slush from his face. From his ragged breathing, Ronnie deduced he was close to tears. He looked back once at the doorman, who stood watching to make sure he left the premises.

Stumbling blindly, Charlie reached the place where Waite stood watching. The cop leaned back to avoid notice, but when Charlie put his hand against the building for support, Ronnie jumped to him, leaving Waite in the shadows.

Chicken Charlie saw the world through a blear of alcohol. As Ronnie adjusted to his fuzzy thoughts and the slight reel in his gait, she tried to pick from his thoughts what he knew about the Hanrahans. It wasn't easy. While every person's mind is a constant roil of subjects,

Charlie's was also fuddled by years of drink. In addition, he actively suppressed his more disturbing thoughts, pushing them out of consciousness because he was unwilling to face them.

Disjointed phrases came in rapid, incomprehensible bursts. *I didn't mean nothing.* Ronnie sensed Charlie was worried about Lee. At the same time, he was angry with her for reasons Ronnie guessed were mostly selfish. *She shoulda helped me—*

Charlie hurried along the streets, his breath short and his gait unsteady. When he stopped at a set of steps leading up to a doorway, Ronnie recognized the address as the one Lincoln Cole had written down for Joe Waite. Charlie climbed to the eighth floor, grunting harder with each successive flight. When he reached his destination, he rapped on the door with his knuckles, waited, and rapped again. "Jackson? Jackson, open up!"

A sleepy-eyed lad of about sixteen opened the door a crack, saw who was there, and stepped back, revealing pajamas too short for his legs and arms. "Geez, Dad. Is somebody chasing you?"

"No, son. I need to talk to Linny."

Yawning, the kid rubbed at his face. "She's at work."

"I know that. I thought I'd wait for her here."

The boy rolled his eyes but asked, "You want something to eat?"

Charlie waved the suggestion away. "I could use a beer."

"You know Linny doesn't allow it in the house."

He shook his head. "Hard to see how a daughter of mine could take such ideas."

"I'm going back to bed," Jackson said. "I got sidewalks to shovel tomorrow." He turned toward his bed but stopped to add, "I'll be checking to see if anything comes up missing."

"Don't talk like that to your father, son." Though his tone was resentful, Ronnie knew Charlie had at that very moment been wondering where Linny had hidden the jar of change she kept for emergencies. When Jackson returned to bed, Charlie sat in a tattered rocking chair, the only space available since a second teen slept on the couch. Crossing his arms on his chest, Charlie dropped his chin forward. Before he dozed off, Ronnie heard the questions that plagued him. *Where's Lee? Why did she run away?* And when his inner defenses slipped momentarily: *What did I do?*

***

When Malloy crawled into bed, treating his bruised groin with great care, Seamus barely waited for him to drift away before he called, "Ronnie?"

"Here!" she replied. "I'm with Charlie Cole. He's Linny's father."

"Interesting. What's he like?"

"One of those guys who's always going to get rich someday when things come together. Even his family doesn't trust him."

Seamus told Ronnie what had happened to Malloy at Danny's, and he heard her whistle softly. "Okay, this is way beyond your wife seeing some other guy. Charlie Cole, who is her friend Linny's dad but not exactly a straight shooter, was spying on her for some reason. Charlie works for Danny Proust, at least sometimes. Neither Charlie nor Proust seems to know where Lee is, but they both want to know. Why?"

"Somebody at that club must know something," Seamus said. It wasn't an answer. It was more like a desperate hope.

Chapter Fifteen

Malloy slept late Sunday morning, but at 9:00 his mother rapped on the door. "Deanie, you'd better get up or you'll be late for mass."

Without thinking, he rolled out of bed then winced as his groin objected. Seamus felt it too, but it wasn't as bad as he'd feared.

"Deanie?"

"Coming, Mom."

Biting his lip, Malloy tested his legs. They held, and he told himself, *It's a bruise, like other bruises, just in a more sensitive place.* Pulling down his shorts, he examined the spot in some detail. Seamus wished he could look away.

After practicing to hide any sign of the injury in his walk, Malloy went downstairs. His mother was already dressed for church in a pale gray suit with navy edging on the lapels. On the stand in the hallway were her hat and gloves, a clean handkerchief, and a small clutch bag. "I'm going in early to put up signs for the rummage sale," she told him. "You and your father can come later in your car."

"Okay." Taking a bowl and a box of cereal from the cupboard over the sink, he shook out a liberal portion of Puffed Wheat then turned to the round-topped refrigerator for milk. Pulling the paper cap off the bottle, he poured milk on the cereal and added a liberal spoonful from the sugar bowl that sat on the table.

"Did Joe have a good time at the poetry reading?"

"I think so."

"And did you have a good time?"

He suppressed a grim smile. "I'm not much for poetry."

"You remember we're going to the Stuarts' for Sunday dinner, don't you?"

Malloy groaned. "Mom, do I have to? With all their kids and *their* kids, nobody will miss me."

"Of course they'd miss you, Deanie. Miranda specifically asked on Thursday if you were coming."

No surprise there. Miranda Stuart has been after me for three years. A picture of the perfectly nice Caroline's wide, blank eyes appeared in Malloy's mind. *She's dying to find a husband and start having babies, but I've got things I want to do before I turn into my father.*

Realizing he'd never win an argument with his mother on the matter, Malloy agreed he'd make an appearance at the Stuart home by noon and headed for the shower.

***

Charlie woke at 7:00 a.m. to the sound of Linny's key in the lock. She looked exhausted, but when she saw her father with his feet propped on a small table he'd pulled from a corner, her expression turned dark. "What are you doing here?"

"There's my girl!" Charlie rose, crossed the room, and hugged her thin shoulders. When Linny merely abided it he chided, "No sugar for your old dad?"

"When you show up not wanting something, I'll be happy to see you." Setting down her tattered shopping bag, Linny took off her coat and hung it on a peg near the door. She pulled off a thin pair of galoshes and set them on a mat of old newspapers, aligning them precisely in the center. "I'll ask again, Daddy. What do you want?"

"I heard last night that Lee's missing."

"She is." Linny's eyes narrowed. "Did you know she was married?" Charlie opened his mouth to deny it, but her finger almost connected with his nose. "Don't lie to me, old man!"

He raised his hands, palms out in a gesture of surrender. "I didn't know it at first, Lincoln, I swear. All I knew was she was singing at the club one day and gone the next." In an aside typical of narcissists everywhere he complained, "After all I done for that girl, she slipped away without sayin' boo."

"After all you did for her?" Linny's pretty face twisted in a sneer. "You talked her into working at a place she hated."

Charlie tried for outrage. "That job coulda supported all you children and your momma, too. If Victoria hadn't been so stuck-up about it, things woulda been easier for all of us."

"You knew Momma wouldn't take a cent of money that came from other people's sin." Linny's eyes narrowed. "But I'll bet you had your hand stuck out every time Lee got paid."

"She helps me out from time to time." Charlie smoothed his shirt front. "It's what a girl does for the man that raised her."

"You never raised any of us!" Linny spat at him. As a word he'd used caught her attention, she paused. "She *helps* you out, you said? You've seen Lee lately?"

"It was a accident, you know?" Charlie wiped the sides of his mouth with a finger and thumb. "After Lee ran away from Danny's, I didn't see her for two years. Then one day I was walking down Maxwell Street, and there she was, stepping off a bus." His eyes misted with the memory. "She looked different, but I knew she was my Lee right off. Still beautiful." He waved a hand as if to conjure the image he saw in his mind.

Linny folded her arms. "What'd you do about it?"

"I followed her to this building with a sign out front that said, L. K. DOBBLEMAN, ATTORNEY, and below that, S. HANRAHAN, PRIVATE INVESTIGATOR." Charlie's manner became more animated as he told the story. "Through the window I saw Lee sit down behind a desk in the private eye's office. I hung around, and pretty soon a white man came along and went in there. What I saw between him and Lee let me know she was his lady." He smiled knowingly. "I guessed that white man didn't know he was kissing a colored girl."

"And then you guessed you could make some money on it."

Charlie stood a little straighter, though he was never perfectly straight. "That gal run off and left you and me to fend for ourselves. I figured she could help her old daddy out now she was all set up good."

"Stepdaddy."

He looked down his nose at her. "I'm the only daddy she ever had."

"And that wasn't much!" Linny shook her head angrily. "I can't count the times I told my sister not to listen to you, but your sweet talk always got to her."

Ronnie lost a few seconds of the conversation as its meaning hit her. Chicken Charlie was Lee Hanrahan's stepfather. Linny Cole was her half-sister. Seamus was apparently unaware of it. He'd guessed she was giving money to her family, but he hadn't guessed who that family was.

It's no big deal, Ronnie tried to tell herself, but she knew that wasn't true. "Passing," as it was called, offered advantages for those light-skinned enough to appear to be white. Though Lee was probably of mixed blood, the operating premise in 1950's America was that any drop of Negro blood classified a person as Negro and therefore inferior. Laws on the books in many states forbade blacks and whites to marry. Though Illinois had repealed its interracial marriage ban in the late 1800's, efforts were still widely in place to keep the races separate. Neighborhood associations were often formed, and though the practice of "racially restrictive covenants" was declared unconstitutional by the Supreme Court in 1948, whites simply proclaimed the organizations social and continued using them to keep blacks from moving into predominantly white areas. Many people of both races believed these separations were not only desirable, they were morally right.

Though his marriage to Lee was legal, the social stigma of having a black wife might well have cost Seamus customers, friends, and more. His lawyer landlord might have insisted he vacate the building in order to save his own practice from being tainted by Seamus' situation. He'd have been a social pariah, despised by some, pitied by others, and joked about behind his back.

Lee's race explained many of the things she'd done. If she'd loved Seamus, she must have agonized over whether to tell him her secret. If she confessed he might walk away, unable to resist society's prejudices. Ronnie didn't see Seamus as a bigot, but he'd had half a century to change his views. Had the 1950s Seamus been the kind of guy who'd reject Lee for her race, or would he have accepted the animosity of the world in order to remain with the woman he loved?

That brought to mind a question for Ronnie: What was she going to do with her new-found knowledge? She'd promised to be honest with Seamus, but they'd suspected a love affair, not this. He claimed he'd come to terms with Lee's infidelity. How would he handle this unexpected turn?

Ronnie returned her attention to Linny, who asked her father, "Where's Lee now?"

Charlie raised his hands again, palms up this time. "That's what I come to ask you. I don't read no newspapers, so I didn't know about her husband getting killed and all that."

"They found him in the lake. I told the police Lee didn't have anything to do with it."

Charlie turned away. "No. Of course she didn't."

"I told the detective in charge of the case that Lee's no killer, but he doesn't believe me." Linny gave a disgusted huff. "And she didn't have no boyfriend do it for her, neither."

Charlie chewed at the side of his lip, and Ronnie read in his thoughts the question of how much he could tell his daughter without revealing his own dirty deeds. "That part's true, Sissy."

"What do you mean?" Linny took a step toward him. Charlie cringed but didn't back away.

"Calm down, now, Lincoln! Lord, you remind me of your mother when you get like that." He smoothed his shirt front again. "There was someone Lee was seeing on the side—another white man."

"I don't believe it," Linny said. "If Lee got married, she'd stay that way."

Charlie's graying brows rose high on his forehead. "That just shows you don't know everything. Lee has this big old boyfriend, and he's a cop. She even set him on me." His shoulders shifted nervously as he recalled the incident. "I was just walkin' around like a normal citizen, and all of a sudden that man shoved me up against a building and told me all he'd do if I bothered Miz Hanrahan anymore."

"You deserve it," Linny said angrily. "You had no right to shake Lee down for money."

Charlie's expression turned sly. "But she didn't send her husband to scare me off, did she?"

Linny had no answer for that, and after a moment he went on. "Her and that cop used to meet up in the park. Even when it got cold, they'd sit there talking for a long time. Once I saw him reach out and put his arm around her, right in public, like he didn't care who saw."

"Lord!" Linny breathed the word.

Charlie seemed pleased he'd convinced her. "Like I said, they used to talk till my feet started freezin' to the sidewalk."

"It doesn't matter," Linny said stubbornly. "Whatever Lee did, she's in trouble, and we don't know where she is or how to help her."

Ronnie decided Linny could be helpful to her now. As she jumped from Charlie to his daughter, she picked up Linny's thought, which was in the form of a prayer: *Lord, please guide Joe Waite. Let him find my sister and prove that whatever sins she committed, she's no murderer.*

Ronnie had forgotten that Linny Cole worked nights. As soon as her father left, she woke Jackson, replaced him in their only real bed, and slept for six hours while Ronnie twiddled her mental thumbs and wished she'd stayed with Chicken Charlie. At least he was on the move—and semiconscious.

Chapter Sixteen

When the shrill clang of metal hitting metal sounded at five a.m. Monday morning, Malloy woke and shut the alarm off with a well-practiced, in-the-dark movement. He fumbled for the bedside lamp and turned it on, giving Seamus a window on the conglomeration of sports trophies, photographs, and other memorabilia Malloy had collected in his twenty years. A small phonograph with a stack of records beside it sat on the dresser, and a pile of clean clothing that should have been put away last Monday still rested on the seat of a chair. Pulling on his exercise shorts, Malloy made his way downstairs to the bathroom.

The workout was much the same as before, and he went through the steps unconsciously, his thoughts on the last few days' events. Malloy was angry at the treatment he'd received at Danny's Place. Seamus was more concerned with Danny's request that Malloy bring any information he found on Lee to him. Whatever his reason, Seamus guessed it would be bad for Lee.

"Help Joe," Seamus whispered, and Malloy was more than willing. As the jump rope tapped the garage floor in rapid rhythm, the young cop muttered, "I'm going to look for evidence to give the bunco squad, too." Dean Malloy wanted to put the Proust boys completely out of business.

Once he finished his workout, Malloy breakfasted, this time on Wheaties, fetching two fresh bottles of milk from the porch when he heard the clink of the milkman's delivery. With his cereal he had a quarter cup of raisins and two pieces of toast smeared with jam. Then he went back upstairs to get ready for work.

Seamus hadn't heard from Ronnie, but he had little to report anyway. Malloy's Sunday of church services, polite conversation over fried chicken and biscuits, and avoiding alone time with the amorous Miss Stuart hadn't left much of an impression. He resolved to wait and hear what Waite had to say about the weekend's events.

The two cops didn't get a chance to talk until Monday meeting was over. They were brought up to date on current cases and recent events, given their duties for the week, and cautioned to be on the lookout for two wanted men thought to be in the area. When they finally got to their patrol car, Malloy started with his visit to Wilma Jameson Collins' home. "She was pretty quick to inform someone about my visit," he said in conclusion. "I think you're right and she paid Danny Proust to have that girl set her husband up."

"Then how did the two of them end up dead?"

Malloy shrugged. "Accidents happen, I guess."

Waite told Malloy about his Saturday night activities, the card game from which he'd followed Chicken Charlie to the night club. "Charlie was pretty upset about Lee Hanrahan being missing," he concluded. "He went directly to Danny's Place to ask about where she might be."

"See? He thought they'd know. Something's all wrong about that place." Though he hadn't been sure he was going to, Malloy told Waite what had happened to him at the club.

"You should have called me," Waite chided.

"Why, Joe? You gonna go down there and beat the stuffing out of those goons for me?"

Waite's grin conceded the point. "Okay, probably not. Tell me again everything that happened the first night you went there. Something you did or said must have set off their alarms."

Shrugging, Malloy counted off points on his fingers. "I talked to the waitress, who's new and never met Lee. I talked to the singer, Patti LaFlame, who didn't like Lee and claims she doesn't care where she is. I talked to Sandra, the hat-check girl, and Addie, the club photographer. They liked Lee but claim they haven't seen her since she left."

Waite frowned. "Doesn't sound like enough to make anybody want to scare you off."

Malloy huffed disgustedly. "They didn't scare me off. They made me more interested in finding out what's going on."

Waite shook his head. "It can't have anything to do with Lee. If she was going to tell on them for some crime, she'd have done it when she ran away from there two years ago."

"Maybe something changed." Malloy shook his head. "Proust is up to something."

"So notify the sergeant you suspect there's criminal activity down there. He'll pass it on to the bunco squad, and they'll look into it. You and I need to keep looking for Lee."

Malloy didn't argue, but he found the situation at Danny's more intriguing than helping Linny Cole's friend. Joe had an attractive girl to spur him on. Malloy had a bruised groin and an equally bruised ego.

By the time his shift was over for the day, Malloy had decided to talk to Sandra again. He might be able to convince her to tell the police what she knew about Danny's Place. It was a longshot, since she'd probably lose her place of employment, but she seemed like a decent girl.

When he knocked on Sandra's door, however, she wasn't pleased to see him. Wearing an over washed chenille robe, she stood behind the door, hunched over like her back hurt. "I can't go out today," she said. "I have to wash my hair."

"Your hair looks fine," Malloy told her. "We can go to the drugstore and—"

"I'm not going anywhere with you." She tried to sound authoritative, but her voice shook a little, and she glanced behind him as if expecting to see someone there.

"Why, Sandra? I thought you liked me."

She pressed her lips together for a few seconds, but her chin quivered. "You got the wrong impression," she said stiffly. She tried to close the door on him, but Malloy stopped it with a hand.

"Sandra, listen—"

Her eyes met his, and he saw fear in their depths. "Please go. And stay away. I mean it."

As she pressed again on the door, Malloy saw four round, dark bruises on her upper arm, left by fingers closing hard on the soft flesh. Perhaps because of his own recent experience, he guessed those fingers belonged to Herb, the new bouncer at Danny's Place.

***

As soon as Malloy drifted off to sleep that night Seamus called, "Ronnie?" No answer. "Ronnie?"

So softly he wasn't sure he heard it, a word came. "Linny."

Matching her low volume he replied, "Got it." Linny Cole worked nights, which meant he would have to wait for a time when Ronnie could communicate without Linny hearing their conversation in her head. It was frustrating, but sooner or later she'd contact him and he'd learn what she knew.

***

For her part, Ronnie was relieved to have an excuse not to talk. What was she going to tell Seamus, or rather, *how* was she going to tell him? Because she knew she had to reveal Lee's secret before he found it out somewhere else.

Chapter Seventeen

Eager to discover if the detective in charge of his case was making headway, Seamus jumped his way to Grulke's desk Tuesday morning. He still hadn't heard from Ronnie, but he wasn't worried, since Linny Cole was probably just now going to sleep.

Grulke was dialing the telephone, using the eraser end of a pencil. The jump from a passing cop to the detective was tricky, since Seamus' host was hurrying to the mimeograph machine. His landing was rough, and a plaque on the desk teetered and then fell over with a crash. Grulke righted it with his free hand as he waited for his call to go through, letting out a soft belch. "Sausage Clarice made for breakfast must be a little off," he mumbled to himself.

Having learned that Seamus was a Chicago cop before the war, Grulke was calling his old station house to get an impression of the man from those he'd worked with before the war.

"This is Officer Berman at the 18th," said a voice on the other end of the line. "How can I help you?"

"Grulke down at the 8th. I'm looking for someone down there who remembers a cop named Seamus Hanrahan. He didn't come back to the force after the war."

"Hanrahan. That's the guy they pulled out of the lake?"

"Yeah. Did you know him?"

"Never worked with him. I've only been here two years, but he used to stop in sometimes to see Detective Wellman."

"Great. Can I speak with him?"

There was a pause. "He's not available."

"When's a good time to catch up with him?"

"Uh—Who did you say you are?"

"Detective Peter Grulke. I'm working Hanrahan's homicide."

"Grant's at Cook County Hospital, Detective. In a coma."

"Damn!" Grulke fumbled for a more sympathetic comment. "Is he going to be okay?"

"They don't know. He took a bullet in the chest then crashed his car, which smashed his head into the steering wheel. He's got a lot to recover from."

"Are you telling me Wellman is the cop who was shot last week?"

"Yes, sir."

Ending the call with a request he be kept informed, Grulke dug out the phone book and called the hospital. Once he'd identified himself, he was connected to a doctor who told him what was known of Wellman's injury. His car had hit a light post near the Metropole Hotel, and when the doorman hurried over to help, he saw that the driver had been shot. Transported to the hospital by ambulance, Wellman had undergone surgery but had not yet regained consciousness. "He's lucky to be alive," the doctor told Grulke.

"You don't know where he was when he was shot?"

"No. The police asked me how far he could have driven in his condition, but it's just too hard to say. If he hadn't done it, I'd have said it was impossible he drove at all."

"Thank you, doctor."

Grulke called the 18ᵗʰ again and asked to speak to someone who knew Wellman. After the introductions, during which they discovered they'd met at least once, Grulke told Detective Tony Cannell, "I'm working on the homicide of a private investigator named Seamus Hanrahan. I wanted to speak to Wellman because I understand he knew the guy."

"Hanrahan, yeah. He and Grant were partners before the war. From what I read in the papers, the wife looks like the guilty party."

"Very possible. She'd have had help, though."

"I see." Cannell paused. "You don't think Grant had anything to do with it, do you?"

In a rare moment of enlightenment, Grulke chose to be discreet. "I just want to know what he can tell me about the Hanrahans."

Cannell sighed. "I met Seamus a few times. Seemed like a decent guy."

"And he and Wellman were old friends?"

"Yeah, from back when they were patrolmen."

"What can you tell me about Wellman getting shot?"

Cannell repeated the account of the accident, adding, "We were supposed to take in a Blackhawks game that night, but Grant called and said he couldn't make it." With a sniff of regret he finished, "If he'd been with me, maybe he wouldn't be in a coma right now."

"So something came up last minute?"

"He said he had some personal stuff to take care of."

"And you don't know what that might have been?"

A tinge of irritation colored Cannell's reply. "I'm Grant's partner, not his wife. He isn't required to tell me about his private life."

Grulke hung up, muttering, "At least he didn't have to watch the Hawks lose again." Pulling a notebook toward him, he scribbled some notes: *Wellman & wife plan to murder Hanrahan. He gets suspicious & fights back. W gets wounded, wife disappears.*

He paused, tapping the pencil eraser on his desk blotter. "But how did Hanrahan end up in Lake Michigan if he shot Wellman?" He fell silent, but Seamus heard the rest of his thought. *She cooked up a double-cross, got her boyfriend to kill her husband then repaid him with a bullet through the ribs.*

Seamus was certain Lee wasn't that cold-blooded. She'd been in love with Grant. She wouldn't have betrayed him.

A few minutes later the phone rang, and Grulke got a response to a request he'd made for background information on Lee Hanrahan. As the clerk on the other end read from the record, Grulke copied down the points that interested him. Lee Hanrahan was born Lee Crevier. Father unknown. Mother Victoria Crevier. The identification card she'd obtained in 1948 listed her home address as East Wickett. When Seamus recognized it as a truncated street that ended at the rail yards, his mind began to roil with questions.

Bells went off in Grulke's mind, too, but he kept writing until the clerk covered everything she'd found. Lee had graduated from high school, but after that the records got sketchy. She'd filed income taxes, listing her employer as Daniel Proust, owner of a nightclub called Danny's Place. She'd made pretty good money at it, and the detective smirked as he guessed what sort of entertainment she'd provided.

"She went from working in a night club to marrying a private eye," Grulke muttered. "Maybe somebody down there can tell me how that came about."

Navigating the damp streets, Grulke found the club (after circling the block twice) and asked to speak to the owner. After he'd waited several minutes, Danny Proust came out of his office and down the stairs.

Noting Proust's well-made suit, perfect haircut, and alligator shoes, Grulke leaned toward disliking the guy, but Proust began apologizing before he reached the main floor.

"So sorry to keep you, Detective. I know how valuable your time is, and I wouldn't have made you wait except I was on the phone long distance with one of my suppliers. The time difference between here and Los Angeles makes it difficult—" He broke off abruptly. "But you don't need to hear about my troubles. I'm Danny Proust." He looked past Grulke to the man who'd let him in. "Did you offer the detective a drink, Herb?" Turning to Grulke he said, "Coffee, or something stronger?"

"Coffee's fine." Grulke showed Proust his star, mollified by the apology and the man's friendly manner. "Detective Peter Grulke, from the Chicago 8th. I'm looking into a murder and searching for a missing person—a suspect."

Proust nodded. "How can I help?"

Grulke explained about the fishermen finding Seamus Hanrahan's body in Lake Michigan.

"I read about that," Proust responded. "And I bet I know why you're here."

"You do?"

"Yes, sir. I recognized the photo in the paper of Lee Hanrahan. I didn't know her by that name, but she used to be a singer here."

"When was that?"

He considered. "Most of 1950, if I recall correctly."

"Have you seen or spoken to her since she left your employment?"

"I have not. She just walked out one night." Proust's tone hinted he was still angry about it. "Lili—that's the name I knew her by—was a beautiful woman with a voice like silk, but I found out later that she was dishonest."

Seamus' indignation rose, and he whispered, "Liar!" forgetting he suspected Lee had been dishonest with him. Grulke paid no more attention to his comment than he did to the background noise in the room.

"How did you come to hire her?"

"There's this old Negro who hangs around the place, kind of a Stepin Fetchit who does odd jobs for us. Charlie was determined I should hear the girl sing. He'd seen her in a church choir, and he kept telling me how great she was."

A link connected in Seamus' brain. It had been Charlie Cole who encouraged Lee to take the job at Danny's.

"I finally agreed to listen to her," Proust went on, "and I had to admit she was everything he said she'd be. A little shy at first—at least that's what I thought. Later I realized she wasn't shy, just cold. Lili was one of those women who might as well be made of marble." Shaking his head ruefully he added, "Still, she was one beautiful dame."

"I've seen the pictures," Grulke said.

"And she sang like an angel. Cole claimed he was her agent, and she agreed that he should make the arrangements. We booked her for six nights a week, and in a month the place was jumping." Proust chuckled. "Charlie wasn't her best choice for representation. I'd have paid a lot more to keep Lili Moreno around."

"You say she left without giving a reason."

"That's right, Detective. Not a word. And—well, there was money missing. I should have suspected it, since I came into my office one time and found her snooping. She said she needed a stamp, and I thought nothing of it. When she ran off, though, I found that the envelope I keep for petty cash was gone. I'm not dumb enough to leave large amounts lying around, but it shows what kind of girl she really was."

"And you never saw her again?"

"No, and most of the employees were happy to see her gone. Patti got her old job back as soloist." His brows rose in a man-to-man expression. "There's always another girl, but Patti's all heat. She doesn't have that combination of cool and hot Lili had."

Grulke glanced around. "The club does okay without her?"

"We do great." Proust also looked around the room. "This place used to be a glassmaking factory. I did a lot of work to convert it." Nodding toward the back, he said, "That used to be the batch house. The cold end was down there, and the manufacturing was done here, in the hot end. The sheds along the side of the property are where the raw materials were stored."

Grulke wasn't really interested, but Proust was disarmingly proud of what he'd done, so he said, "Seems like your idea turned out well."

"It's a great location for an evening of dining and entertainment." His tone turned rueful. "Lili helped build our clientele. I'm grateful to her for that, even if the rest of it didn't turn out well."

"Is there anyone here she might have stayed in contact with? Anyone who might know where she is now?"

"I can't think of a soul," Proust replied. "My people are loyal to me, and they didn't take her desertion well." With a small gesture of one hand he invited, "Ask anyone here. No one knows where Lili is, because they'd have come to me when the story broke."

"They'd come to you? Not to the police?"

Proust's lower lip pressed upward. "As I said, my people are loyal and perhaps a little protective of the club's reputation. If one of them had information about Lili's whereabouts, I would of course send them directly to you. The job of a police detective is difficult enough without people keeping secrets."

As Grulke drove back to the station, he decided Proust wasn't a bad sort. He'd been as helpful as he could be, and he'd shown respect for the job Grulke had to do. His revelations about Lili Moreno fit nicely with Grulke's own suspicions. The woman was beautiful, talented, and dangerous. Just the sort who'd arrange her husband's murder.

Seamus hardly noticed Grulke's smug conclusions. The number of questions in his mind had multiplied as he listened to Danny Proust. Lee hadn't had more than a few dollars when she left the club, so his contention she'd stolen from him was a lie. Or was it? Might the scene between Lee and Murray have been about theft? Had the "lesson" he'd come to give her been about keeping her hands out of the boss' cashbox? He knew Lee had taken money from the agency, but he'd told himself she had a right to those funds. Only the fact that she'd taken them secretly had made her seem dishonest.

The real question was what kind of person Lee Hanrahan was. The answer was he didn't know. With a touch of familiar sadness, Seamus admitted he hadn't known anything about her. He only knew how she'd made him feel.

Back at his desk, Grulke looked through the notes he'd made on the case, reading everything he'd garnered with renewed interest. After some time he sat back in his chair, staring into space with a hand over his mouth. The man at the desk across the aisle said teasingly, "You look like you just discovered the cure for cancer, Pete."

"Nothing like that," he replied, "but it's interesting just the same. The address that woman named Cole gave me the other day is the same as the one on Lee Hanrahan's original ID card. It's an apartment right in the middle of the Black Belt, and her so-called talent agent is a Negro named Charlie Cole."

The other man shrugged. "So?"

"So, I'm thinking Mrs. Hanrahan isn't Lincoln Cole's friend, she's her sister. Lee is a Negro passing for white."

"What? She doesn't look—"

"That's the point."

Now the other man got it. "She made more money as a white woman." He frowned, adding, "You think Hanrahan found out the truth about her?"

"I don't know," Grulke replied, "but if he got wise to her tricks, she had a really good reason to kill him."

Chapter Eighteen

Linny Cole was a bundle of worry. She wasn't sure she could pay the upcoming month's rent. She didn't know where her brother Jefferson had spent the night on Monday. She fretted about her father's recent visit to her home, knowing he'd probably taken anything of value he could carry away and sell to feed his gambling habit. Most of all she worried about her sister. *Where is Lee? How much trouble is she in?*

Ronnie had put herself in a terrible position. In the first place, Linny had no idea where her sister was or where she might go next. In addition, having Linny as her host isolated Ronnie from everyone investigating the case, especially Seamus. She couldn't talk to him because Linny's schedule was the reverse of everyone else's.

Linny had heard nothing from Joe Waite. By the time she got home from work Wednesday morning, she had decided to take the bold step of contacting him.

"Jackson, before you leave for school today, call this number from Mrs. Allen's phone downstairs. Make sure to ask her real polite if you can use it, hear?" As Jackson took the slip of paper she went on, "Tell whoever answers that Linny Cole would like Officer Waite to stop by at her home when he can."

Jack's eyes widened, but he didn't question her. "I'll take care of it, Sissy."

Before he turned away, Linny caressed his face. Jack went to school, got good grades, and wanted to make something of himself. His older brother Jefferson, on the other hand, was headed for trouble, and there was little she could do about it. She was gone nights, their oldest brother Doug worked on the railroad and was away almost all the time, and their father's only interest in his children was what he could weasel out of them. Jeff had begun emulating Charlie's walk and mannerisms, as well as accepting his philosophy that the world is full of suckers meant to be taken for a ride.

Jeff was currently asleep on the couch. Linny had tried to get him up for school, but he'd simply refused, turning his back and ordering her to leave him alone. In the past Linny would have dumped a glass of cold water on him, but he'd become increasingly aggressive of late. *It isn't worth the fight,* she thought. *He'll just cuss at me and threaten to leave for good.*

Ronnie was appalled by the hopelessness of Linny's life. While she had above average intelligence, there weren't many chances for her to prove it. The majority of jobs available to her were menial, soul-sucking grinds. That made it hard for Linny to convince Jeff he needed to succeed in school in order to build himself a future. "Like you got?" he'd scoffed recently. "That's what I want out of life, Sis, mopping floors and cleaning toilets all night long."

An hour after Jackson left the apartment, a knock sounded on the door. Rising, Linny peered through the peephole she'd drilled in the wood with a screwdriver. Patting her hair and straightening her dress, she let Joe Waite in. He was dressed for work, and she thought he looked even more handsome than she recalled. "Come in, Officer."

"Please, call me Joe." He smiled. "It's not like I'm here to arrest anybody."

Jeff opened one eye and sat up abruptly when he saw a cop in his home. "Sissy?"

"Officer," Linny said, folding her arms. "Jefferson here thinks he shouldn't have to go to school anymore since he turned sixteen."

Joe got it, and he gave her a wink before directing a frown at the boy. "Young man, do you expect your sister to take care of you your whole life? Is that the kind of man you are?"

Jeff's jaw jutted. "Uh, no."

"Then you get yourself dressed and get over to that school. You keep on doing that every day until you get a diploma you can show to me. If I have to come over here five mornings a week and see that you're doing what I say, I'll do it. You want to know why?"

Resentment flickered in the boy's eyes. "Um, yeah."

"Because things are changing for us." Gesturing at his uniform Joe said, "I'm a police officer. There are Negro men in Congress, in business, and in the courts. Now the question is this: Are you going to be the kind of black man makes the rest of us proud, or are you some shiftless punk that makes us all look bad?"

Jeff glanced at Linny. "I guess I want to be good."

"Well, school's the first place to prove it. The work there isn't always fun, but it's important. You dig?"

"Yes, sir." Sweeping up his clothes, Jeff hurried into the bedroom to change.

"Thank you," Linny told Joe softly.

He shrugged. "Lord knows my daddy had to kick my butt every once in a while when I was his age."

Linny led Joe to an alcove with a small gas range, a table with three chairs, and an icebox. As she poured two cups of coffee, keeping the chipped one for herself, Ronnie jumped to Waite.

He wasn't as surprised by the apartment's shabby condition as Ronnie herself had been. The place was neatly kept, and he noted running water, a hanging cord that allowed two appliances to be plugged in, and a radiator under the window. Waite didn't seem to think it was unusual that a space that would serve two people fairly well was home to four. Ronnie made a mental correction. When Lee and her mother had lived there, the number would have been six people.

There were only two rooms. The bedroom was apparently shared, with Linny sleeping there during the day and her brothers taking turns at night. Ronnie wondered briefly where the bathroom was and concluded it must be down the hall somewhere. How did they manage?

Linny and Joe said little until Jeff emerged from the bedroom and headed out the door. When he was gone, she said, "Sometimes I think maybe I should throw that boy out. I don't want him to influence Jackson, the one who called you. He's still doing all right in school."

"I'll do what I said," Joe promised. "I'll stop by sometimes on my way to work and see that Jefferson goes to school."

Ronnie knew Waite was less interested in Jefferson Cole than in his sister, but it was nice of him to help her out. Of course Waite admired Linny's determination to do the best she could with what she had, but in addition, she was pretty, at least when she smiled. Each time she looked directly at him, a surge of warmth went through Officer Waite.

Hang on, Ronnie thought. *It's about to get hot in here.*

As they sipped coffee, Linny told Joe everything, starting with the fact that Lee Hanrahan was her half-sister and ending with what she'd learned from her father. "If he couldn't squeeze money out of Lee," she finished, "you can bet he figured out how to profit from knowing her secret some other way."

"You don't think she would have gone to him if she was in trouble?"

She made a dismissive gesture. "Daddy can't be trusted with a secret. The only time he keeps his mouth shut is when somebody pays him to."

He told her about the poker game, adding, "Charlie was surprised to hear Lee is missing. When the game ended he went directly to Danny's Place and asked about her, but they said she hasn't been there."

"Lee only planned to work there until Doug finished school." Linny stared into space, remembering. "After Momma kicked her out, Lee and I would meet at the library once a month, and she'd give me money. She didn't want me or Douglass to have to quit school, but things were hard with the boys growing so fast and prices going up and up."

Shifting her body in the chair, Linny went on. "When Momma figured out where the money was coming from, she threatened to set me out on the sidewalk, too. She said it was dirty money, and she called Lee a whore. I told her it wasn't like that, but Momma had her mind made up."

"She made you cut ties with your sister."

Linny nodded. "Lee said she'd get the money to us somehow." A small line appeared between her brows. "I guess she couldn't figure out how to do it, but Doug was lucky. He got a job right after graduation. We'd have been all right, but then Momma got sick."

"I'm sorry," Waite said. "My mother passed when I was eighteen."

"I'm real sorry to hear it."

"Daddy's not the same without her. When he isn't playing his music, he mostly just sits in a chair by the window." Ronnie felt Joe's surprise at the ease with which he made the revelation. He didn't usually share such things with others, but Linny was different from other girls he knew. Mature. Strong.

Pretty.

Turn down the heat, Ronnie thought. *What are you, fourteen?*

Staring at her cup, Linny said, "It's hard to turn into the one in charge when you're not quite grown up your own self." She took a sip of coffee. "Momma always was hardest on Lee. Once she was gone, we weren't even allowed to say her name." Tears filled her eyes, but she blinked them away. "She was just doing what she thought was right. Lee always did right, that's why I don't believe she killed her husband."

Waite rotated his cup on the table. "Where would she go if she was in trouble?"

"She'd come to me." Linny corrected herself. "Except she maybe doesn't know Momma's gone."

"If she couldn't come to you, who might she go to?"

Linny's face lit. "Aunt Evelyn. She always liked Lee." Her voice turned wistful. "Since Uncle Hank died, she has a whole apartment to herself. Lee could maybe stay with her."

Standing, Joe set his empty cup in the sink. "If you give me her address, I'll talk to her after shift. You should get some sleep now, while it's quiet."

"If my head will let me." Linny rose to find paper. "I know I have to try."

She wrote down the address and handed it to Joe, who pocketed it. With his hand on the doorknob, he paused. "Miss Cole, are you seeing anyone?"

Linny blushed but met his gaze squarely. "No."

"If I asked you to go to a movie sometime, is that something you might do?"

"I have Sundays off—Joe." Ronnie felt another surge of warmth through Waite's body.

"Let's plan on it then. Maybe I'll have word on your sister by then." Linny followed him into the hall, and Ronnie would have bet she stood watching until he made the first turn and disappeared.

Putting thoughts of his upcoming date with Linny Cole to one side, Joe managed to perform adequately during his shift. Malloy's brows rose when Joe revealed that Lee Hanrahan was Linny's half-sister.

"I've heard of people passing," Malloy said, "but I never understood it. I mean, there's lots of Negro entertainers these days. Why would somebody pretend to be white when Ella and Duke and all the others have made it?"

Waite didn't try to explain, which frustrated Ronnie. She'd have given the white boy a lesson on what it's like to always be second-class, to use the back entrance and to be judged an anomaly if you're bright or talented or well-spoken. Apparently Waite didn't even want to attempt it.

When work was done for the day, Waite located the address Linny had given for her aunt. Ronnie read his thoughts easily, for Waite had an uncommonly orderly mind. He wanted to be the one who found Lee Hanrahan, and he had three strong reasons for doing so. The first was that justice needed to be done. A cop's whole purpose was to right the wrongs of the world, and a great wrong had been done to Seamus Hanrahan. It made no difference if Lee was black or white, if she'd killed her husband, she should pay.

A second reason was that finding an accused killer would attract notice from his superiors. Waite intended to move up in the ranks of the Chicago P.D., and the case was a perfect opportunity to demonstrate what he could do.

The third reason was Linny Cole. While she wouldn't like it when her sister was arrested and charged with murder, he could do no less as an officer of the law. If by some miracle he could prove Lee hadn't killed her husband, the bonus would be double: approval from his superiors and Linny's eternal gratitude.

Evelyn Adair lived in one of the new high-rise apartment buildings the government had built on Chicago's South Side. As the Negro population grew and threatened to take over traditionally white neighborhoods, residents had become alarmed. The solution—at least someone's idea of a solution—was to expand what was known as the Black Belt upward rather than outward. Though the high-rises were mainly cheap, ugly boxes of concrete, Mrs. Adair probably felt lucky to have gotten a place in one. Despite their plainness and shoddy construction, they were still better than the shabby apartment the Cole family crowded into.

Peg Herring

When Waite knocked, Linny's aunt opened the door a crack, peering at him suspiciously. She was about fifty, and when she swung the door wider and showed herself, Ronnie noted she seemed to have been flattened in a mangle: no bosom to speak of and no rear, either. Even her face had a flat look. Friendly once she learned Linny had sent him, she invited Waite inside. "You're a policeman?" she asked in amazement. "A colored boy that's a policeman. My, my!"

Waite had to give a brief recital of how he'd become a cop, assure the lady that yes, his father was very proud of him, and insist he needed neither a cup of tea nor a cookie. When he was finally able to tell his hostess why he'd come, she expressed surprise. "Our Lee's missing? Lord above, what a terrible thing!" Dropping her chin to her chest, she said a brief prayer. Ronnie immediately concluded that Mrs. Adair wasn't the type who could hide anything. Waite agreed. Not only was she completely shocked by the news of Lee's disappearance, Mrs. Adair was one of those people who have no talent for deception.

"Amen." She raised her eyes to Waite, ready to hear the details. As he described the situation, cries of "My Lord!" and "God have mercy!" interjected. When he finished she sat for a few moments, letting the story sink in.

When she spoke, her tone was rueful. "Once my sister threw Lee out, I didn't hear no more about her."

Ronnie wondered briefly how people in the Black Belt seemed uninformed about the goings-on in the city, but on reflection she answered her own question. In her time there was 24-hour news, and it was everywhere. In an age where the six o'clock news was all there was and TV sets were by no means universal, people could and apparently did ignore the media, for the most part.

Evelyn's lips moved in prayer again. "Poor child!" she said after a moment. Looking pointedly at Waite she asked, "Are you a Christian man, Officer?"

"I hope so, ma'am."

"That's good. That's real good." Her lips pursed, making her chin wrinkle. "But some Christians are a little too hard on their fellow men and women. Do you know what I mean?"

"I do," he replied. "I got an uncle who'll smack you with the Bible any chance he gets, literally and figuratively."

Though her brow puckered at the comment, she apparently got the gist of it. "My sister, bless her soul, was a Christian woman, but the world did terrible things to her. She turned into one of them Christians that only sees one way to be."

"You mean how she treated her daughter."

The older woman clasped her hands in her lap. "Lee's got a good heart, and she did what she did for her sister and her brothers." Evelyn shook her head. "When Lee left and Victoria died, things got bad for the family, but by the Good Lord's grace, those children keep going. Linny works hard, and so does Douglass." She frowned. "Jackson's too young to help out much, and that Jefferson is going straight to Hades if he don't change his ways."

Waite steered the topic back on track. "Lee sang at the night club in order to support her family."

"That's right. She made more money there than anybody I ever heard of, but they thought she was a white girl, you see. If my sister Victoria wouldn't have been like she was, she and the children could have done all right on Lee's money. Linny might have gone to secretary school and got a job someday where she'd make a decent living."

"Why did your sister reject Lee's help?"

"Because she couldn't accept it, young man. She just couldn't!" Evelyn rubbed her arms, apparently trying to decide whether to go on. "When she was nineteen and I was twenty, Victoria and me got jobs taking care of white people's children. I got mine first, with this real nice couple over in Lake Zurich. I took care of all their babies, and when those children grew up, Mr. and Mrs. helped me get a job with another family."

Waite made a guess. "Victoria wasn't so lucky."

"No." Evelyn's mouth turned down. "The man she worked for took advantage of her—you know, like some men do. When she got pregnant, he told his wife Victoria stole things and he had to fire her."

"And the wife believed it."

Evelyn's shrug indicated that either way, the result was the same for Victoria. "Mister gave her some money and told her he never wanted to hear from her again."

Waite's indignation didn't match Ronnie's, but he'd probably heard such stories before. "The baby was Lee?"

"Yes, sir. Victoria never could forget how her first child came to be, especially since Lee came to this earth as light-skinned as one of that man's own childrens."

"Does Lee know where she came from?"

"Lord, no." She massaged her shoulder absently. "Victoria said we should forget it ever happened, but she was the one couldn't do it. My sister blamed poor Lee for any bad thing that happened." She rubbed her arms again, and Ronnie could almost feel the arthritis that plagued her. "I tried to help, but nothing makes it right when a girl's mother can't stand the sight of her."

"But Victoria married and had more children."

Evelyn made a sound of disgust. "Rumor got out Victoria had a little money. Along comes Charlie Cole, smooth as honey and twice as sweet. Before his face got all cut up in a knife fight, he was one good-looking man." She paused for a moment as if picturing the Charlie of twenty-odd years before. "First he swept my sister right off her feet. Then he went to spending the money she got from Lee's father."

"Gambling?"

Evelyn waved a hand. "That and any other devil-made way folks ruin their chance at Heaven. Charlie's got a golden tongue, and for years Victoria believed him when he said this time he'd straighten up, this time he'd get a job, this time he'd be the husband she always wanted." Evelyn gestured at the other pictures on the wall. "In five years he gave her four babies. When the money was gone, he took himself off to greener pastures."

"But he comes back now and then to sponge off his family."

She shrugged. "Linny shoos him away most times, and that man knows to stay clear of me." She looked out the window at a matching building fifty feet away, where laundry hung from balconies the size of playpens. "It was Charlie talked Lee into working at that place."

"Lee gets along with her stepfather?"

Mrs. Adair frowned. "He's all the daddy she ever knew, and he didn't treat her bad like her mama did. Charlie thought it was something grand that Lee looked white, and he was always bragging on her singing." She sighed. "I guess Lee was grateful he didn't take her momma's word she was trash."

"Lee has people she might come to now that she's in trouble: you or Linny or Charlie."

She raised a crooked index finger. "Not Charlie. He don't care about nobody but Charlie."

"You said he got her the job at Danny's Place."

"Oh, you know he got a chunk of money out of it, one way or another." Shaking her head, Evelyn repeated, "One way or another." She pulled her thoughts back to the topic. "I felt real bad when Lee ran off, but I told myself she was better off without her momma swearing she was headed to Hell and her stepdaddy using her to get what he wanted."

Waite rose to go, and she followed him to the door, wringing her hands. "When Lee didn't come back all this time, I hoped she'd found a way to be happy. I pray to Jesus she ain't in trouble now."

"I do too, ma'am."

Ronnie realized Waite meant it. He was starting to like Lee Hanrahan, despite his earlier assumption of her guilt.

"When you find her, young man, tell her Aunt Evelyn loves her, no matter what. And so does Jesus."

"I'll do that, ma'am. Thanks for your help."

Chapter Nineteen

After leaving Evelyn Adair's apartment, Waite made a decision. Malloy's account of the treatment he'd received at Danny's Place had been bothering him all day. He liked the kid, and it made him angry that a couple of overstuffed goons had shoved him around. If the club was on the up-and-up, they had no reason to threaten Dean. Waite thought he'd go down there and reprise the role of a guy looking for work.

"You again?" the burly doorman said when Waite came across the parking lot toward him.

"You said you might have work for me, boss. I come to see 'bout it."

Herb considered. "Well, I might be able to give you something tonight. The boy who usually helps us out got handed his walking papers."

"What he do wrong?" When the bouncer frowned Waite showed his palms defensively, "I'll just make sure I don't do that, boss. I don't want no walking papers."

Herb thought that was funny. "He stuck his nose in where he shouldna. It don't pay to be too curious, understand?"

"Sure, boss. I understand good."

Waite spent three hours at the club, doing Herb's bidding. First he hauled more empty kegs down to the old boathouse, stacking them in front of the two rows already there.

"When they gonna pick those kegs up, boss?" he asked Herb on his return. "There's lots of 'em."

Herb shrugged. "There's still chunks of ice in the river, so probably not for a while longer."

The other job Waite was given was bagging up the trash from the kitchen and bathrooms. He wasn't allowed into the customer areas, but he glimpsed the stage and the dining room as he passed the doorway. Herb kept a watchful eye on him, so he didn't linger, but what he saw was intriguing: small round tables circled by glittering patrons, a half-round stage populated with pretty girls in sequined costumes. Above it all, a man stood like a Colossus, feet spread as he surveyed his domain. Danny Proust, no doubt.

In the second when Waite paused in the doorway, Proust's gaze found him. He frowned, and Waite went on, hanging his head like a beast that understands only labor and obedience.

Waite packed the week's trash into bags, readying them for pickup by the horse-drawn garbage scow that would begin weekly trips up the river once all the ice melted. He was startled when a voice behind him said, "Who's your new friend, Herb?"

Glancing sideways without turning his head, Waite saw that the speaker was Danny Proust. Behind him was another man who could only be his brother Frankie.

Herb looked nervous, but he answered in a casual tone. "To tell you the truth, boss, I don't know his name. He did some toting for me a few nights ago, and he showed up again tonight, wanting work. I figured now that Charlie's gone, we could use a boy to help out."

"You might have let me know." Proust's tone was mild, but there was rebuke in it nonetheless.

Frankie stepped in. "Herb's not used to things yet, Danny." Officiously he turned to the bouncer. "Danny likes to know who's inside his establishment."

"Um, sure. Sorry, Danny—Mr. Proust." He turned to Waite, who acted as if he were not the subject of the disagreement. "You. You can go now."

"Not so fast," Danny said, approaching Waite. "What's your name?"

"Reggie, boss. Reggie Combs."

"And how did you hear we needed a man here?"

Waite kept his eyes averted, his head down. "I didn't hear nothing, boss. I just go places where there's people and ask if anybody got work for me."

"I see." Proust examined him for a few seconds. "You look like a strong fellow. Why can't you find steady work?"

Waite knew the answer was important, and he took on the manner of petty criminals he'd met on the job. "Spent a little time in prison, I guess. Makes it hard to get work."

"Prison. What for?"

"I didn't hurt nobody, boss. They said I stole some stuff."

"You wouldn't steal from me, would you, Reggie?"

"Oh, no, boss. I never would."

"That's good, because if you did, I'd hunt you down and kill you real slow." Proust's voice was like a blade, but in the next instant, he was almost friendly. "Now you go ahead and finish the job like Herb told you. If he's happy with your performance, we'll try to find you something a little more permanent."

***

Seamus thought Grulke would never go to bed that night. He watched his snowy television until late, snorting at Milton Berle's antics while he emptied several beers and ate half a dozen of the peanut butter cookies his wife had made.

Clarice, the type of woman Seamus had often met in his lifetime, was her man's help-meet, her son's anchor, and content to be nothing more. After she tucked the boy into bed, she returned to the living room, sat down in a rocking chair, and began embroidering roses onto some pillowcases she planned to give as a wedding gift. During the commercials, while packages of cigarettes sang and danced, she told Grulke about their son's day at school and reported gossip she'd picked up from the neighbors. He paid little attention, merely grunting at appropriate moments. Finally she asked, "Anything interesting going on at work, Pete?"

"They pulled one out of the lake last week. He was a white guy, but today I found out his wife was a Negro."

"A Negro? Really?" Her shock reminded Seamus of what he and Lee would have faced if the truth had been known.

"Her sister's black as the ace of spades, but we have a photograph of the wife and you'd never guess what she was. It looks like the husband didn't know."

Clarice's nose wrinkled. "How could he not know?"

Grulke scratched his abdomen. "They met at this club where she used to sing. Nobody down there knew either, so they couldn't tip the poor sap off." He sniffed. "She probably told him she was an orphan or something."

Mrs. Grulke touched her own pale face. "What if they'd had a baby?"

I'd have loved it, Seamus wanted to shout. *Boy, girl, dark or light, I'd have loved that child.*

Unable to tolerate the Grulkes' discussion of his wife's supposed sins, Seamus tuned out for a while and considered how Ronnie would react to what he'd learned. She no doubt knew about prejudice firsthand, but as the product of a different era, her experiences wouldn't be—couldn't be—the same as Lee's must have been.

He struggled with his thoughts, sometimes sympathizing with Lee's decision and other times angry with her for keeping secrets from him. Trying to be completely honest with himself, Seamus admitted he didn't know what his reaction would have been if she'd told him when they met at the club that first night. Would he have backed away? Of course she couldn't have taken the chance he'd tell her employers the truth. But later, when she'd known him better, shouldn't Lee have trusted him?

Seamus had begun interpreting events from the past differently. Lee had tried to discourage him from pursuing her. She'd avoided physical contact in the early days. He'd thought it was cute, a combination of shyness and a feminine tendency to play hard to get.

Why hadn't she confessed when he asked her to marry him? Recalling her desperate situation: a job she hated, no friends, no family, no place to live, and the threat from Murray, he knew the answer to that. Even if she'd only liked him a little, his offer of marriage must have felt like a life raft in a sea of trouble. Could she risk losing the chance at a new start by confessing she was a Negro?

And once they were married, how could she have told him? He recalled her tears on their wedding night, how he'd kissed them away, and how sweet their lovemaking had been.

He'd never seen himself as one who'd turn away from love for such a silly thing as skin color, but which of us knows what he'll do until he's faced a real-life decision. As an interracial couple in the '50s, their lives would have been difficult. Would he have urged Lee to keep her race a secret? Would he have asked her to deny her sister, her family, her true self for the rest of her life?

He hoped he'd have encouraged Lee to be honest, but that would have meant facing prejudice from blacks and whites alike. Had their love been strong enough to withstand it? It was impossible to say, but he wished he'd been part of the decision. Lee had shut him out of the pain, doubt, and fear she faced every day. Lee hadn't trusted him, which led Seamus back to his earlier conclusion. She hadn't loved him. He'd been convenient when she needed help, but once she met Grant, true passion had entered the picture. After all, Grant was everything a woman could want in a man.

That brought up another question. Had Grant known Lee's secret? Had she shared with him what she couldn't share with her own husband?

Seamus told himself to stop asking questions he had no answers to. He'd tell Ronnie everything, and they'd talk it over together. The kid was smart, and she certainly had more insight into Lee's situation than he could ever have.

After the late news "The Star-spangled Banner" played, and a black-and-white test pattern replaced the moving images on the TV screen. The Grulkes went to bed, turning back the covers on identical twin beds with blond headboards. In mirrored movements they reached out and turned off identical white ceramic lamps with ruffled shades that sat on matching night stands. Seamus waited impatiently for Grulke to relax and for his regular breathing to signal that he slept.

"Ronnie?"

She answered immediately. "Here."

"Where are you?"

"Back with Joe Waite. I spent some time with Lincoln Cole—" There was a pause as she apparently considered how to finish.

Seamus did it for her. "My sister-in-law."

"Yes." Her relief was obvious. "How are you feeling about that?"

"I think I'm okay." Seamus said something he'd never said aloud to anyone except Lee herself. "I loved her, Ronnie. I loved her more than any difference between us could have affected."

"Good for you, Seamus," she said softly. "The world needs more of that."

Embarrassed by his emotion, he got back to business. "Tell me what Linny told Waite."

"Well, she doesn't believe Lee would have anything to do with murder. She didn't see her much because of the mother's anger and the—uh—passing. For a while Lee still gave money to Linny, but when the mother found out, she threw a fit."

"Great parenting."

"Yeah, you have Charlie on the one side, a self-absorbed grifter, and Victoria on the other, about as fanatical as a person can be about sin and the wages of sin."

"But the money Lee got from me. Where did it go if not to Linny?"

"I don't know. Linny quit school when their mother got sick, and she and the brother have been supporting the family ever since. I don't understand why Lee gave up on them."

They were silent for a few seconds, thinking. "What if Lee sent Charlie Cole the money," Seamus asked. "What if she asked him to give it to the family? Money her mother wouldn't have taken from Lee might have been acceptable coming from her husband."

"But Charlie kept it for himself." Ronnie sniffed disgustedly. "The man can justify almost anything in his own mind. I have no doubt he gambled every cent away and told himself that when he hit it big, he'd pay it all back."

"That kept him from bothering Lee for a while, but then he found out about us and followed her to where we lived. He started harassing Lee for more money."

"A little blackmail, a little guilt. Charlie swears he'll keep her secret and her family will get the benefits."

"Like I said, great parenting."

"Why'd she keep lying, Seamus? Why didn't she just tell you the truth?"

"I think you know the answer to that."

"I've heard the stories. It's just hard to imagine people of color masquerading as white to get better jobs, better pay, better lives. It's terrible."

"Terrible they did it, or terrible they felt they had to?"

"Let's just say it's terrible what people do to other people."

"It certainly is."

Ronnie's tone was hesitant as she went on. "Charlie did tell Linny that he saw, um, something when he was watching Lee."

"He saw her with Grant."

"Yes."

"It's okay, Ronnie. I knew it was true." Seamus sighed. "What's Waite going to do next?"

"After his shift tomorrow, he intends to find Chicken Charlie again. He's pretty sure the old goat has more to tell if somebody squeezes it out of him."

"That's one good thing about the '50s," Seamus observed, trying to lighten the mood. "Not every chump on the street hollered for his civil rights, so a cop could do a little squeezing and maybe get at the truth."

Chapter Twenty

When he got in Thursday morning, Grulke called Tony Cannell, the detective at the 18th, to check on Grant Wellman's condition. "There's been a little change for the better," Cannell reported.

"He's awake?"

"Not that much change, but the nurse said he stirred a few times in the night, like he was trying to come to." Cannell seemed to realize his enthusiasm wasn't shared. "They said it was a good sign."

"I hope he wakes up soon. If he knows where the wife went—" Recalling that Wellman and Cannell were friends, Grulke reworded his thought. "He knows them, so he might be able to tell us where she'd go."

Cannell's tone darkened as he said, "Our guys found a suitcase in the back of Wellman's car. It's likely it belongs to Lee Hanrahan."

"Really." Grulke pressed the corners of his mouth with his fingers, glad Cannell couldn't see the smug smile that appeared there.

"Grant might have given her a ride to the train station. She could be visiting family down South somewhere, unaware that her husband's dead."

"And she left without her suitcase?"

"I don't know!" Cannell seemed desperate to find an explanation that didn't cast shadows on Wellman's reputation.

And the facts of the case, Grulke thought disdainfully.

"The three of them could have been waylaid somewhere. Grant was shot but managed to drive away, the husband was killed, and Mrs.

Hanrahan—maybe she was abducted. I mean, she's a good-looking woman."

Grulke lost patience with Cannell's attempts to paint Wellman as an innocent party. "Or maybe Wellman and the woman were leaving town together. Hanrahan caught up with them somewhere downtown, and there was a fight. Wellman got shot, but Hanrahan was subdued in the end." For the sake of Cannell's friendship, he gave Wellman all the latitude he could manage: manslaughter rather than first-degree murder. In his own mind, the fact they'd been prepared with a boat to use to dump Hanrahan's body didn't indicate an accidental killing. "However it happened, the woman got away, and she left Wellman injured and bleeding."

"Maybe she panicked."

Grulke rolled his eyes at Cannell's maybes. "Anything in the suitcase that's of interest?"

"Clothes. A few toiletries. Fifty dollars in an envelope." Cannell sighed heavily. "Grant would not do what you're thinking, Detective. I know the guy, and he wouldn't treat a friend that way."

Grulke suppressed a sigh of impatience. "Okay, say Wellman didn't intend to kill the husband but the wife did. He wouldn't be the first guy some dame used as her patsy."

"Then who shot Wellman? If it was Hanrahan, how did the wife subdue him, load him into a boat, take him into Lake Michigan, and toss him overboard? Judging from her photographs, the woman hardly weighs a hundred pounds."

Grulke tapped his pencil against his blotter. "Just keep me informed about Wellman's condition. The sooner he wakes up, the sooner we get some idea where our little *femme fatale* has gone."

After he hung up the phone, Grulke took out the photo of Lili Moreno the newspaper had printed when Seamus' body was found. "A woman like that probably has men lined up on a string, like fish," he muttered. "She had Wellman get rid of her husband, and then she got rid of Wellman, at least she tried to."

***

"Grulke's worse than you, Seamus," Ronnie said that night. "Now he's convinced Lee shot Grant Wellman *and* murdered you."

"She wouldn't hurt Grant."

Ronnie was clearly irritated. "You believe your wife would kill you but not your friend?"

"It's hard to understand, but yes. Lee fell in love with Grant, and that started all this. But she isn't some man-eater who talked Grant into killing me then shot him and went on her way with a third guy."

"From what I've seen she isn't the type who'd kill anybody, least of all you. Your wife loved you, Seamus."

He made a derisive sound. "In spite of the lies and the sneaking around behind my back?"

"Sometimes people lie to those they love the most, because they're afraid the truth will drive them away."

"And the secret meetings? Was that so Lee and Grant could discuss how much they both admired me?"

Hearing the raw emotion in Seamus' voice Ronnie thought, *Maybe coming back wasn't a good idea.*

Facing the truth was worse than Seamus had imagined, and there was nothing she could do to help. Grulke certainly thought the two people Seamus cared about most were behind his murder. Ronnie didn't want that to be true, didn't want the detective's cynical conclusions to be borne out by the next few days' investigation.

Too bad wanting something to be true isn't the same as making it so.

***

Once again, Waite had a difficult time finding Charlie Cole. He'd been everywhere a few hours earlier, according to people Waite questioned, but now he was nowhere. A little before midnight, when Waite was about to give up, a man on the street said he'd seen Charlie. "Saw his hat, anyways." A little unsteady on his feet, the man gestured loosely behind him. "In the alley back there."

"His hat?"

"The one he always wears. With the feather. Musta lost it." He chuckled, his jaw drooping. "Prob'ly running from a jealous husband."

A sense of dread gripped Ronnie, and she whispered, "Look!" Waite obeyed, hurrying in the direction the man had pointed. The hat lay in the slush at the side of the alley, a wet stain already stealing up its crown, turning the purple to black. Waite headed down the alley, dipping to scoop up the hat as he passed.

There was a sharp turn fifty feet down, and around it Charlie Cole lay slumped against a brick wall, his face all but obscured by blood. His left arm lay in his lap at an odd angle. "Mr. Cole!" Waite called, kneeling beside him. "Mr. Cole, can you hear me?"

Charlie opened his eyes, but there was no recognition in them. Waite looked around, unsure what to do. "Will you be all right if I go for help?" When Cole managed a nod, he said, "I'll be back as soon as I find a phone."

Ronnie was frustrated by the fact that Waite had to search out a way to call for help. Unaware of other possibilities, he hurried to a bar a few blocks down and demanded the startled owner let him use the phone stored under the counter. *How did people survive before cell phones?* she asked herself as he dialed. *And how many people died while some desperate friend entered one number, then another, then another, waiting in agony each time while the dial returned to its starting point?*

Once he'd made the call, Waite returned to the alley and waited with Cole until an ambulance wailed up to the narrow entrance. After a brief examination and a few questions Waite couldn't answer, one of the attendants went back to the street, hauled a stretcher out of the ambulance, and returned. Gently lifting Charlie onto it, they carried him to the street and put him into the back of the vehicle.

"Where are you taking him?" Waite asked. Since some hospitals didn't take Negroes, it would either be Provident, which had been created for black patients, doctors, and staff, or Cook County.

"He'll be at County," the attendant replied, slamming the back door and hurrying to join his partner.

"I'll get his daughter," Waite called after them. The man waved a casual acknowledgment, unconcerned with that part of the process.

An hour later Waite and Linny, with Ronnie in silent accompaniment, arrived at Cook County Hospital. They were sent upstairs to where Charles Cole dozed in a room of unrelieved white. As they paused in the doorway, a nurse in white shoes, white stockings, and a white dress of stiff fabric approached. Her cap had one black stripe along its folded brim, signifying she was an RN. "Yes?"

"This is Mr. Cole's daughter," Waite said. "May we see him?"

The nurse looked them up and down before answering. "We've given him medicine to help him sleep. You can see him, but I doubt he'll make much sense."

They tiptoed into the room where Charlie lay on a metal-framed bed. His arm was casted, his head bandaged. One eye was swollen shut and his nose was crooked, but the blood had been cleaned away, and he was recognizable. "Daddy!" Linny said, hurrying forward. She took his undamaged hand in hers, and Charlie reacted with a feeble squeeze. Linny looked to Waite with relief in her eyes. He knew she was there.

Waite tried some gentle questions about the cause of Charlie's injuries, but he got no answer. Watching Cole shake his head in response to each question, Ronnie concluded fear kept him silent, not his injuries.

"Mr. Cole," Waite said, "we can't catch the people who did this if you don't tell us what happened."

No answer.

Linny joined her urging to Waite's, but Charlie merely gave her a mournful look, begging for understanding.

After only a few minutes, the nurse returned and shooed them out. "Visiting hours are long over," she told them. "I shouldn't have let you in at all, but I knew you'd want to assure yourselves he'll recover."

Leading Linny away, Waite asked, "Can we go somewhere and talk?"

"I should go back and finish my shift."

"I'll call your boss in the morning and tell him the police came for you because of an emergency."

"And how will I make up the hours I lost?" she asked, but she seemed resigned—and tired to the point of exhaustion. Ronnie felt Waite's desire to make Linny's life easier, to see her smile more and worry less.

Less than a block from the hospital, they found a restaurant that stayed open all night. There were only white people inside, and Waite looked at the waitress for signs they weren't welcome. Though Ronnie knew what he was feeling, she guessed the result of ignoring such signs were more serious in this era than in her own. When the bored waitress only glanced at them, they made their way to a table at the back.

The woman came with coffeepot in hand a few seconds later, and Waite ordered scrambled eggs for them both, since Linny seemed unable to make a decision.

Two men in coveralls sat at the counter, and at three separate tables, people ate alone, their faces blank. As Linny toyed with her coffee mug she asked, "What happened to my father, Joe?"

He put his hand over hers. "I'd say somebody meant to teach him a lesson."

"About keeping his big mouth shut?"

"Yes." Waite smiled to take the sting out of it.

Her answering smile was grim. "That 'somebody' must know Daddy's always telling things he shouldn't."

Waite met her gaze squarely. "My partner thinks there's illegal stuff going on at the club where your sister used to sing. I guess Charlie still works there?"

"That's what he says. I don't know much about the place."

"It looks like some of the girls there trap guys in compromising situations."

She frowned. "What does that mean?"

"They get pictures of men with the girls—you know—breaking their marriage vows. Then their wives divorce them and get a big settlement."

After some thought Linny said, "That could be why Lee hated the place so much."

"And why she left so suddenly."

Linny bit her lip. "You think Daddy helps them?"

"It would explain the beating he got tonight. When my partner went there asking questions about Lee, he got a pretty strong warning to keep his nose out of their business."

"But why would Daddy tell what he knows now if he didn't tell it before? What changed?"

Waite's eyes narrowed. "The thing that changed, the thing that might make your father tell what he knows, is that your sister is missing."

"I don't see what difference it makes."

"Neither do I," he admitted. "But when Charlie heard what happened to Lee's husband, he went directly to Danny's Place. It looks like they're worried about what he might tell." He added, mostly to himself, "Malloy might be on the right track after all. The goings-on at that club connect somehow to Lee's disappearance *and* to the murder of Seamus Hanrahan."

Chapter Twenty-one

Waite escorted Linny home, which meant two bus rides and a substantial walk. It was almost 5:00 a.m. by the time he reached home. After an hour of doubtful consideration, he called Malloy. He'd never telephoned his partner at home before, but someone at the department had typed up a list of numbers to be used in times of emergency. Despite several strikeovers, most of the list was readable.

Malloy was a white man, living in a neighborhood that Waite imagined had stately trees, homes with neatly-painted front porches, and fair-sized lawns. Waite doubted people like Malloy chatted on the telephone with their Negro acquaintances. Still, he thought his partner would want to know what he'd found out as soon as possible. It was time to discuss whether they should go to Grulke with what they'd discovered before they started their shift.

"Malloy residence," a woman's voice answered. When Waite explained who he was, she said, "Oh, you're Joe! We've so wanted to meet you, but Deanie always forgets to invite you over."

Deanie?

When Waite hesitated, she went on. "As long as I've got you on the telephone, I'll just go ahead and ask. Would you like to come to dinner some evening? It would just be the four of us: you, me, Deanie, and his dad, but we'd love to get acquainted.

I'm talking to Dean's mother. Ladykiller Malloy lives with his parents!

"He says you're quite the athlete," she went on. "We'd love to hear about it."

"Was, ma'am. I pitched a little in high school."

"City champion, Deanie says. That's impressive."

"I'd enjoy meeting you and Mr. Malloy some evening. Right now I need to speak with Dean, if that's okay."

"Is it about the woman you're trying to find? He told us about it, and I think it's very nice of you boys to help find that poor widow." Ronnie winced at her use of the term *boys* until she realized Mrs. Malloy meant both Waite and "Deanie."

"Ma'am, that's exactly what I want to speak to Dean about. I found out some things we have to report to Detective Grulke first thing this morning."

"Well, that's good, although Dean says Detective Grulke is kind of grumpy. Let me see if he's done in the garage. He's very dedicated to his exercise routine."

The phone made a clunk as she set it down, and Waite heard soft footsteps and a door opening. "Deanie?" The rest of it was muffled, but in a few seconds Malloy came on the line. "Hello?"

"It's Joe. Sorry to call you at home."

After the slightest of hesitations, Malloy said, "That's okay."

Waite told him what had happened to Charlie Cole. "I think Lee Hanrahan's disappearance is connected to the divorce scheme at Danny's Place."

"Yeah?"

"They gave you a hard time when you asked about Lee. It's pretty obvious Charlie's been warned to keep his mouth shut, and I can't see Lee beating her stepfather half to death."

"No, I guess not."

Waite felt frustrated at his partner's apparent lack of interest. "What's the matter, Malloy? I thought you suspected the Proust brothers of all kinds of illegal doings."

"Um—" Suddenly Malloy's voice changed. "There. She's gone upstairs." With the air of a kid keeping secrets he explained, "My mom likes to listen in, but eventually she gets bored and drifts away."

"I didn't realize you lived with your parents."

Malloy chuckled. "Not the kind of thing a guy likes to admit."

"Hey, I get it. My dad's asleep in the next room right now."

"Did she ask you over for dinner?"

"Um, yes."

"She's been bugging me to do it, but I—I didn't know if you'd want to come here."

That surprised Waite. "Why?"

"Your dad's a musician, for Pete's sake. My dad sells plumbing parts, and Mom bakes cookies."

Waite's face relaxed into a smile. "I like cookies, Dean." He almost said "Deanie," but it would have been too much.

"Yes, but—Are you saying you might want to come for dinner?"

"How would the neighbors take it?"

"To heck with the neighbors."

Easy for you to say. Waite didn't verbalize that thought. "So will you go to Grulke with me this morning?"

"Sure. We'll tell him what we know and see what he thinks. He can't do more than kick us out of his eight square feet of office space."

Chapter Twenty-two

While Detective Grulke was surprised to see Officers Malloy and Waite approach his desk, Seamus was relieved, having not heard from Ronnie in a while. Noting Waite's red-streaked eyes, he concluded the young man hadn't slept last night. From their serious expressions, he guessed they intended to lay out everything they knew. Seamus resolved to see that the detective paid attention.

When Malloy explained they had "stumbled on some things" that might help with the Hanrahan case, Grulke's first response was to dismiss the two officers with a reprimand.

"Listen," Seamus whispered, and Grulke grudgingly obeyed. With an abrupt gesture, he indicated the two younger men should sit.

Malloy pulled a spare chair from an empty desk, allowing Waite the one already there. Malloy did the talking, and Seamus guessed the two had consciously chosen to do it that way. Grulke was a racist, though he didn't see himself that way. By the time it was Waite's turn to speak, Grulke might be interested enough to give him a fair hearing.

Malloy left out his visit to Mrs. Collins and the fact that he'd masqueraded as Jim Cooper, Private Eye. He said only that he'd gone to Danny's Place and met a hatcheck girl who knew Lee Hanrahan when she was singing as Lili Moreno. He described Sandra's abrupt shift from helpful to frightened and the threats he'd received when he returned to the club a second time.

"You're saying Danny Proust is crooked?" Grulke asked. "The guy seemed okay to me, at least for someone who owns a night club."

"I called a friend who works over there," Malloy responded. "He says they've got their eye on Danny and his brother Frankie."

"Why's that?"

"A couple of their employees have shown up in the hospital looking like they've been beaten. Both claimed they got their injuries in a fall, but the investigating officers don't buy it."

"Maybe they got caught with their hand in the till."

Malloy's expression revealed frustration. "Frankie Proust has a history of violence from the time he was a teenager. He's been in several scrapes but never got convicted of anything. Each time, his mother pleaded with the judge to show clemency. The last time he was arrested, it was because he lost a boxing match. He caught his opponent in an alley afterwards and beat him with a club of some kind."

"And what happened to that case?"

Malloy made a *tsk* sound. "The victim decided not to press charges. Danny promised to give his brother a job at his dining club to keep him on the straight and narrow."

"And has Danny been successful at rehabilitating his brother?"

"My friend says Danny just found a way to channel Frankie's love of violence into something that benefits him. The word is he terrorizes anyone who gives Danny trouble."

"He seemed like such a gentleman," Grulke murmured.

"If you mean Danny, he can afford to be now that his brother's willing to be the bad guy."

"All right. Let's say the Prousts are violent and slightly criminal. What has that got to do with my murder case?"

Malloy looked to Waite, who told his part of the story. He also left out some things, like the illegal poker game in the back room of the chair factory. When he finished, they both waited to hear what the detective would have to say about their amateur investigation.

Grulke stared at the two young officers. "You two have certainly been busy."

"We followed some leads that seemed worth looking into." Malloy's expression was earnest. "After what's happened, we knew it was time to bring what we know to you."

"Well, you guys might think us detectives just sit on our hands up here, but we stumbled onto some interesting stuff too." Grulke told them about Grant Wellman's relationship to the Hanrahans and his current condition.

Waite's expression turned somber. "You think Detective Wellman is the guy Chicken Charlie mentioned, the one Lee was seeing on the side?"

"Yup. Pretty telling connection, huh?"

"And he got shot the same night Seamus Hanrahan died."

"We didn't know where he was coming from that night, but the spot where the car crashed is just a few blocks from Danny's Place."

"That's where Hanrahan was killed?"

"It's certainly possible." Grulke leaned back in his chair. "Here's what I think happened. Lee Hanrahan soft-soaped Wellman into killing her husband, but Hanrahan managed to shoot the detective before he went down. Somehow Wellman made it to his car and escaped, leaving Mrs. H with a half-dead husband to dispose of. She can't do it alone, but Danny's Place isn't very far. She figures her old friends there will get rid of the body and help her get out of Chicago. I didn't know why the Prousts would agree to it, since she left them high and dry a few years back, but you two just added that piece. She knows about their little divorce-for-hire scheme."

"But Linny—Miss Cole—says Lee would never trust anyone at that club," Waite protested.

"When a criminal's in trouble, you can bet she'll call on other criminals to get her out of it."

"Did the bullet that hit Wellman come from Hanrahan's gun?" Waite asked.

Grulke ran a hand through his thinning hair. "No guns have been found yet. We're not even sure Hanrahan owned one." He returned to the scenario he'd formed. "The question we have to answer is who at that club helped Lee finish off her husband?"

"Danny's the obvious choice," Malloy said. "But there are at least two other candidates, Frankie and the bouncer, Herb."

Waite shook his head. "Herb's new, remember? He wasn't working at Danny's the night Hanrahan died."

"Frankie or Danny Proust, then. Maybe both of them."

"You need to talk to them." Malloy spoke without thinking and immediately reworded. "I mean, will you talk to them, Detective?"

Grulke leaned forward, setting his elbows on the desktop, and pointed his index fingers at them. "The woman lied about being white. She arranged for her boyfriend to murder her husband. And she either shot Wellman herself or she didn't much care if he bled to death in his car. Lee Hanrahan left a big mess behind, so she's the one I want, not some two-bit pimps that run a night club."

The phone on Grulke's desk rang, and he picked up the receiver. "Grulke." After listening for a few seconds he said, "Thanks, Cannell. I'll meet you there." Turning to the young officers he said, "We'll know the details soon, boys. Wellman is awake and ready to tell what he knows."

"Will you keep us informed?" Waite asked.

Grulke was already up and putting on his coat. "Check with me at the end of your shift," he said. "I should know it all by then."

As Grulke left the station, Seamus felt torn. He was about to learn the truth about Lee. After all this time, would knowing bring peace to his mind or simply more unhappiness?

***

As they left Grulke's office, Waite stopped at the desk and said to the duty officer, "We're going out to do some work for Detective Grulke. Should be about an hour."

"Got it." The officer wrote it down while Waite ignored the jab in the back he got from Malloy.

As they left the building, Malloy said, "He didn't send us anywhere, Joe. Did you just get us both into hot water?"

"I doubt it. We'll be back before Grulke, and he'll be happy if we get information on where Lee Hanrahan is."

"And where we gonna find that out?"

"From Charlie Cole's cousin." After a second he added, "I hope."

When they pulled up at the chair factory in their patrol car, Malloy said, "How are we going to approach this?"

"You do the talking," Waite replied. "Tell the owner you need to interview one of his employees, Pickles."

The man who'd been wearing the eyeshade the night of the poker game was at work in the shop, sweeping up wood shavings and cigarette butts. When he saw Waite his eyes widened for a second, then his head drooped almost to his chest and stayed there.

The owner looked up, saw two police officers in his store, and placed a protective hand on the cash register. Waite wondered who might be shaking him down for protection money. Cops?

The man dragged up a smile. "Officers, what can I do for you?"

"Good morning, sir. We're investigating an automobile accident that took place yesterday evening. We were told your employee here might have witnessed it."

The man looked at the Negro, who had stopped sweeping. "Pickles, did you see an accident?"

Pickles hesitated, and Joe Waite made a slight gesture, no more than a shift of his head. The older man's gaze went to him, read something in his expression, and said, "Yessir, Mr. Adams. I seen two cars crash a little bit down on Baker."

Malloy turned to the owner. "Is there someplace we can speak with him and get a statement?"

"Certainly. Pickles, take them to the back and tell them what you know." After a moment he added, "And tell the truth, man. No dancing around the facts." His glance at Malloy telegraphed his belief that

Negroes had to be told such things or they'd automatically lie. Malloy stared at him blankly, tacitly rejecting the opinion.

Pickles led them through the showroom and down a narrow hallway half-blocked by boxes of rungs, spines, and screws. Soon they were seated at the same table where Waite had played cards with Pickles, Chicken Charlie, and the others. Pickles was half-resentful, half-awed. "You really a policeman, son?"

"Yes, sir, I am. I came here last Saturday to find Charlie Cole, because I'm trying to locate his stepdaughter Lee."

Pickles fingered his chin whiskers. "I ain't seen Charlie. He didn't come here last night."

"I know that." Briefly Waite told the older man what had happened to Charlie. His expression turned regretful. "I done what I could for Charlie, because he family, but that man just can't stay away from trouble."

"He sleeps here?"

"Sometime, when he ain't got noplace else. I'm sorta the night watchman, you see. Mr. Adams let me stay back here if I keep a look-out for thieves and such." He gestured at the grim room. "It ain't much, but I can't do no heavy work. I had an accident on a job down in Cicero, and my back ain't been right never since."

Waite looked around the room, noting in the daylight a cot in one corner and some shirts hung from pegs along the wall.

"What can you tell us about Lee?"

"Pretty girl." The man shook his head wonderingly. "Pretty, pretty girl. I guess she up and married some man she met at that place she used to work at. Rich man, I guess."

"He was rich?"

"That what Charlie said. I know she sent him money every month." He grinned widely, and spaces where there weren't any teeth showed. "We'd have a good time when Charlie got his money!" Sobering, he added, "Course it never lasted long with Charlie. Man can't resist drawing to an inside straight, and he couldn't pick a lucky number if God hisself whispered it in his ear!"

"How did this money arrive?"

"Charlie would go to the post office and pick it up. He griped some, because Lee never put a return address on it. He knew she was still in the city, but he didn't know where."

"But he found out."

"Did he, now?" Pickles thought about it then nodded. "You might be right, son. The last few months he been a little different, like he knowed something nobody else did." He chuckled. "Charlie think he real smart, but he can't hide what he thinking. That's another reason he don't never win at cards."

When Malloy and Waite left the store, the owner escorted them to the door. "I trust Pickles was helpful, Officers?"

"He's got excellent observational skills," Malloy replied.

"That's good. I've always found him to be helpful and courteous myself. I wouldn't keep him around otherwise."

"Good day, sir." When they got outside, Malloy buttoned his jacket to keep out the wind. "Do you put up with whites with attitudes like that all the time, Joe? If you're good at your job it's because they know how to keep you in line, and if you're not—well, it's what they expected?"

Waite answered honestly. "Not everybody thinks that way, and that helps a little."

Ronnie smiled to herself. If nothing else, Seamus' case was allowing the two men to relate to each other as people. That, she believed, was the only way to get past the ignorance of prejudice.

Chapter Twenty-three

On the way to the hospital, Seamus had an argument with himself. Would he jump immediately to Grant and find out the truth directly, or would he stay with Grulke and hope the detective asked the right questions? Ronnie had been correct. A person didn't really want to know what his friends were thinking. But Ronnie was with Waite, and Seamus couldn't wait until she could maneuver her way to Grant.

Cannell was waiting when Grulke arrived at Wellman's hospital room. Tall and thin, he moved with a kind of grace that brought Cary Grant to mind. After shaking hands with Grulke, he gestured toward the hospital room. "He's very weak and in a lot of pain, but he's lucid. The doc agreed to let us talk to him if we keep it short."

When he saw his friend, almost as pale as the sheets around him, Seamus knew the answer to the question he'd been debating. Grant was in no shape to be hosting a second soul.

"Detective Wellman, I'm Pete Grulke, homicide detective with the 8th."

"Nice to meet you," Grant replied. His voice, usually rich and tinged with wry humor, was faint and halting.

"Can you tell us what happened?"

The telling took a while, since the patient had to stop frequently to rest. "Lee and Seamus Hanrahan are friends of mine," Wellman began. "One day a few months ago, I stopped to see them one day and found Lee arguing with a Negro man. She was crying, but she was angry too. As soon as he saw me, the guy left. I noticed he had a long scar down one side of his face. When I asked Lee what was wrong, at first she said it was nothing. When I told her I'd heard the man say: 'You don't want your man to find out what you are,' she broke down and told me her secret."

"That she's a Negro," Grulke supplied. Cannell's brows rose, but he said nothing.

Wellman closed his eyes once, signifying an affirmative. "I don't think she'd have admitted it if she hadn't been so upset. Her own stepfather was blackmailing her, demanding money or he'd tell Seamus the truth about her."

"What did you do?"

Wellman licked his dry lips. Taking a cup from the bedside table, Cannell rather clumsily gave him a drink. When he finished, Wellman went on with his story. "Lee didn't want me to do anything. She wouldn't even tell me how to find the guy. I thought I could help. It took a while, but I tracked the guy down and told him it would be better for his health if he left Lee alone." Wellman paused, taking a few shallow breaths. "Lee wasn't happy when I told her what I'd done. She insisted it was better if she paid him off because that was all that would keep him quiet."

"Did she tell you why she was passing for white?"

Wellman's expression revealed that he heard the disgust in Grulke's tone, but he didn't comment. "She thought Seamus would hate her if he knew."

"So you comforted her, which led to the idea of getting Hanrahan out of the way."

"Grulke!" Cannell interrupted angrily. "You've got no cause to say that."

Grulke raised a hand to stop Cannell's protest, but he remained focused on Wellman. "I'm listening, Detective."

Wellman's face revealed stunned surprise. "Is that what you've been thinking? That Lee and I killed Seamus so we could be together?" He tried to laugh, but it was almost a sob. "Lee would never betray Seamus, and for that matter, neither would I. He is—" He stopped, still adjusting to the idea that Seamus was gone. "He was my friend."

Grulke licked his lips, doubting himself for the first time. Inside his head, Seamus too reeled with doubt. Was it possible he'd been wrong all this time?

"What happened, then?"

"For weeks I tried to convince Lee to tell Seamus the truth. I argued that no one else had to know, but she owed it to him." He raised a hand weakly. "Lee thought it would make things harder for Seamus. 'What if I do tell him?' she'd ask me. 'Will he lie to the world for the rest of our lives, like I do?'"

"It's how people get along in this society," Cannell said softly. "We share who we really are only with the few who understand."

The shift from *people* at the beginning of his comment to *we* at the end led Seamus to wonder about Detective Cannell. What secret about himself did he share only with a few?

Focused on his own thoughts, Grulke missed it. "She didn't want Hanrahan to divorce her."

"Seamus wasn't the kind of man who'd do that, but he wouldn't have hidden from the truth, either. He'd have accepted being the guy with the Negro wife, with no apologies to anyone."

A tiny jolt of relief went through Seamus' mind. Grant saw him as the person he hoped he'd have been. Why couldn't Lee have been that certain?

Wellman paused for a few seconds, staring at the blank wall beside him. "Lee insisted he'd lose friends and business because of her, and I couldn't argue with her on that. I just kept repeating that Seamus wouldn't care."

"What did she say to that?"

He turned his gaze away for a second. "She said *she* cared. She cared enough for him that she didn't want him to have to live like that."

"What did that mean?"

"She was going to leave."

"Leave Hanrahan?"

"Leave Chicago." His expression turned rueful. "In trying to help Lee, I'd actually made her situation worse. Lee knew if her stepfather wasn't getting paid to keep her secret, sooner or later he'd find another way to profit from it."

"Great guy," Cannell opined.

"Yeah," Wellman agreed. "Lee said if she left Chicago, Seamus would never have to know the real story."

"And what was your reaction to that?"

"I argued every which way against it. I didn't think he'd ever recover if Lee left him."

"So what did you do?"

After another brief rest, Wellman replied, "I decided to talk to the stepfather again. If I could convince him to keep his mouth shut, I thought Lee might stick around. Then I could work on convincing her to tell Seamus the truth." His eyelids drooped. "The last time we talked about it, she said Seamus knew something was going on. I hope he didn't think—"

Noting his friend's anguish, Seamus felt ashamed. He'd been an idiot, suspecting the two best people in his life of betraying him. Lee had read his thoughts and seen the mistrust in his eyes.

Grulke was only interested in what happened. "So you went to find the guy with the scar."

"Charlie Cole. He works at Danny's Place downtown—at least, when he works."

"Gentlemen, you have to step out for a few moments." Grulke and Cannell turned to find a nurse with a tray on which a large hypodermic needle lay.

"We're in the middle of an interview," Grulke said, his voice a growl of discontent.

"And you can pick it up again in just a few minutes," the nurse said. Her tone was sweet, but the pure steel behind it indicated there was no use arguing.

In the hallway, Grulke told Cannell, "The guy he mentioned, Charlie Cole? One of my cops found him in an alley last night, beaten pretty badly. I think they brought him here to County."

"Who beat him?"

"He won't say, but he works at the club where Lee sang before she married Hanrahan."

Cannell considered for a few seconds. "What if I go down there and tell him I'm Wellman's partner? I can hint that I know more than I do and maybe get the truth out of him."

"It's worth a try," Grulke said. "I'm going to have the owner of that club picked up. Somebody there is involved in this, and it's time we found out who."

***

Malloy was excited when the call came on the radio to pick up Danny Proust. "Grulke asked for us," he told Waite. "He must think we're on the right track."

"But he's still looking at Lee as the main suspect," Waite replied. "Do you think she killed her husband?"

"Honestly? Yes. There's no reason for Proust to want Hanrahan dead."

"So what are they hiding at Danny's Place?"

"Maybe Proust or someone who works for him helped Lee dump the body so she wouldn't tell about his moneymaking scheme. They probably helped her leave town too."

"Then why did he ask you to tell him first if you found her?"

"Trying to throw me off, so I wouldn't suspect him."

Waite sniffed. "It feels wrong to me. I don't think we know everything yet."

Malloy shrugged, willing to let his partner have his opinions. "Then anything Grulke gets out of Mr. Proust should help."

Danny Proust's place of residence was an apartment building a few blocks from the club. The building had pretensions to grandeur, but on closer inspection, the corners were dirty and, as Malloy commented on the way up, the elevator wheezed like a dying walrus.

When they knocked on the door of Proust's apartment, no one answered for some time. Knocking again, Waite called, "Chicago police, Mr. Proust. We need to talk to you."

When the door finally opened, it took Malloy a second to recognize the woman standing there. Patti LaFlame's shiner rivaled one he'd once seen on the loser of a match with Rocky Marciano. Her undamaged eye narrowed when she took in his face and the uniform. "Weren't you at the club a while back?"

"Maybe."

She seemed unable to connect Malloy with the fictional James Fennimore Cooper. "What do you want?"

"We need to talk to Mr. Proust."

Her mouth curled in a bitter smile. "He ain't feeling so good today."

"That's too bad, but we still need to see him."

Patti rolled her eyes—actually one eye—and stepped back to let them in. "You might want to be careful what subjects you bring up."

Malloy took a guess. "Like Lili Moreno?"

Patti touched her swollen eye in subconscious revelation. "Yeah, like that."

"Who's out there, Patti?" Proust appeared in a doorway, wearing a smoking jacket draped over one shoulder. The change in him was shocking. His skin was pale, with a sheen of sweat on his forehead and cheekbones. Even his voice seemed less forceful than before. "What is it?"

"Detective Grulke would like to see you down at the 8th," Malloy said. "We're here to escort you."

"I can't go anywhere," Proust replied. "I'm not feeling well."

He looked like he meant it, but Malloy glanced to Waite for an opinion. It was generally understood that white cops dealt with white suspects, but Waite was the senior officer. Waite shook his head minimally, and Malloy interpreted that to mean they weren't going to be talked out of this. Turning back to Proust he said, "Sir, you're going to have to come with us."

Proust's expression revealed both anger and dismay. "I told you, I'm sick."

"He didn't have nothing to do with killing that guy." Patti unconsciously touched her blackened eye again. "He was here with me all that night."

"Shut up." Proust's voice was weak, but Patti winced.

"Did he give you that mouse, Miss LaFlame?"

"No." The response was a little too quick. "I'm clumsy sometimes."

"Yeah, well, I bet you won't be so clumsy once we take this guy downtown."

"He can't leave," Patti insisted. "He's real sick, and it's cold out there."

"It won't take long," Malloy said. "A few questions, and we'll bring him back and let him use you for his punching bag some more."

"He didn't mean it." Patti forgot she'd denied being hit. "Maybe you got a doctor down there who could give him something for the pain."

"We'll see what we can do," Malloy said. "Mr. Proust, come with us."

"Don't cuff him. He fell on the ice and hurt his shoulder real bad."

Malloy looked at Waite, who shrugged. "He's not under arrest. The detective just wants to talk to him."

Taking a coat from a hall tree near the door, Patti draped it over Danny's shoulders, careful to avoid touching the damaged side. "I'll call your lawyer, Baby. Don't you worry about a thing."

As they ushered Proust out, Patti's confidence evaporated. "He'll be back, won't he? You ain't gonna lock him up."

Since neither man knew the answer to that, they didn't answer. Patti stared after them, her face taut with fear. Proust didn't give her any reassurance. In fact, he didn't even glance back at her.

As they entered the elevator, Malloy reached out to press the button and accidentally brushed against Proust. "Son of a bitch!" he gasped.

"Maybe you should see a doctor once Grulke's done with you," Waite advised.

"Or maybe you should stop beating your women," Malloy added. "I hear that's hard on a bum shoulder.

Chapter Twenty-four

When Grulke returned from using the telephone, the nurse was exiting Wellman's room. "You can go back in now," she said magnanimously. He glared as she went off down the corridor, her white shoes soundless on the checkered tile floor.

As he wondered if he was obligated to wait for Wellman's partner to return, Cannell came around the corner, his face pinched with frustration. "Cole checked himself out," he reported. "The doctor tried to stop him, said he probably has a concussion, but Cole wouldn't listen."

"We can track him down later if we need to," Grulke said. "I have his daughter's address. Let's see what more your friend can tell us about this mess."

The detective wasn't happy that his neat explanations were under attack. If Lee Hanrahan wasn't sleeping with Wellman, he was determined to find out exactly who she had been cheating on her husband with.

They entered Wellman's room together, where he lay with eyes closed as machines that monitored his condition beeped and burbled.

Cannell touched Wellman's arm. "Grant? Do you feel like talking some more?"

"Feel terrible," he mumbled, but he opened his eyes. "I want to help."

"Okay, that's good." Cannell looked to Grulke.

"You were telling us about the second time you spoke to Charlie Cole."

"Yeah." Wellman swallowed. "The guy's pretty slippery, and it took me a couple of trips to the neighborhood to find him. I waited outside a place somebody told me was his favorite card-playing spot. Some furniture store on Duncan."

"This was Saturday the 12th?"

"Yes. When Cole saw me he tried to run, but I chased him down. He started babbling about how he didn't tell them where she was, so they couldn't have hurt her. 'Who's they?' I asked him."

"Indeed," Grulke murmured.

"It took a while, but in the end I got most of it. Cole insisted he accidently mentioned he'd seen Lili Moreno recently."

"Why did The Prousts care?"

Wellman frowned. "When Lee left the club, word went around that she'd stolen money from Danny, and anyone who could tell them where she was would get a reward. Nobody knew where she went, so the offer was never accepted."

Grulke nodded at the first thing Wellman had said he could whole-heartedly agree with. "Mr. Proust said when she left, the girl took cash from his desk."

Wellman made a grimace of disgust. "If you knew Lee, Detective, you'd know how ridiculous that accusation is."

Grulke raised a doubting brow. "What other reason would he have to pursue her?"

"Lee said her life might be in danger."

"She knew something about the Prousts?"

"There was no proof of anything. Lee thought she was safe with a new name and address, but then Charlie happened to see her on the street one day."

"And he told the Prousts."

"Accidentally." The sarcasm in Cannell's tone indicated he'd formed an opinion of Chicken Charlie.

"He had the nerve to blame me," Wellman said. "He blackmailed Lee into paying him to keep quiet about her new life. When I shut off the flow of cash, he remembered the reward Proust had offered." In a tone of disgust he finished, "No accident about it."

"So Cole sold out his own daughter?"

"Stepdaughter, but yeah. That's Charlie." With a slight gesture of the hand that was free of IV's Wellman said, "In his defense, Charlie believed Proust when he said he only wanted Lee to repay the money she'd taken from him."

"But you knew it was more than that." Cannell folded his arms tightly, anticipating the revelations that would follow as if he knew how chilling they would be.

"I knew Lee would never have stolen money from a guy like Proust. She isn't stupid."

"What did you do?" Cannell asked.

"First I hunted up a telephone and called the house. Lee said Seamus had gone to meet someone. When I told her what Charlie had confessed, she said the call he'd gotten was a trap."

Seamus remembered every word of that phone conversation.

If you want to know the truth about your wife, meet me at Danny's Place after closing tonight.

He'd been leery at first, but the husky-voiced woman claimed she'd moved into the upstairs room Lee used to stay in. *There's a bunch of stuff up here she left behind. You need to see it for yourself.*

Grulke rubbed his jaw. "Who made the call?"

"Lee didn't know." Cannell offered more water, which Wellman sipped gratefully. "She said she had to find Seamus, because the Prousts were setting him up."

"Maybe she was afraid of what her husband was going to find out."

At Wellman's look of confusion, Grulke explained. "You say it wasn't you Mrs. Hanrahan was having an affair with. What if she was seeing someone at Danny's Place, and that's what the caller intended to tell him?"

"I'm telling you, there was no other man!" Wellman rolled his head on the pillow in agitation. "Lee was going to leave Chicago that night—alone. She had her things packed when I got there."

Cannell glanced at Grulke. "She asked you to drive her somewhere?"

"To the train station. I agreed, mostly to get one more chance to change her mind."

"And did she change her mind?" Grulke's tone was mild, but he watched Wellman's face intently.

"Not about leaving Chicago, but she said she had to stop Seamus from going to Danny's Place before she could go."

"Was she going to tell him the truth?"

Wellman coughed weakly then winced at the pain it caused. "Once we made sure he was safe. She thought Danny would leave Seamus alone once she was out of the picture."

Grulke made a sound of impatience. "Detective Wellman, you're saying Danny Proust intended to harm Mrs. Hanrahan's husband? Why would he do that?"

"To get to her," he replied. "To get Lee to come to the club—" Wellman coughed weakly, then coughed again. "She was—" He coughed again, harder this time, and his face contorted with pain. A monitor on his right beeped, and the nurse who'd shooed them out earlier returned.

"You're going to have to step out for a while," she ordered. Grulke's impatience manifested this time in an audible groan.

"He's helping us with a murder case, Nurse."

"And he's full of mucous. I need to sit him up and let him cough it out."

"When can we come back?" Cannell asked.

Glancing at her watch, she said, "He's scheduled for some tests. It will take two hours at least."

Wellman's continued coughing was clear evidence they had no choice. Cannell's eyes met Grulke's and he shrugged. "We'll be back."

Outside the room, Grulke told Cannell, "I sent a couple of guys out to pick up Danny Proust. Want to sit in on the interview?"

"You don't have to ask me twice," the younger detective said. "I have a feeling he can tell us everything we need to know about what happened that night."

***

In a generous mood, Grulke invited Waite and Malloy to watch through the one-way glass as he and Cannell interrogated Danny Proust. The club owner wasn't looking any better, but he played the role of outraged citizen. "What is this about, Detective? I've done nothing that merits this high-handed treatment from the police."

"First, Danny, we know you're running an illegal scheme out of your club." Seamus approved of Grulke's technique, beginning with the small stuff and saving more serious accusations for follow-up.

"What scheme would that be?"

"It seems you arrange divorces—"

A laugh interrupted Grulke's sentence, though Proust's face didn't form an amused expression. In fact, he looked like an actor in a Kabuki mask. "And how would we do such a thing?"

"That isn't important right now."

Proust spoke, his lips stiff and his voice jerky. "I'll—tell you what, Detective. You show—me evidence that—I've done—anything wrong. No—one in the city will—come forward and accuse me."

Grulke had hoped to break Proust down using the scraps of information Malloy and Waite had gleaned, but the man had a point. Who would testify about the divorce scheme? Certainly not the hat-check girl or Charlie Cole, who'd been warned off with violence. And certainly not the women actually involved in the scheme. In addition to being afraid of the Proust brothers, they'd also be incriminating themselves.

While Grulke groped for a way to make Proust talk, Seamus made a decision. He wanted to learn what Proust knew, even if he couldn't help the detective prove it. When Grulke walked behind Proust in an attempt to make him nervous, Seamus jumped to the nightclub owner.

And felt immediate, excruciating pain. The man was using every iota of concentration just to sit erect in the chair and appear calm. His head seemed to be splitting into shards. His neck and jaw throbbed. His shoulder burned. The rest of his body seemed rigid and sore in sympathy. Danny Proust was a very sick man.

"Mr. Proust," Grulke asked, "Where is Lee Hanrahan?"

Proust summoned all his energy to make a response, but his mouth barely formed the words. "She was—close to our former—bouncer, Murray Dobbs. He—disappeared—the night her husband turned—up dead."

"If you're lying, we're going to find out—" Grulke began, but Proust could take no more.

"Doctor!" he said through his teeth.

"What?"

Proust's body began to spasm, and Grulke backed away in surprise and horror. "Hey!" he shouted. "Get some help in here! This guy's having a seizure!"

Malloy ran out of the observation room, calling for assistance. The desk officer hurried in and bent over Proust, assessing his condition as Grulke looked over his shoulder. Seamus jumped back to him, using the man between them as a stepping stone.

Focused on loosening Proust's clothing, the man in the middle hardly noticed Seamus' entry and immediate exit. Feeling something under the writhing man's shirt, he pulled the fabric back. "Look—his shoulder's bandaged." Checking under the wrappings he added, "I think he's been shot."

"What happened to you?" Grulke asked, but Proust was beyond answering. His body arched in pain, and his muscles stood out like ropes under his skin. Sounds came from his throat, but his teeth were clenched, his lips drawn back.

Clatter on the stairs signaled the arrival of ambulance attendants. A few minutes later they had an initial, though amateur diagnosis. "Lockjaw," the older of the two attendants said. "Something dirty got into the wound, a wood splinter, maybe, or bird manure."

"Lockjaw?" Cannell repeated. "Isn't that, um, fatal?"

The attendant nodded as he and his partner lifted the stiff body of Danny Proust onto a stretcher. He grunted in pain, and judging from the glazed look in his eyes, he was beyond understanding what was being said.

"Most of the time it is," the attendant said. "There's a vaccine for tetanus now, but a lot of people haven't had it." Fastening the straps tightly around Proust's convulsing body he added, "Once you see somebody die this way, you'll get the shot, believe me."

After Proust was taken away, things settled down. Malloy and Waite got orders from Grulke to find Frankie Proust and bring him to County Hospital. "I'm going to finish the interview with Wellman," Grulke told them, "then we'll see how Proust is doing. If he can't tell us what's going on, maybe his brother can."

Chapter Twenty-five

As they waited for the desk sergeant to locate Frankie Proust's address for them, Malloy and Waite picked at what little Proust had revealed in the interview. "He made it sound like Lee killed the bouncer too," Waite said.

"She might have called him when her plan to murder Hanrahan went wrong."

Waite frowned. "So now you think she took off with What's-His-Name?"

"Murray. Sandra says he was always chasing women. A pretty woman like Lee could have got him to help when her plans went wrong."

Ronnie had to fight the urge to jump to Malloy and tell him how wrong he was, but she knew Lee had despised Murray only because Seamus told her. Waite's orderly thought process would be enough to dispel his partner's half-baked theory—she hoped.

"Linny said her sister had no use for any of the men at Danny's Place. Everyone I've talked to says Lee isn't the type to kill, but you're saying she murdered or tried to murder three men in one night."

Ronnie wanted to pat Waite on the back. He'd come over to Lee's side. Seamus himself had been on the wrong side for too long, but a part of him must have held onto hope. Why else had he been unable to let go of Seamus Hanrahan and leave the ship behind?

Malloy wasn't convinced. "Just because her aunt and sister think she's sweet and innocent doesn't mean it's true, Joe."

"But you said the hat-check girl liked her."

"On a cold night, Lee let her stay in her warm room and made her cocoa. That's not proof of anything except she likes cocoa." Taking the slip of paper with the address from the sergeant, he led the way to the doors. "The one thing our three victims have in common is Lee."

As they left the building, Malloy stopped abruptly. "Look there."

Standing outside the door was Pickles, the guy from the chair factory. In his hand was a crumpled envelope, and on his face was evidence of an inner struggle, probably whether to go inside the station or return home.

"Let me handle this," Waite said. Malloy stepped aside, and Joe approached the man.

"What you got there?"

Instead of answering, Pickles said, "Charlie came to the factory a while ago. He was a big old mess."

"Yeah."

"He said you saved his life, got him to the hospital." When Waite didn't respond, he went on, "He wanted money so he could get out of Chicago, but I didn't have none."

"Where is he now?"

He looked at Waite, his expression earnest. "We had a truck leaving for Shreveport. The driver's a good guy, and he said he'd take Charlie along for comp'ny. I don't know what he did, Officer, but Charlie, he family. He said there's men wanting to kill him. I just had to help him out."

Dead to Get Ready—and Go

Waite glanced at Malloy, who made a grimace of resignation. Charlie could exit the truck anywhere between Chicago's South Side and the Gulf of Mexico. They would probably never find him.

"We appreciate you coming down here to tell us, Pickles. At least we won't waste man-hours looking for him in the city."

"Well, I brought this, too." He held out the envelope. "Charlie didn't take it with him, so I guess he don't want it no more."

As soon as they got into their patrol car, Waite examined the envelope. *Charlie,* he read aloud as Malloy drove, *Please give this to Linny without Momma seeing.*

"I guess that never happened," Malloy said.

The flap had been torn open. "Somebody read the letter." Taking the single sheet from the envelope, Waite scanned it. "It's dated September 21st, 1950." He read aloud:

> *Dearest Linny,*
>
> *I don't know when I will see you again. I have married a wonderful man who loves me as much as I love him, and because of his kindness, I've found a way to help you and Momma out. Each month I will send money in your name in care of General Delivery at the main branch of the Chicago Post Office. All you have to do is go there and ask for a letter for Lincoln Cole. It won't be as much as I used to send, but I hope it will be enough that you can stay in school until you graduate.*
>
> *I had to leave Danny's Place. I told you I believed the Proust brothers are dishonest, and I found proof*

of that in Danny's office. Hidden inside a hollowed-out copy of the book Kon-Tiki *is a register where he keeps track of their illegal activities. I was copying pages from it into my own little notebook whenever I got the chance. I am not sure what I would have done with it, but Danny became suspicious and sent Murray to find out what I was up to.*

The man who is now my husband saved me from the beating Murray intended to inflict on me. We left Danny's Place together, but I wasn't able to take the evidence I'd been collecting. Now I have no proof of Danny's crimes, only the word of a dishonest Negro who has been passing as a white woman. We both know how little weight that would carry with the police against a prosperous white businessman.

I am terrified Danny will find us. He is the type of man who might hurt my husband, knowing that would bring me more pain than anything he could do to me.

No one knows where I've gone, and no one but you knows I have married. I will be careful not to call attention to myself, and I have put Lili Moreno completely in the past. I pray the Prousts will conclude I am no danger to them when time goes by and their crimes remain secret.

It is not my place to tell Charlie what to do, but you might warn him to stay away from Danny's Place and everyone associated with it. If he continues to deal with the Prousts, he will surely suffer at some point.

Dead to Get Ready—and Go

Please do not try to find me. For the first time in my life I am completely happy. I love you, and of course I miss you and my brothers every single day, but this is how it must be.

Your Loving Sister,

Lee

"Wow," Malloy said as Waite refolded the letter and put it back into its envelope. "She definitely laid it all out, didn't she?"

"But Charlie Cole ruined her plan."

"He didn't pass this letter on to Linny like Lee asked him to."

"It was too good for a guy like him to pass up." Waite put the envelope into his jacket pocket. "Charlie's an opportunist. When he read Lee's letter, he realized she'd never know if her family got the money or not. He went to the post office every month and presented himself as Lincoln Cole."

"How would he get away with that?"

Waite shrugged. "He probably picked up something from Linny's house to convince them of identity, like a bill with her name on it. *Lincoln* certainly sounds more like a man's name than a woman's."

"And Charlie got a nice little sum of money every month to gamble away as he pleased."

"While his own children scrambled to pay the rent." Waite shook his head at Cole's heartless actions. "I guess he knows now he shouldn't have ignored Lee's warning. I could tell that his arm was broken in more than one place."

"Serves him right if he's got permanent damage," Malloy said. "Now it's up to us to make sure nobody else has to suffer because of the Proust brothers."

Chapter Twenty-six

After Danny Proust's collapse, Grulke and Cannell returned to the hospital. As they entered Wellman's room, a very young nurse was adjusting the sheets on his bed, and her eyes sent all kinds of messages to her oblivious patient. When she left the room Cannell observed, "Even half dead you still pull in the ladies, Grant."

Wellman chuckled weakly. "Wish I didn't feel half dead. I might care."

A look from Grulke pulled Cannell back to the point of the visit. "Grant, you told us Lee was afraid of Danny Proust. Do you know exactly why she thought that?"

Wellman grimaced. "Lee had a room at the club. One night she heard noises and stepped into the hallway to see what was happening."

"Her room was where?"

"In a loft over the stage. Danny's office is at the front, and behind it are two rooms, one where the bouncer stayed and then Lee's."

"And how did Mrs. Hanrahan pay for her living quarters?"

The suggestion in Grulke's voice angered Wellman. "For the last time, Detective, Lee wasn't like that. When her mother disowned her she wanted to quit the club, but Danny offered her the room for free. She had nowhere else to go."

"It's hard to believe the relationship was platonic," Grulke said smoothly. "Night club owners aren't usually philanthropists."

"Lee made it clear she wasn't interested in sleeping with him or anyone else at the club, employee or patron. They made it rough on her, but they never pushed her so far that she'd quit, since her singing brought in new customers."

"Okay, back to what she saw. She came out of her room—"

"Frankie was standing near the stairs, and when he saw Lee, he said something to someone in Danny's office. She thought it was, 'Hold on a minute.' She asked what was going on, and he said it was nothing and she should go back into her room and shut the door. She did as he said, and that was it, as far as she knew."

"But she changed her mind later."

"One of the dancers, Tina, was missing the next day. Danny told everyone she'd quit, but a week later the police found the girl's body in the Chicago River."

"With a guy named Arthur Jameson," Grulke supplied.

Wellman blinked agreement. "Tina was one of the few who'd treated Lee decently. It was because she was worried about her that Lee spoke to Seamus when he came to Danny's. She hoped he was looking for Tina, but he'd been hired by Mrs. Jameson to find her husband."

"There was nothing suspicious about the accident," Grulke said. "The car slid on the icy road and crashed in the river."

"That was the official conclusion, but several months later, Lee went into Danny's office to use his stapler. Reaching for it, she knocked something off the desk and onto the floor. When she bent down to retrieve it, Lee noticed something shiny back in the corner. It was a bracelet Tina had made for herself, one of a kind. She'd been wearing it the last time Lee saw her."

"Okay. Tina was in Proust's office the night she died. So what?"

"The bracelet was too far back for her to reach, so Lee pulled on the rug under Danny's desk to get it away from the wall. Under the rug was a large stain, and she was pretty sure it was blood. The bracelet and the bloodstain brought back the memory of the night Tina supposedly left, and the noise she heard in Proust's office that Frankie said was nothing."

"She thinks Proust killed one of his employees? Why would he do that?"

"The real question is if Tina died in Proust's office, how did her body get into the river in Jameson's car with Jameson dead beside her?"

"He killed them both." Cannell sounded convinced, but Seamus felt Grulke's resistance to changing his mind. He didn't want to believe Lee was innocent. He wanted to hold onto his belief that when a husband dies, the wife is the most likely suspect—especially if she's a Negro pretending to be white.

Unaware of Grulke's thoughts—or perhaps in spite of them, Wellman replied to Cannell's comment. "Lee had no proof of any wrongdoing. As you said, there's no reason Tina shouldn't have been in Proust's office on the night she supposedly quit. The bloodstain on the floor could be explained a dozen ways. But Lee had seen the Proust brothers operate, and she had no doubt they were capable of murder."

"Why would they have killed a patron?" Cannell asked.

"Lee figured Arthur Jameson found out he was being set up for divorce. He made a fuss and they killed him."

Cannell got it. "The girl died because she was unlucky enough to be a witness."

Grulke still wanted to blame Lee for something. "If she had evidence of a crime, why didn't Mrs. Hanrahan go to the police?"

"She didn't think they'd believe her."

"Why not? Other people might have seen the girl wearing the bracelet that night. She could testify to the commotion in Proust's office in the wee hours. And there was the bloodstain—if we accept her story."

"Proust would have invented his own explanation, and once an investigation began, Lee's background would have been revealed. She'd be the Negro singer who passed for white and made up lies about her boss."

"So she's a Negro," Cannell said, "That doesn't mean she can't tell the truth."

Wellman smiled grimly. "Danny's employees had to keep quiet or lose their jobs. Besides, Lee had seen enough to understand that talking about what you see at Danny's gets a person nothing but pain."

Aware of what had happened to Charlie Cole and Sandra, neither Cannell nor Grulke argued the point. After a moment, Wellman went on. "Lee was a nervous wreck. She couldn't look either Danny or Frankie in the eye without picturing Tina's body on his office floor. To try to stop them, Lee started snooping."

"What happened?"

"Lee was no detective, and Danny got suspicious. He sent Murray to put a scare into her, but Seamus happened along and saved her."

"So she married him to get away from Proust."

"She married him because she loved him." Wellman's tone was firm. "Lee was in a bad spot, but marrying Seamus was not a convenient escape. Seamus was the best thing that ever happened to her."

Something that could only be called joy flooded Seamus Hanrahan. He'd never been so happy to be proved a complete idiot.

"So she got away, and she had it good," Grulke said, "until Proust found out where she was."

"Right. Lee felt guilty enough that she'd lied to Seamus about her race, but when he walked into danger on her account she had to try to fix it."

"So she could run away from Chicago and let a couple of murderers go unpunished? You were going to let her do that?"

Wellman chuckled weakly. "I didn't know all the things I just told you until that night. The story came out in the car on the way to the club. I told Lee she should stay in Chicago and tell what she knew, but she couldn't deal with it all at once. I figured we'd talk about it once we found Seamus and got him out of there."

"Why did they lure him down there?" Cannell asked. "Why not her?"

"Because Lee wouldn't have gone anywhere near either Proust. I think they meant to kill them both, in case Lee had told Seamus what she knew. If they captured him then called Lee she'd have gone anywhere they said. She'd have bargained for his life, even if it meant losing hers."

Grulke wasn't interested in hearing more about the Hanrahans' love for each other. "Okay. You and Lee went to Danny's to stop Hanrahan from walking into a trap."

"We were still arguing about what we should do when I pulled into the parking lot. I remember there was a black DeSoto alongside the building, but it was cold and covered with snow. I got out of my car. It was snowing lightly, and we listened for a few seconds to see if we heard anything. When there was no sound, I concluded we'd arrived before Seamus. We had the car, and he was using public transport, which meant he had to walk a good part of the way."

"What did you do?"

"I told Lee to wait in the car while I looked around." Wellman's voice changed as he relived the experience. "I drew my gun and started around the building. It was slow going, because there was crusty snow piled under the eaves and it was slippery. I had a flashlight in my pocket but didn't think I should advertise my presence until I figured out what was going on.

"When I got almost all the way around the building, I came up on the black DeSoto. Beside it, two men were bent over a third man, who wasn't moving." His voice caught. "Seamus' fedora was lying on the ground a few feet away. They had the car's trunk open, and as I came closer, they lifted Seamus into it. I stepped up and called for them to freeze, but someone fired at me. When I ducked, the two men disappeared into the shadows."

Wellman's voice got tighter and his words came faster. "I couldn't tell where the shot came from, but I heard the trunk lid snap shut. One of the men got into the car. I couldn't fire at him for fear of hitting Seamus.

"Since I didn't know where the shooter was, I was stuck along the wall of the club. Someone tried to start the De Soto's engine. It rolled over but didn't fire."

Wellman licked his lips again, and Cannell gave him a sip of water. Nodding thanks, he continued, "My car headlights came on, and I realized Lee was trying to blind the shooter so he couldn't locate me. I started to circle toward her, but there must have been a third man. He fired from somewhere in front of me, and I went down."

The others waited until Wellman was able to go on. "The driver was still having trouble getting the DeSoto started. I heard the starter grind again, heard the gas pedal thump as it hit the floor. My chest hurt like hell. I couldn't breathe, and I fought to stay conscious. I kept thinking about Seamus, shut up in that trunk, and Lee, waiting in my car. I wanted to get them both out of there, but all I could do was gasp for air like a carp on a dock."

"Then what?"

"My car's headlights went out, and the parking lot went dark. In a few seconds I felt someone pulling at my coat. Lee whispered, 'Grant? Can you walk?' I meant to say I'd try, but I think all she got was a grunt. She helped me up, and we started for my car." His eyes looked bleak. "She pretty much had to carry me, but I did what I could."

"And your attackers?"

"They must have heard us. They fired twice more, but the bullets missed. Lee made a little squeak each time, but she kept going. Then the guy in the DeSoto finally got it started. He drove off, not past us, but toward the back of the club."

"Where would that take him?"

"To the river." Cannell and Grulke fell silent again, melding what they knew of Seamus' death with what Wellman was telling them.

"What did you and Mrs. Hanrahan do?"

"We got to my car, and she helped me into the driver's side. She said, 'Grant, you have to go and get help. Can you do that?'" Wellman paused again, his face haggard. 'No,' I told her. 'I can't leave you here!' Lee had picked up my gun. I saw her put it into her coat pocket before she closed the car door. 'I know where they're going,' she said. 'Get help, and I'll meet you back here when I know for sure where they've taken Seamus.'"

"She intended to follow them on foot?" Grulke's disbelief was apparent in his tone.

Wellman's brows met. "I'm not sure what she intended, Detective. I was doing my best to keep breathing."

"If she used to work at that club," Cannell observed, "she'd know where that road led."

"Okay," Grulke said. "What happened next?"

"That's all I remember," Wellman said. "I guess I tried to do what Lee told me to."

"You made it several blocks before you hit that lamp post," Cannell said. "Pretty tough."

"Not tough enough." Grant's face twitched with emotion. "All I have after that are vague impressions of an ambulance and doctors putting their faces close to mine and asking if I can hear them." He

257

made a weak gesture at Cannell. "Tony told me Seamus is dead. I went there to help him, and I failed."

Cannell shifted his feet. "You didn't know those men were willing to kill to protect their secrets."

Wellman couldn't let himself off so easily. "I met Danny Proust and his thug brother Frankie once, and I remember thinking they were slimier than the bottom of a soap dish." Turning to Grulke he begged, "Detective, you've got to find Lee. She's in real danger."

Seamus heard Grulke's thought: *Criminal or victim, Lee Hanrahan's good at not being found.* Aloud he asked, "You don't have any idea where we might start looking for her?"

"You need to squeeze Danny Proust," Wellman said. "Hard."

"We'd like to, but we can't." Grulke filled Wellman in on Proust's condition. "I sent some officers to find the brother. I promise you, we'll get one of them to talk."

As they left the hospital Cannell said, "Did you warn your men that Frankie Proust might be a killer?"

Grulke snorted his porcine laugh. "We've only got Wellman's word for that." He raised a hand as Cannell took breath to object. "I know, he's a regular boy scout, but you can tell how he feels about Lee Hanrahan from the way he talks about her. We don't know who shot Wellman in the dark. It could have been her."

"What about the men who attacked Hanrahan?"

"She could have arranged it. She wants both her husband and her boyfriend dead, so she makes up a story that gets them both down there where it's easy to dispose of the bodies."

"She helped Grant get away."

"He was hurt. He might have imagined it."

"I don't buy it," Cannell said. "Wellman's too smart to be taken in like that. I think the Prousts are behind this, and that means Frankie's dangerous."

Grulke snorted again. "Word is the guy's a fruit. How tough can he be?"

Cannell said no more, but Seamus noted the look in his eyes. He wanted to.

Chapter Twenty-seven

Malloy was again pleased when Grulke called on them to find Frankie Proust. "He might as well come out and say we've helped on this case. I tell you, partner, we're in the catbird seat with Detective Grulke."

Waite huffed doubtfully while Ronnie hoped the younger cop's enthusiasm didn't make him careless.

"He wants us to pick him up and bring him to the hospital?" Malloy asked as his partner navigated the slushy streets.

Waite nodded. "He probably wants to question the two of them together."

"It didn't look to me like Danny's going to be ready to be questioned any time soon."

At the address they'd been given for Frankie, they found only an empty terrace apartment. Peering in the window Malloy asked, "What now?"

"He could be at the club."

"Then let's go see what we can find there."

When Waite turned down the side street leading to Danny's, Malloy pointed to a black DeSoto parked near the club entrance. "There's a car. Somebody's here."

Malloy's tone became businesslike "How do you want to do this?"

Waite regarded the building. "There are windows toward the back. Let's peek in and see if anyone's moving around in there."

Exiting their vehicle, the men separated and went around the building on opposite sides. When they met at the back Malloy said softly, "All the windows over there are either shuttered or glass brick. I didn't see any movement."

Waite grimaced. "Kitchen's the only view I got to the inside, and it's empty."

Malloy regarded the outside stairway. "There's a window in the door up there. If you cover me, I'll go up and take a look."

Waite followed Malloy to the staircase and took up a position where he could see if someone came out the door at the top. Malloy took the wooden stairs quickly and lightly, his gun drawn but held at his side. Peering through the foot-square window in the door, he turned his head this way and that then shrugged, indicating he could see nothing. He came back down the stairs.

"Go knock at the front," Waite ordered. "I'll stay here and watch, in case somebody doesn't want to talk to us."

In seconds Malloy pounded on the front door, calling, "Chicago police! Open up!"

At first nothing happened. Then the door above Waite opened with the tiniest squeak of hinges. Herb looked out, saw that his escape was blocked, and with only a second of hesitation, drew a gun from his waistband. He was going to shoot his way out. Waite stepped back, brought his own weapon up, and shouted, "Stop! Police!"

Herb's answer was a bullet that whined past Waite's head and sent him scrambling for cover.

Ronnie was at first surprised, then confused, then terrified. Someone was shooting at her—at her host, which was every bit as bad.

The cop was a sitting duck, and not only did she worry for his safety, she had to consider her own. If Waite received a fatal gunshot, she had no one to jump to.

"Cover!" she urged. "Take cover!"

Behind him was the row of sheds, and Waite backed between two of them, firing twice to force Herb to retreat into the club. The space between the slanting, rough walls was just big enough for him to slide into. The dry boards pulled at his clothing, and he got only a few feet when a debris pile blocked his way. Still, he was no longer exposed to easy shots from the man above.

Movement to his right caught Waite's attention, and he saw Malloy round the building, his back to the wall.

"I'm okay!" Waite called out. "Stay back!"

Malloy obeyed, remaining at the corner of the building. His gaze followed Waite's and he saw Herb, now prone in the stairway door, aiming at the spot where Waite crouched.

"Give up, man!" Malloy shouted. "You won't get away."

Herb fired once at him before returning his attention to Waite.

"Call for help!" Waite ordered, and Malloy backed away.

"More cops on the way," Waite called to Herb. "You might as well surrender."

Instead of answering, Herb fired once more then crawled backward through the doorway and closed the door. At that moment Waite noticed smoke coming from the roof of the club.

Waite left his place of refuge and headed to the car, where Malloy sat in the passenger seat, talking into the radio microphone. "Suspect is armed, I repeat, armed."

"He's set the place on fire!" Waite pointed to the smoke.

"Send fire trucks too," Malloy said into the mic. "Repeat, fire at this address." Setting the receiver in its cradle he said, "We've got to stop him."

Guns ready, the two men approached the front door. It was securely locked and sturdy enough to resist attempts to break it down that didn't involve crowbars and sledgehammers. "Let's try the one at the back," Waite said.

The back door, too, was secure. "They must have figured they'd have to repel you and me at some point," Waite said in a halfhearted attempt at humor.

"That leaves the upstairs door," Malloy said. "I can break the window and let myself in."

"He'll hear it and leave by one of the other exits."

"We can't wait," Malloy argued. "The fire will destroy whatever evidence is in there. I'll flush him out, and you can catch him."

After a momentary glance at the smoke wisping from the eaves, Waite nodded. "Go."

As Malloy climbed the stairs, Waite looked for a spot where he could see both the front and back doors. That wasn't possible, but gambling that Herb wouldn't use the front door, where police cars would soon be showing up in large numbers, he focused on the back.

Ronnie saw a flaw in the young cop's plan. "Windows," she whispered. "Windows!"

At her urging, Waite realized the shuttered windows on the building's sides blocked entry but didn't prevent someone inside from coming out.

He looked up. Malloy was no longer visible. His presence on the second floor should drive Herb to the main floor. It seemed that human nature would influence Herb to exit the opposite side of the building from where he'd last seen the two officers. Moving quickly around the back, Waite took up a position at the corner and watched the three shuttered windows, waiting. Sure enough, the one nearest him twitched a few times as someone inside worked quietly to displace the covering. Waite moved closer, crouching along the wall.

When the quiet method didn't work, there was a crash, and the shutters burst open.

Taking a steady stance, Waite raised his gun and calmed himself with a deep breath. A large rear end emerged from the window. The gun stuck in the hopeful escapee's waistband presented itself to Waite, and he plucked it easily from its resting place. "Stop!" he commanded, Herb surrendered with only a muttered curse word.

Waite steered the bouncer to his car, cuffed one of his hands, ran the other cuff around the post between the triangular vent window and the larger driver's window, and fastened it onto Herb's other hand. Once he was secured, Waite went back to the window and leaned in. "I've got him, Dean." He heard sirens in the distance, but nothing from Malloy. "Dean? Are you okay?"

Nothing.

Pulling himself onto the sill where Herb had exited, Waite twisted his legs around and stepped into Danny's Place.

He was in the dining room, and the open window cast a harsh light on battered tables and cigarette-smoke-dulled walls. The upper story crackled as the flames ate at it, and he heard the low hum of oxygenation, but as yet there wasn't much more than a taste of smoke in the air downstairs. Waite moved cautiously through the room, waiting for his eyes to adjust. Where was Malloy?

On his right was the stage, which he skirted, heading for a staircase marked EMPLOYEES ONLY. A velvet rope spanned the bottom step, emphasizing the privacy of the loft. Waite looked up. Black smoke rolled ominously above as air currents moved it this way and that.

Where was Malloy?

He found him at the top of the staircase, his body limp and his head bleeding. "Dean! Dean, can you hear me?"

Much to Waite's relief, his partner groaned and stirred. "Fr—" he mumbled. "Watch Fr—"

Focused on Malloy's condition, Waite failed to pay attention to what his partner was saying. "Come on. Let's get you out of here."

"Fra—" Malloy repeated. Finally he got the whole word out. "Frankie."

The warning registered just in time, because the man himself came at Waite, holding a baseball bat aloft. Waite managed to get a hand up to deflect the blow, though it felt like the whole building landed on his shoulder. He felt his collarbone crack as he almost fell down the stairs, catching himself at the last second by grasping the newel post with his left hand.

Ronnie felt the pain resound through Waite's body, but there was no time to give in to it. "Up!" she ordered. "Up, up!" Scrambling out of reach and using the wall for support, Waite rose to face his attacker. His right arm hung limp at his side. Behind Frankie, flames licked at the old wooden walls and sent out heat waves that made his form seem to waver. Acrid smoke burned Waite's eyes, and it hurt his lungs to breathe.

"You'd better help your friend." Frankie, too, felt the effects of the approaching fire, and he coughed as he added, "He looks bad."

Waite didn't glance at Malloy, aware that Frankie would kill them both if he got the chance. Reaching across his body, he took out his gun with his left hand. It was a clumsy move, but Ronnie approved. *A gun beats a club like Rock breaks Scissors.* Proust switched the bat threateningly but didn't swing it, aware he couldn't connect before Waite fired.

"You're under arrest," Waite said. "Drop the weapon." At that moment, sirens wailed above the roar of the fire. Help had arrived.

The half-second's distraction the sirens caused was exactly what Frankie had been waiting for. He swung the bat at Waite, hitting the barrel of the gun hard enough to knock it from his hand. As it thumped down the stairs, Frankie turned and disappeared into the smoke.

Waite hesitated, unsure whether to stay with Malloy or pursue their quarry.

"Go after him!" Malloy urged. "I'll be okay until the good guys get here."

Waite gave his shoulder a squeeze. "Okay, but your mom owes me a dinner, so don't die on me."

Malloy's grin was weak. "I won't if you don't."

The fire was gaining fast, and the initial combustion point was easy to spot. The room at the front of the loft—Proust's office—was engulfed in flames.

Where was Frankie?

As Waite made his way down the smoky corridor toward the outside stairway door, Ronnie again worried that her host would be killed. Frankie could be lurking in one of the doorways he had to pass, waiting to finish him off. What could she do to help?

Waite assessed the situation more calmly than she did, and he saw two possibilities. If Frankie was confident the fire would destroy the evidence, his instinct would be to escape. He might already be hurrying away from the club, devising a plan to leave Chicago and begin somewhere new. Frankie was a criminal, however, and criminals don't always do what makes sense. In that case, he might be waiting in one of the rooms along the hallway with the bat raised, intent on murder.

Ronnie couldn't shake the feeling that Frankie was still there. "Careful!" she whispered. Though she heard with Waite's ears and saw with his eyes, she somehow sensed the movement beside him before he did. "Duck!"

She misunderstood Frankie's intent. He wasn't there to kill Waite. He meant to make pursuit impossible.

At Ronnie's warning Waite crouched, protecting his head and damaged shoulder, but the blow came low, not high. The bat slammed into his knee, sending him to the floor. For a few seconds he was beyond reason, his eyes closed in anguish.

"Look!" Ronnie urged, though she felt the injury as strongly as Waite did. "Danger!"

Fearing there could be another blow coming, Waite forced his eyes open. The smoke was thinner near the floor than above, and he saw Frankie's feet turn away from him. There was a clunk as he tossed the bat away, and his feet turned toward the exterior stairs.

With a painful lunge, Waite put out his good hand and caught one leg of Frankie's pants. Frankie kicked out viciously, but the cop held on. Grunting with effort, Waite tried to lift Frankie's leg high enough to unbalance him and send him to the floor.

Ronnie felt the pain that stabbed through her host's body as the two men struggled. He felt piercing jabs along the collarbone and down his arm each time Frankie kicked at him. It was all he could do to push back enough to keep the blows from connecting. Though Waite's attempts to down Frankie were unsuccessful, they weakened the force he could direct into his kicks. Neither man was able to subdue the other. Neither was willing to stop trying.

Sounds downstairs indicated that help had arrived. Something rammed against the door once, twice, and a third time, causing it to give way with a huge crash. Voices called out, first Malloy shouting, "Over here!" then others, asking questions. "My partner's up there," Malloy shouted. "He went after the guy."

In a final, desperate act, Frankie twisted his leg sharply, jerking the fabric of his trouser leg out of Waite's grasp. In no time he was gone, disappearing completely into the thickening smoke. Waite heard the exterior door slam against the wall as he threw it open and left the building.

"Outside!" Waite called to the officers below, but smoke choked his voice, making it raspy and weak. The firemen outside weren't likely to detain someone escaping a burning building. Waite coughed some of the smoke from his lungs. He had to go after Frankie.

Pulling himself to his feet—*foot*, Ronnie corrected—Waite rose. Putting weight on the left leg was agony. Limping painfully along the corridor, Waite held himself erect by bracing his good hand on the wall.

It was a slow process, and Ronnie had to force herself not to urge him to hurry. Waite was doing the best he could with the injuries he had, but she was afraid Seamus' killer was getting away.

"There's a cop up here that's hurt!" Proust was on the platform outside, shouting to those on the ground. "Somebody help him!"

Ronnie imagined the firefighters craning their necks as they tried to see through the smoke. Frankie's voice faded as he started down the steps, repeating his supposed cry for help. "Help him! Up here!"

As Waite staggered on, using the wall for support and dragging his left leg, his foot hit something. The bat Frankie had dropped. "Use it!" Ronnie urged.

Bending to pick it up, Waite set the knob in the palm of his good hand and used the bat as a crutch. He moved a little faster, but not much, and she wasn't sure he knew what he'd do if he did catch up with Frankie.

When Waite reached the doorway, Frankie was just setting foot on solid ground. Several firemen rushed to him, asking questions. Frankie shook them off, pointing up at Waite, who stood half-blind and coughing as smoke billowed out behind him. "Hold him!" Waite croaked, but the roar of the fire and his smoke-clogged lungs defeated his attempts. Someone led Frankie to the rear of a firetruck and gestured for him to sit while they turned to complete the rescue.

As soon as the firemen turned their backs, Frankie stood again. Giving Waite a cocky little wave, he started at a trot down the road that led to the river.

Waite tried to gesture at Frankie, but his damaged arm managed only a weak wave. One of the firemen began climbing the stairs toward him. The others looked up at the burning building and the man in need of rescue, no longer concerned with the man who'd escaped. No one else saw Frankie Proust leaving the scene.

"Stop!" Waite croaked. The faces below reflected confusion.

Suddenly Ronnie recalled Waite's days as a baseball player. She'd seen bats fly out of the hands of professional players and circle into the stands or the dugouts. Could Waite stop Frankie with his improvised crutch? She whispered, "Throw it!"

Waite fought the idea briefly. His right arm was useless. He could barely stand. "Do it!" Ronnie urged. Waite looked toward the river, where the boat Frankie had used to dispose of Seamus Hanrahan's body waited. In minutes he'd use it to escape arrest and disappear.

"Stop him!" Ronnie urged, and Joe Waite acted. Balancing clumsily on his good knee, he used the platform railing to hold himself upright. With his good hand, he spun the bat in an arc, as he'd seen aborigines on television do with boomerangs. It circled in the air for what seemed like forever then traveled outward and down, hitting Frankie a glancing blow on the head. He let out a cry of pain and outrage, and two firemen ran to him, stopping his exit from the scene.

By that time, a fireman had reached Waite's side. "Arrest that guy," he whispered as the man put a shoulder under his arm to support him. "He tried to kill me and my partner."

Chapter Twenty-eight

Seamus was surprised to note that Grulke felt a moment's guilt when he saw Malloy approach, leading a handcuffed Frankie Proust. Standing outside the hospital room where Danny lay near death, he acknowledged that the two young cops should have been warned they were dealing with murderers. *Nobody died*, he comforted himself, *so it worked out okay.*

Seamus couldn't look at it that way. Waite had been Ronnie's host, and the fact that he wasn't with his partner indicated something bad had happened to him. Surely Ronnie would have jumped to someone else if Waite were seriously injured. Despite Grulke's careless dismissal of his own shortcomings, Seamus hoped Waite wasn't dead or dying.

Better not to think about that. Seamus had never lost a host, but he imagined it was as bad as one's own death, maybe worse. Ronnie would no doubt feel she should have been able to save him. Seamus knew he would, in a similar situation.

"Waite's okay," Malloy said, ending Seamus' painful speculation. "This guy bushwhacked both of us."

Evidence showed in the huge knot bulged under a bandage on Malloy's forehead. The eye below it was bloodshot, and darkening bruises surrounded it.

It pleased Seamus to see that the suspect was in as bad a state as the arresting officer. Congealed blood showed around a cut on the back of Frankie's head, and stains on his shirtfront indicated he'd taken a header in a slushy, muddy spot. Both men smelled of smoke, which made Grulke's nose wrinkle.

"What happened?"

Malloy gave a recap of the events at Danny's Place, ending with, "I have a hard Irish skull, I guess. The doc downstairs insisted he should look Waite over, just to be sure."

"This is all a misunderstanding," Frankie said. "I resent—"

"Save it," Grulke interrupted. "We know about your divorce-for-hire scheme."

Frankie considered that for a few seconds. "I'm thinking any evidence you mighta found concerning a so-called scheme would have been at the club." His tone turned sneering. "Too bad the place went up like a Japanese lantern."

Malloy cleared his throat a little theatrically. "Detective Grulke, you might want to know that before this ape attacked me, I located the book where Danny Proust kept track of his illegal activities."

"You're a damned liar," Frankie growled.

Grulke looked to Malloy questioningly, and he explained. "The book was in Danny's office, right where Lee said it would be."

"Lee Hanrahan told you where to find evidence against the Prousts?"

"Yes, sir."

"Then you found her?"

"No, but Joe got hold of a letter she wrote." He explained Pickles' visit. "She was trying to get proof of the divorce scheme, and she was pretty sure the Prousts killed Arthur Jameson. She found the book in

Danny's office, and she was copying down parts of it whenever she got the chance. Danny caught her in there and got suspicious."

That's why Murray came after her that night, Seamus realized. She must have felt lucky to get out of there alive.

"Knowing where the book was, I was able to get to it before the fire took hold," Malloy said. "I stuffed it inside my shirt and started downstairs to meet Joe, but that's when this jerk whacked me." As he handed the book to Grulke he told Frankie, "I hope it's enough to fry you."

Grulke also turned to Frankie. "You need to tell us what's been going on at that club, Proust."

Frankie sniffed disdainfully. "I ain't telling you nothing."

"You haven't seen what I have to show you in here." Turning, he went into the patient room. Malloy gave Frankie a shove, compelling him to follow.

Danny Proust lay like a dead man on the hospital bed. His chest rose and fell due to a tube down his throat that attached to a pump beside the bed, sucking and hissing as it breathed for him. "Your brother has tetanus, Mr. Proust. The doctors have paralyzed him with curare so the muscle spasms he's experiencing don't break every bone in his body." It was impossible to tell if Danny heard, but Grulke added coldly, "They don't hold out much hope that he'll live."

Frankie stared at his brother for some time. Grulke hoped the shock of seeing Danny so ill would soften him, but Seamus noted the man's flinty eyes. Frankie wasn't in shock. He was trying to figure out how to turn the situation to his advantage.

"Look," Seamus urged, trying to get Grulke to see that his ploy wasn't working. If they didn't get Frankie to talk now, he'd ask for a lawyer and they'd lose the chance to learn the truth. Frankie knew what had happened that night. He knew what Lee had done, and maybe even where she'd gone.

Grulke briefly resisted Seamus' command. He was unused to a difference of opinion inside his own head, and he tended to ignore thoughts that contradicted his established beliefs. "Look!" Seamus said a little louder, and this time Grulke took better note of Frankie's demeanor. His gaze, feral and rapidly shifting, was focused on a point beyond Danny. As Frankie stared past his dying brother, Grulke saw what Seamus already knew: Frankie's concern was only for himself.

Unwilling to completely give up on his plan to shock Frankie into confessing, Grulke said, "We know Danny was shot, probably last Saturday night or early Sunday morning. Wherever he was when that happened, there was germy stuff, and he got tetanus."

Frankie said nothing.

"We have a man named Charles Cole in custody," Grulke lied. "He told us how you and your brother planned to lure Hanrahan to the club that night."

"Danny mighta done that," Frankie said calmly. "I can't say, because I didn't know nothing about it."

Recognizing the game Frankie had chosen to play, Grulke went on building a story he hoped would undermine the man's confidence. "Two women who work at the club will testify against you. And before he was taken ill, Danny said the two of you planned everything together."

Frankie remained calm. "I think what you have, Detective, is evidence against my brother. I just ran the club for him. I have no knowledge of any illegal activities he might have been conducting."

Anger got the better of Grulke. "You were right beside him every step of the way."

Frankie's eyes glinted as he answered innocently, "If I did things Danny told me to without knowing their true purpose, I guess I'll take my punishment. The sentence for aiding and abetting can't be much though." Meeting the detective's eyes Frankie said, "Like you said, Danny won't be around much longer, so he can't testify against me, can he?"

***

Ronnie knew Frankie Proust was every bit as guilty as his brother, because she was inside his head. As the police finished up at the burning night club, she'd left Waite, who had a lot to deal with due to his injuries. He needed to recover, and she'd been curious about what went on in a killer's mind once he was caught.

She knew it all now. The Prousts had set up the divorce scheme together. After Danny killed Arthur Jameson in the heat of anger, Frankie had killed Tina in cold blood. It was Frankie who'd shot Grant Wellman, and he'd helped murder Seamus, too. Ronnie felt no speck of guilt in the man for what he'd done, only the instinct for self-preservation. He could *not* get away with a slap on the wrist.

Joe Waite stumped into the room, one arm in a sling. "I'm sure glad to be done with doctors," he said. "It took the guy twenty minutes to find the right size for me." He indicated the cane that served as support for his damaged knee. "Had to promise to come back tomorrow for X-rays," he said. "Doctor thinks the collarbone is cracked but not displaced, and the knee is just badly bruised."

Malloy turned to Frankie. "You won't get out of attacking me and my partner."

Frankie remained unruffled. "When the club caught fire, I went upstairs to try to save my brother's papers. I heard someone break in, but the smoke was so thick I couldn't see very well. Naturally I defended my brother's property with the first weapon I could get my hands on."

"We were in uniform," Waite pointed out.

"As I said, it was smoky. All I could make out was a very black face. I assumed we were being robbed."

Suddenly there was a second presence in Frankie's head. A wave of nausea passed through the man, and Ronnie realized it was the result of hosting two angry spirits. *He deserves everything he gets,* she thought, *and everything he's going to get*. She'd been planning a way to get to Frankie, using something Sandra had said. As evil as they were, the Proust brothers had never wanted their mother to know how truly criminal they were.

"Tell the truth, son." Ronnie said in a voice slightly higher than her normal one. "You need to confess your sins."

Frankie jumped as if he'd been swatted with the proverbial rod. "Who said that?"

"Who said what?" Grulke asked.

Though Ronnie had started it, Seamus immediately joined in. "You know you were with me every step of the way," he said in a fair approximation of Danny Proust's voice.

"I was not!" Frankie shouted.

The four cops looked at him in puzzlement. "Wasn't what?" Cannell asked.

"I didn't know what he was—"

"Son, don't lie," Ronnie piped. "These men need to know what happened to Danny. Help your brother so the doctors can save him."

"Stop it!" Frankie shook his head, and Ronnie smiled to herself. The man with no conscience was confused by the betrayal coming from within.

"Calm down, Proust," Grulke ordered. "What's the matter with you?"

"Voices!" Frankie replied. "They're talking in my head!"

"Who is?"

"I don't—I don't know." He tried to regain his composure, but Seamus wasn't about to let that happen.

"Tell them," he urged. "Tell them everything."

"No!" Frankie's whole body shook. "Stop it. Go away!"

Those were the words, though he couldn't have known it. Since a host had ordered them to go, Seamus and Ronnie were required to leave. Seamus went first, returning to Grulke. Ronnie left reluctantly, knowing how close they'd come to making Proust tell what he knew.

As she lingered, she heard a snippet in his mind that intrigued her, something about the boathouse. As she jumped to Waite, who was closest, she knew she'd garnered something the police could use.

Frankie calmed, but he didn't regain the smug expression he'd worn earlier. They'd shaken his confidence.

"Boathouse," Ronnie whispered to Waite. "Gun."

He got it immediately, though he'd later attribute the idea to the mind's ability to sift through experiences and make conclusions without conscious thought. "Where's your gun, Frankie?"

"What?"

"Your gun. Is it in that boathouse you keep locked up so tight? Should we look there?"

Grulke followed Waite's lead. "You know, Chicago has the oldest and finest crime lab in the world. When ballistics matches the bullet they took out of Grant Wellman to your gun, you're going to be looking at attempted murder of a Chicago police detective."

Frankie's shoulders slumped and he let out a gust of breath. "What do I have to do to get a deal?"

It was time to offer the carrot of hope. "We know Danny's the brains behind everything. If you tell us what you know, we'll see what we can do for you."

Frankie hesitated so long that Ronnie considered jumping back and giving him one more prompt from his "mother." She wasn't supposed to do that, so she was relieved when he said tersely, "Okay."

Grulke moved in quickly, taking advantage of the suspect's possibly transitory weakness. "First tell me what happened to your brother."

"The girl shot him." Frankie glanced at Danny, who seemed vaguely aware of what was happening. His face was a frozen mask due to the drugs he'd been given, but Seamus thought he detected understanding in his eyes. Frankie shuddered involuntarily. "We didn't think it was bad. I took him inside and bandaged him up real tight, and the next day he seemed okay."

"Which girl shot him?" Grulke asked.

"The one that used to sing for us, Lili."

"Why did she shoot him?" When Frankie hesitated, Grulke said, "The truth, or the deal's off."

Frankie swallowed. "The girl knew about something that happened back when she worked for us. Danny figured she'd told her old man about it, so we—um, *he* was gonna take care of the two of them."

"You mean kill them."

Frankie thought about how to reply. "*I* said we could just talk to them, you know, and get them to leave the state or something. Danny said husbands and wives murder each other all the time, so if they came floating up in the lake, the cops would think they iced each other."

"She hit him over the head and he shot her before he died? Something like that?"

"Danny said a few days in the lake would cover a lot, and it would be hard to tell what happened."

"I guess you learned that trick with Jameson and the dancer."

Frankie's lips tightened. "I don't know anything about that."

"You were there the night they died. Lee told Wellman—that's the cop you shot—and he told us."

Realizing he was out of options, Frankie seemed to deflate like a balloon. "Jameson found out Tina was setting him up. He dragged her into Danny's office and started shouting that he was going to see that we all went to jail. Danny hit him with the bat he kept beside his desk." He made a weak attempt to defend himself. "He made me help him get rid of the bodies."

"That bat was the same one you used on Joe and me, I bet." Malloy unconsciously touched the bandage on his head.

Shooting the young cop a look to remind him not to interrupt, Grulke prompted, "So Danny killed Jameson."

"Yeah, but when Danny whacked him, the girl went crazy and started crying like old Billy. We had to shut her up." Licking his lips, Frankie added, "Danny did."

"You're just the cleanup man."

Frankie indicated agreement with a twitch of his shoulders.

"What about shooting the cop who caught you trying to kill Hanrahan?"

"That was an accident. We had the P.I. down—" Remembering his claim to innocence he amended, "We were gonna take him inside so we could talk to him, you know?"

"How did you take him by surprise?" Cannell interrupted. "From what Grant said, Hanrahan was no greenhorn."

"We were above him, on the staircase," Frankie replied. "We heard the car pull in, and we came down the steps real quiet."

"And attacked him."

Frankie glanced at his brother, who seemed to have lost the ability to focus. "Danny's orders."

"And where was Danny?"

"Inside. He came out to see if we'd done like he told us to, and that was lucky, because the cop didn't see him there." He turned his wrists, trying to relieve the strain on his cuffed hands. "Danny did the cop shooting. It wasn't me."

Grulke's sigh said he was sick of Frankie's innocent act. "How did that happen?"

"We were tying Hanrahan up, and this guy comes up behind us and hollers, 'Stop! Police!' There's a shot, and Murray and me took off. It got crazy then, but there was another shot, maybe two. The cop staggered for a few seconds and then fell."

"You were the innocent bystander again."

With an expression that hinted he could be nothing else, Frankie replied, "I'm telling you, it was Danny did the shooting."

"With your gun."

Frankie pressed his lips together. "I don't know how he got it. You'll have to ask him."

Cannell wasn't having any of it. "I think you did the shooting, Frankie, but it doesn't matter. You were in on at least three murders. Your goose is cooked, no matter how many excuses you invent."

Grulke stuck with the account. "What happened next?"

"The bastard—I mean, he didn't stay down." Frankie huffed disdainfully. "The cop got up and started running away. Afterwards I figured out the woman must have helped him, but at the time we didn't know she was there. All I heard was him groaning and some whispering."

"What did you do?"

"Danny finally got into the DeSoto and tried to start it, but the engine wouldn't turn over. In the meantime, the other car turned around in a big circle and started away. 'Stop him,' Danny hollered to me and Murray. Then he took off."

"Danny drove down to the river with Hanrahan in the trunk?"

"There's a boat there we use for...stuff."

"It was how you planned to get the bodies out into Lake Michigan," Grulke said.

"I didn't know that." Frankie's voice rang with false righteousness. "I did what my brother told me to do. Danny runs things."

Everyone looked down at Proust, who was no longer able to run anything.

"Murray and me followed the car all the way down to Wacker. It was weaving like crazy. Murray said Danny got that cop good and he wouldn't make it far before he bled to death."

"You're lucky he didn't," Cannell told Frankie. "If you'd killed my friend, I'd strangle you myself."

Eager to finish his confession, Frankie forgot to protest his own innocence for the final segment. "Murray said he'd go help Danny with Hanrahan. Once we got rid of him in the lake, nobody could tie us to it. I was supposed to clean up the scene and then join them."

"What about the woman?"

"I told you, we never saw her." Frankie bit his lip. "I got a flashlight from the club and went over the parking lot. I picked up Hanrahan's hat and the cop's, too. I found his badge where he dropped it when he fell. While I was stuffing them into a trash can, shots came from down by the river, two or maybe three. By the time I got there, everything was a mess."

"Your brother had been shot."

"Yeah. He said the girl came out of the dark with a gun. She wanted her husband. Danny tried to laugh it off, but she said he better do what she said or she'd kill him."

"Danny refused and she shot him?"

Frankie frowned. "I only know what Danny told me. Murray came along right then and yelled something. That startled Lili, and she fired, hitting Danny in the shoulder. After that, he isn't real sure what happened."

"She ran away?"

Frankie glanced again at his brother's lifeless figure on the hospital bed. "All I know is when I got there, Lili was gone, Danny was bleeding like a pig, and poor old Murray was stone dead."

Seamus knew it wasn't right, but hearing the odious Murray hadn't outlived him brought a little glow of satisfaction. He was too interested in hearing the end of Frankie's story to waste time chiding himself for it.

"I took Danny back to the club, got him bandaged up, and then I went back to, um, take care of things."

"I can't imagine you disposed of two bodies by yourself," Grulke said. "Who helped you?"

"I called Herb." Frankie shrugged. "That's how he took over Murray's job at Danny's Place."

Chapter Twenty-nine

Grulke called for two additional officers to take Frankie Proust to jail, commenting that Malloy and Waite were too beat-up to handle the job. Once that was taken care of, he made a proposal. "If you men are okay, we could all go take a look at the scene of the crime. You've both been there before, so you can serve as tour guides for Detective Cannell and me."

Seamus saw Malloy grin at Waite as Grulke turned away, pleased they'd gone from a couple of thorns in his side to his two favorite cops. Ronnie saw it too, but a thought overshadowed her enjoyment of the two young officers' moment of glory.

Nothing they'd learned told them where Lee Hanrahan was. Her family didn't know. Her enemies didn't know. Where was Lee?

They arrived at what had been Danny's Place to find the fire crew still cleaning up. Grulke and Cannell got out of Cannell's Chevy and joined the two cops, who'd come in their own car. Grulke frowned at the sight of the devastation that was once Danny's Place. "Not much sense looking for evidence here. The whole place is just trampled, wet ash."

"Good thing the kid here got that book out," Cannell said, pointing at Malloy. "Nice work, officer."

"Thanks," Malloy replied. "But it was my partner who stopped Frankie."

"You two are a regular mutual admiration society, aren't you?" Grulke observed, and Malloy shot Waite a grin Grulke didn't see.

"We need to have a look in the boathouse," Waite reminded them. "That's where this all ended."

Ronnie knew what it would cost him to make the slippery trip down the sloping road on his injured knee, but he was determined. Malloy insisted on supporting Waite as they made their way to the water, for which he was both embarrassed and grateful.

"Got a call on the way over." Cannell was holding his coat tightly as he shivered in the brisk March air. "Danny Proust died just after we left the hospital. They said his heart couldn't take any more."

Grulke added dryly, "Nice of him to save the state the cost of a trial."

"Now if Frankie gets what's coming to him, the scales will balance out—at least a little," Malloy said.

"If Waite here is correct and there's a gun in that boathouse, I think he will. Frankie can say all he wants that Danny's responsible, but I'm betting he was the guy who carried a gun. He shot Wellman."

"Is the detective going to recover, do you think?"

Cannell slipped, then recovered his footing. "Like the doc said, my partner's a strong man. I'm willing to bet on it."

The river was pale with cold. Several factory buildings on the opposite shore showed their less beautiful sides. On their right was the spot where Waite had stacked empty kegs against the boathouse in his role as Herb's helper. He recalled the bouncer saying he couldn't find the key. No doubt they hadn't wanted anyone inside until the weather broke and they could clean the boat and hide the evidence of what they'd done.

"It's all locked up," Malloy said.

"I came prepared," Grulke said mildly. Ronnie was horrified when, without a second thought about the Bill of Rights, the detective broke the padlock on the boathouse door with a tire iron he'd brought with him from his car. Inside, a small boat floated directly under the hoist that had held it out of the water until recently. "Frankie must have left it like this after his little trip out into the lake that night." Climbing clumsily into the boat, Grulke examined the interior with the flashlight he'd brought along. "Might be blood on this rope."

Cannell walked to the edge of the walkway and leaned over. "Yeah."

"We need more light." Grulke handed the iron to Cannell, who obligingly went outside to the front, broke the second padlock, and rolled an eight-foot sliding door up on its tracks, allowing sunlight to flood the whole structure.

Malloy moved forward, craning his neck to see what Grulke saw. Waite stood back, resting his throbbing knee by leaning against the boathouse wall.

"Look here," Grulke said triumphantly. Reaching under the boat seat, he took out a pistol that had been wedged between the boat wall and the seat board.

"Evidence," Malloy said. "We can prove they killed Seamus."

But where was Lee?

Ronnie was trying to imagine the scene that night: Danny Proust would have been readying the boat as he waited for Frankie and Murray to join him. Seamus would have been in the trunk of Danny's car, dead or close to it. Lee had been somewhere in the shadows, desperate to save her husband's life. She'd have made her way down the icy road carefully to keep from alerting Proust. According to what Frankie said, she'd caught Danny unaware. She'd ordered him to release Seamus. It might have worked. She might have won.

But Murray had done the same thing Lee had. He might have seen her ahead of him, or if he'd had a flashlight, he might have seen her footprints in the snow. He must have reached the boathouse quietly and come up behind her, spoiling her rescue attempt.

How had she gotten away?

Ronnie tried to get Waite to picture the scene with her: Danny was in the boat, or at least near it. Lee would have stepped through the door and pointed the gun at him. Murray had surprised her, and she'd shot Danny then turned to face him, shooting a second time. That shot had been lethal. The question was if Lee had been able to kill Murray and disable Danny, why had she left Seamus to die at Frankie's hands?

"Look!" she urged, and Waite scanned the boathouse again. In front of him there was only the water, the boat, and a few boat-related items. Beside him were the kegs. As his eyes passed over them without interest, Ronnie understood. Lee had not left Seamus to die. She wouldn't.

"Kegs," she told Waite. "Kegs." She was pleased when he started along the line, peering behind each one.

"What are you doing, Joe?" Malloy asked.

Reaching the end of the row, he leaned in to look behind the last two kegs. "Here!" he called to the others. "She's here."

Lee lay where she had fallen, and except for the blue tinge to her skin, she might have been asleep. One hand was under her body, the other rested on the ground, still grasping a police .38. Malloy rolled a keg out of the way, and they saw the pool of blood that stained the wood beneath her.

"She's been here the whole time."

"Murray shot her, but not before she killed him, too."

"Proust was in the boat, injured and bleeding. He didn't see what happened, so the Prousts concluded Lee got away."

"Poor thing." Waite's thoughts went to Linny Cole. She'd be sad to learn that her sister was dead, but he promised himself he'd do his best to help her get through it. Linny was a woman he'd be proud to spend time with—maybe a lifetime, if things worked out. Inside his head Ronnie whispered, "They will."

Seamus experienced a range of emotions, but none of them was pity. He'd had a long time to think about how a person should leave this world, and this way wasn't so bad. He and Lee died the same night; neither had been left alone. Unaware of what happened to him, Lee was spared the worst of fear and grief. And she'd loved him to the end, which is all anyone can ask for.

And now? Lee already knew death wasn't the terrible thing so many fear. Better able than he to accept that life didn't play fair, she'd no doubt left the ship long ago and gone on. Seamus had foolishly clung to his questions, unable to believe his wife had loved him. But she had.

Despite the fact he'd doubted her, Seamus guessed Lee would have said they were lucky to have found each other, no matter how short the time they had together. *Love is always lucky, always.*

Chapter Thirty

Coming out of her stateroom, Ronnie almost bumped into a woman she'd met several times on the ship. Anna was trying to get up the nerve to become a cross-back, but she seemed more interested in murder's lurid details than in actually helping others. Ronnie doubted she'd ever get to the point of making the crossing, but she tried not to show it. Who was she to judge?

After the obligatory apologies for the near-collision, Anna asked, "Is it true you went on a cross-back with Seamus?"

"Yes."

"Well, what was it like?"

Ronnie shrugged. "The case was really interesting."

"Was it a murder?"

"Yes. Actually, several of them."

Anna's eyes glowed with interest. "Did you help them locate the killers?"

"We did."

"And what's Seamus like? I mean, you can tell by looking at the guy that he's something else. I always wonder how he died, you know? The St. Valentine's Day Massacre, maybe."

"Seamus died in his sleep."

The woman's eyes widened. "Really."

"That's what I heard." Ronnie took Anna's arm confidentially. "Now me? I would have been grateful to nod off. I was an aid worker, and I got captured by terrorists. They wouldn't let me sleep. If I drifted off they'd pour cold water over my head or turn on a siren. I was water boarded, had several sessions with a cattle prod—I can't even remember all I went through before my heart gave out."

"That's awful!"

"I know. Let me tell you—dying is the most welcome thing in the world sometimes."

Anna seemed at a loss for words, but Ronnie patted her arm. "I'm good now. It's all in the past."

"I know that, but I can see why you haven't gone on. You must need time to process."

"Exactly. Well, it was good chatting with you." Chuckling at the response to her latest story, Ronnie went to find the person she really wanted to talk to.

She found Seamus at Artie's, hunched over a plate of Salisbury steak and mashed potatoes. "How you doing?"

"Good, good." Avoiding her gaze he added, "Didn't want to miss out on a last chance at Artie's cooking." He gestured at the seat opposite him. "Join me."

She sat down, silent for a moment. When she thought she could speak in a casual tone she asked, "You're going on?"

He nodded without looking up. "It's how it's supposed to be, right?"

"Right. You're ready."

He chuckled. "I've been Seamus Hanrahan for a very long time, and God knows I wasn't perfect. Like you said, I was always thinking I wasn't handsome enough or tall enough or something. It made me doubt Lee, and that was wrong."

"She made mistakes, too. She should have been honest with you." Raising a hand to stop his objection she continued, "I know. Different times. I can't possibly understand. I still think after two years she should have found a way to tell you the truth."

"You see? That makes my point. Everybody's got flaws. As long as we're who we are—*what* we are—we're going to screw up."

"You think it's time to become something better."

Setting his fork down, Seamus regarded her directly. "You could go on too. I mean, it won't be like when we go back to Life and we're us and can help each other out, but you don't have to hang around here on your own."

"You don't have to feel bad about leaving me behind," she said softly.

He sighed. "I know I don't *have* to, but—"

"Look. It's been great knowing you, and I'll always be grateful for the things you've taught me, but—you've waited your whole death for the right time to go on."

He grinned. "Funny. Very funny."

Now it was Ronnie's turn to sigh. "I'm going to tell you something I haven't told anyone else here: the truth."

Seamus pushed his plate away. "About how you died."

It was some time before she spoke. "I killed myself."

He didn't respond right away, and Ronnie wondered how disappointed he was in her. She'd thrown away the gift of life, the greatest thing a person is given. It was shameful, and she couldn't forgive herself for it.

"Why?"

Ronnie toyed with the basket of condiments on the table, setting the bottles in order according to height. "A diagnosis I didn't want to deal with." She raised her eyes to his. "People say how strong you have to be to fight an illness, how brave you are to keep living when every day's a struggle." She shook her head. "I couldn't do it."

"It's got to be tough."

She nodded. "I couldn't stand seeing my family give up their lives to take care of me."

"I bet they'd have done it without even thinking about the cost."

"That's why I couldn't let them." She smiled shyly. "I managed to make it look like an accident—at least I think I did."

"That's why you haven't gone on?"

"Yeah. I don't feel like I deserve it, you know?"

Seamus folded his arms and leaned them on the table. "You're here, Ronnie. That means you deserve it."

"But how can I?"

"You were told suicide is the unforgivable sin, right?"

She nodded.

"Things are different here, and you have to admit, they know a lot more than we did back there. We're still not the slowest students in the class, but we aren't the valedictorians, either."

"You're right, but—"

"Hey, Mike says each person knows when it's his or her time, and I trust him."

"So I just stay here and wait for the right time?"

"No. You go back a few more times. You help other people figure out what happened to them. You learn from the living, who don't know you're there, and you give them a word or two of advice when they need it. In other words, you carry on the work we started together. Can you do that?"

Her smile was tentative, but her voice was firm. "I think so."

"Good. Now order yourself some lunch. I heard somebody say the corned beef is really good." He rose from the table and gave her a pat on the shoulder that might have been a caress.

And then Seamus was gone.

****

Acknowledgments

The author would like to thank everyone who has read and enjoyed the Dead Detective Series.

Here are some people who went above and beyond the call:

Rasheed Siddiqui, a pharmacist who attempted to return to the 1950s with me and imagine what tetanus symptoms and treatment would be. Any mistakes are mine, either because I misunderstood or because the plot called for something other than strict reality.

My good friend Donna and Coz Kelsey, who provided perspective on what daily life was like in a large city in the early '50s.

P.J. , who helps wherever she can; Connie, who reads and critiques long before a book is ready for public view; and John and Kay, who listen patiently to my ramblings on plot-knots and time sequences.

<u>The Dead Detective Mysteries</u>

#1-*The Dead Detective Agency*

Tori Van Camp wakes up on what appears to be a cruise ship, but she never booked a vacation, and she remembers being shot point blank in the chest. In order to find out what happened, she engages the help of Seamus, Dead Detective.

http://www.amazon.com/Dead-Detective-Agency-Mysteries-ebook/dp/B010MF5J9E/

#2-*Dead for the Money*

Wealthy William Dunbar fears he was murdered by a family member, so he engages Seamus to find out how he fell from a cliff along Lake Michigan. With a trainee along, Seamus' investigation becomes more complicated. How can a guy sort through murderous family dynamics when Mildred the Trainee interferes at every turn?

http://www.amazon.com/Dead-Money-Peg-Herring-ebook/dp/B010R101XM/

#3-*Dead for the Show*

Cassie Parker refuses to believe she's dead, and Seamus is sent back to get proof. Along with investigating what happened to Cassie, he soon must protect Cassie's sister Christy, also a target of the killer. In addition, Seamus senses an odd presence in the small Toronto theater. It makes him wonder: Can a guy be haunted if he's already dead?

http://www.amazon.com/Dead-Show-Detective-Mystery-Mysteries-ebook/dp/B00UX9UL4S/

Other books by Peg Herring

<u>The Simon & Elizabeth Mysteries</u> *(Tudor Era Historical)*

Her Highness' First Murder

Link to Amazon: *http://www.amazon.com/Highness-First-Murder-Five-Mystery-ebook/dp/B003RWSB3Q/*

Poison, Your Grace

The Lady Flirts with Death

Her Majesty's Mischief

***

<u>The Loser Mysteries</u> *(Contemporary Mystery/Suspense)*

Killing Silence

Link to Amazon: *http://www.amazon.com/Killing-Silence-Loser-Mysteries-Book-ebook/dp/B00A87IAQG*

Killing Memories

Killing Despair

***

<u>Clan Macbeth Stories (medieval Scotland)</u>

Macbeth's Niece

Link to Amazon: *http://www.amazon.com/Macbeths-Niece-Peg-Herring-ebook/dp/B004ASN9ME/*

Double Toil & Trouble

Link to Amazon: *http://www.amazon.com/Double-Toil-Trouble-Macbeths-Nieces-ebook/dp/B01AI4GB0U/*

***

Standalone Mysteries

Somebody Doesn't Like Sarah Leigh (contemporary cozy mystery)

Go Home and Die ('60s-era mystery)

A Lethal Time and Place ('60s-era paranormal mystery)

Shakespeare's Blood (thriller)

***

Writing as Maggie Pill

The Sleuth Sisters Mysteries (cozy Michigan)

If you like lighter mysteries, and if you have sisters, had sisters, or know a little about sisters, you'll love Maggie's series.

The Sleuth Sisters

http://www.amazon.com/gp/product/B00IJZZLV6/

3 Sleuths, 2 Dogs, 1 Murder

Murder in the Boonies

Sleuthing at Sweet Springs